DEATH OF THE DEMON

DEATH OF THE DEMON

ANNE HOLT

Translated by Anne Bruce

ISIS
LARGE PRINT
Oxford

First published in Great Britain 2013
by
Corvus
an Imprint of Atlantic Books Ltd.

Published in Large Print 2014 by ISIS Publishing Ltd.,
7 Centremead, Osney Mead, Oxford OX2 0ES
by arrangement with
Corvus
an Imprint of Atlantic Books Ltd.

CIP data is available for this title from the British Library

ISBN 978–0–7531–9288–7 (hb)
ISBN 978–0–7531–9289–4 (pb)

Printed and bound in Great Britain by
T. J. International Ltd., Padstow, Cornwall

To Erik Langbråten,
who has taught me so much about
The Important Things

Alone

From childhood's hour I have not been
As others were — I have not seen
As others saw — I could not bring
My passions from a common spring.
From the same source I have not taken
My sorrow; I could not awaken
My heart to joy at the same tone;
And all I loved, *I* loved alone.
Then — in my childhood — in the dawn
Of a most stormy life — was drawn
From every depth of good and ill
The mystery which binds me still:
From the torrent, or the fountain,
From the red cliff of the mountain,
From the sun that 'round me rolled
In its autumn tint of gold —
From the lightning in the sky
As it passed me flying by —
From the thunder and the storm,
And the cloud that took the form
(When the rest of Heaven was blue)
Of a demon in my view.

— EDGAR ALLAN POE

CHAPTER
ONE

"I'm the new boy!"

With resolute stride he stomped to the middle of the floor, where he remained standing while the snow from his enormous sneakers formed little puddles around his feet. His stance wide, as though to conceal the knock-kneed cross formed by his legs, he threw out his arms and repeated, "I'm the new boy!"

His head was clean shaven on the one side. From just above his right ear, raven-black spiky hair was combed in a curve across the crown, slicked over his round cranium and ending with a straight trim several millimeters above his left shoulder. A single thick lock draped his eye, matted like a leather strap. His mouth formed a peevish U as he tried to blow the strands into place, over and over again. His oversized quilted parka fit loosely around the waist, half a meter too long and with the thirty centimeters of superfluous length on the sleeves rolled up into a pair of gigantic cuffs. His pants hung in folds on his legs. When he managed with considerable difficulty to open his jacket, it was obvious that his pants were nevertheless stretched like sausage skins as soon as they reached his thighs.

1

The room was spacious. The boy thought it could not be a living room; it wasn't furnished as you would expect a living room to be, and there was no TV. Along one wall stood a long kitchen work top, with a sink and stove. But there was no smell of food. He stuck his nose in the air and sniffed a couple of times, concluding that there must be another kitchen somewhere in the house. A proper kitchen. This room was a recreation area. The walls were covered with drawings, and small woolen characters the children must have crafted hung from the unusually high ceiling. A gull made of cardboard and woolen yarn flapped directly above his head, gray and white with a fiery red beak that had partly fallen off and was hanging like a slack tooth from a flimsy thread. He stretched out toward it but could not reach up far enough. Instead he ripped down an Easter chick fashioned from an egg carton and yellow feathers. He pulled off all the feathers and threw the egg carton on the floor.

Beneath two vast windows with crossbars was a massive worktable. Four children seated there had stopped what they were doing. They stared at the new arrival. The eldest, a girl of eleven, skeptically looked him up and down, from head to toe. Two boys who could be twins, wearing identical sweaters and with chalk-white hair, snickered, whispered, and poked each other. A four- or five-year-old redhead sat terror stricken for a few seconds before sliding off her chair and racing toward the only adult in the room, a plump woman who immediately lifted the little one up, caressing her curls in reassurance.

2

"This is the new boy," she said. "His name is Olav."

"That's just what I said," Olav said, annoyed. "I'm the new boy. Are you married?"

"Yes," the woman replied.

"Is it only these children who live here?"

His disappointment was apparent.

"No, you know that perfectly well," the woman said, smiling, "there are seven children living here. The three over there . . ."

She nodded in the direction of the table, sending them a stern look at the same time. If they noticed, the boys did not let on.

"What about her there? Doesn't she stay here?"

"No, this is my daughter. She's only here for the day."

She smiled, as the child buried her face in the hollow of her neck and clung more tenaciously to her mother.

"Oh, I see. Do you have many children?"

"Three. This is the youngest. She's called Amanda."

"What a show-off name. Anyway, I thought she must be the youngest. You're too old to have children."

The woman laughed.

"You're quite right about that. I'm too old now. My two other children are almost grown up. But won't you say hello to Jeanette? She's almost as old as you. And to Roy-Morgan? He's eight."

Roy-Morgan was not at all interested in saying hello to the new boy. He squirmed in his seat and thrust his head dismissively toward his buddy's.

Frowning, Jeanette drew back in her chair as Olav approached with outstretched hand, dripping with dirty, melted snow. Before he had come right up to her and long before she had made any sign of taking hold of the outstretched fingers being offered, he started to take a deep bow and declared solemnly, "Olav Håkonsen. Pleased to meet you!"

Jeanette pressed herself against the chair back and grabbed on to the seat with both hands, drawing her knees up to her chin. The new boy attempted to pass his hands down through the side, but his body shape and clothing caused his arms to remain fixed diagonally, like a Michelin Man. The offensive posture was gone, and he forgot to spread his legs. Now his kneecaps kissed beneath his stout thighs, and his big toes pointed toward each other inside his mammoth shoes.

The little boys fell silent.

"I know why you don't want to say hello to me," Olav said.

The woman had managed to steer the smallest child into another room. When she returned, she spotted Olav's mother in the doorway. Mother and son were strikingly alike: the same black hair, the same wide mouth and conspicuous bottom lip, seemingly unusually soft and a moist dark red, not dry and cracked as one would expect this time of year. On the boy it appeared childish. On the adult woman the lip seemed repellent, especially since she kept shooting out a similarly bright red tongue to wet her lips. Apart from her mouth it was her shoulders that aroused most interest. She did not possess shoulders. From her head, a smooth curve ran downward, as on a bowling pin or a

4

pear, a curved line that culminated in incredibly broad hips, with hefty thighs and skinny legs to hold all this up. The body shape was more pronounced than on the boy, probably because her coat fitted. The other woman tried to make eye contact with her, without success.

"I know well enough why you don't want to say hello to me," Olav repeated. "I'm gross and fat."

He stated this without a trace of bitterness, with a slight satisfied smile, almost as though it were a fact he had just stumbled upon, the solution to a complicated problem he had spent the last twelve years working out. He wheeled around, and without glancing at the director of his new foster home, asked her where he would be living.

"Could you show me to my room, please?"

The woman extended her hand to shake his, but instead of grasping it, he made a gallant and sweeping motion with his arm and made a little bow.

"Ladies first!"

Then he waddled after her up to the next floor.

He was so big. And I knew that something was wrong. They laid him in my arms, and I felt no joy, no sorrow. Just powerless. A tremendous, heavy powerlessness as though I had something imposed on me that everyone knew I would never manage. They comforted me. Everything was completely normal. He was just so big.

Normal? Had any of them tried to squeeze out a five-and-a-half-kilo lump? I was three weeks beyond my due date, I knew that, but the doctor insisted that it was wrong. As though she could know that. I knew exactly when he had come into being. One Tuesday night. One of those nights I gave in to avoid trouble, when I feared his outbursts so much that I didn't have the strength to resist. Not just then. Not with so much alcohol in the house. He was killed in a road accident the next day. A Wednesday. Since then no man had come near me before that baby tub of lard came smiling into the world. It's true! He smiled! The doctor said it was only a grimace, but I know it was a smile. He still has the same smile, has always had it. His best weapon. He hasn't cried once since he was eighteen months.

They placed him on my stomach. An unbelievable mass of new human flesh that already there and then opened its eyes and groped with its wide mouth over my skin to find my breast. The folk in white coats laughed and slapped its bottom one more time. What a guy!

I knew there was something wrong. They said that everything was normal.

Eight children and two adults sat around an oval dining table. Seven of the children said grace together with the grown-ups. The new boy had been right. It was not the kitchen he had entered earlier in the day.

They were now in a room farther inside the capacious converted turn-of-the-century villa. The room had probably served as a pantry at the time the house was built. It was homey and cozy, with blue cabinets and rag rugs on the floor. The only aspect that distinguished it from a private home apart from the unusually large bunch of kids were the rosters hanging on an enormous notice board beside the door leading to one of the living rooms: the dayroom, as the new boy had found out. In addition to the names there were little photographs of the staff on display. This was because not all the children could read, the boy had learned.

"Ha, they can't read," he muttered scornfully. "There's nobody here under seven years old!"

He had not received any reply other than a friendly smile from the plump lady, whom he now knew was the director. "But you can call me Agnes. That's my name."

Agnes was not present now. The adults at the supper table were far younger. The man even had bad acne. The lady was quite pretty, with long blonde hair she had braided in a strange and lovely way, beginning right at the front of her head and ending with a red silk bow. The man was called Christian and the lady's name was Maren. They all sang a short little song while holding hands. He did not want to join in.

"You don't need to if you don't want to," Maren said and was actually really kind. Then they started to eat.

Jeanette, who had refused to say hello to him that morning, was sitting by Olav's side. She was slightly overweight, too, with brown unruly hair in an elastic band that kept sliding out. She had protested about sitting beside him, but Maren had firmly squashed all discussion. Now she was sitting as far over on the opposite side of her chair as possible, causing Roy-Morgan to poke his elbow into her side continually and yell that she had cooties. On the other side of Olav sat Kenneth, who at seven was the youngest in the house. Struggling with the butter, he ruined a sandwich.

"You're even more clumsy than me, you know," Olav said contentedly, grabbing a fresh slice and neatly spreading a generous portion of butter before placing it on Kenneth's plate.

"What do you want on top?"

"Jam," Kenneth whispered, sticking his hands underneath his thighs.

"Jam, you dope! Then you don't need butter!"

Olav grabbed yet another slice, slapping an extravagant tablespoonful of blueberry jam in the center and using the spoon to spread it out with awkward movements.

"Here you are!"

Clattering the spoon onto the plate, he helped himself to the buttered slice and looked around the room.

"Where's the sugar?"

"We don't need any sugar," Maren said.

"I want sugar on my bread!"

"It's not healthy. We don't do that here."

"Do you actually know how much sugar there is in the jam that nitwit there is gobbling up?"

The other children ceased their chatter and listened attentively. Kenneth, scarlet in the face, stopped munching with his mouth full of jam and bread. Maren stood up. Christian was about to say something, but Maren walked around the table and bent over toward Olav.

"You can have some jam as well, of course," she said in a friendly voice. "Besides, it's low-sugar jam, look!"

8

She reached for the jar, but the boy got there first with a lightning flash movement one would not have thought possible of him. Moving so quickly that the chair toppled over, he flung the jar across the room, banging it on the refrigerator door. The impact inflicted a large dent on the door, but amazingly the jar was still intact. Before anyone had the chance to prevent him, he was over at the tall kitchen cabinet at the opposite end of the room, snatching out a large sugar canister.

"Here's the sugar," he screamed. *"Here's the fucking shitty sugar!"*

Tearing off the canister lid and throwing it onto the floor, the boy raced around in a cloud of granulated sugar. Jeanette started to laugh. Kenneth burst into tears. Glenn, who was fourteen and had already begun to grow dark hairs above his top lip, muttered that Olav was an idiot. Raymond was seventeen and a sly old fox. Accepting it all with stoic calm, he lifted his plate and disappeared. Anita, sixteen, followed him. Roy-Morgan's twin, Kim-André, clutched his brother's hand, excited and elated. He looked across at Jeanette and began to laugh uncertainly.

The canister of sugar was empty. Olav made a move to throw it on the floor but was stopped at the last moment by Christian, who took hold of his arm and held it firmly, as in a vise. Olav howled and tried to tear himself free, but in the meantime Maren had advanced and placed her arms around his body. He had incredible strength for a twelve-year-old, but after a couple of minutes she could feel that he was beginning to calm down.

She spoke to him the entire time, gently in his ear. "There, there. Take it easy now. Everything's all right."

When he determined that Maren had control of the boy, Christian took the other children with him out to the day-room. Kenneth had thrown up. A small and unappetizing heap of chewed bread, milk, and blueberries was sitting on the plate he had held hesitantly in his hands as they walked to the other room, the same as all the rest.

"Just leave it," Christian told him. "You can have one of my slices!"

As soon as the other children had gone, Olav calmed down completely. Maren let go of him, and he sank down onto the floor like a beanbag.

"I only eat sugar on my bread," he mumbled. "Mum says it's okay."

"Then I suggest one thing to you," Maren said, sitting down beside him, with her back against the damaged refrigerator. "When you're with your mum, you eat sugar the way you're used to, but when you're here, then you eat what we do. Isn't that a good deal?"

"No."

"Maybe that's what you think, but unfortunately that's the way it has to be, really. Here we have a number of rules, and we all have to follow them. Otherwise it would become quite unfair. Don't you agree?"

The boy did not respond. He seemed totally lost. Gingerly she placed a hand on his bulky thigh. His reaction was instantaneous. He punched her arm.

"Don't touch me, for fuck's sake!"

10

She rose quietly and stood there looking down at him.

"Do you want something to eat before I clear it away?"

"Yes. Six slices of bread and butter with sugar."

Smiling hesitantly, Maren shrugged her shoulders and started to cover the foodstuffs with plastic wrap.

"Do I have to go to bed hungry in this fucking dump, or what?"

Now he looked her directly in the eye, for the first time. His eyes were completely black, two deep holes in his pudgy face. It crossed her mind that he could have been handsome, were it not for his size.

"No, Olav, you don't *have* to go to bed hungry. You're choosing that yourself. You're not having sugar on your bread, not now, not tomorrow. Never. You're going to starve to death if you wait for us to give in before you eat. Got it?"

He could not understand how she could remain so calm. It bewildered him that she did not give in. What's more, he could not understand that he had to go to bed hungry. For a moment it struck him that salami was actually tasty. Just as quickly, he cast the thought aside. He struggled to his feet, snorting with exertion.

"I'm so fucking fat I can't even stand up," he said to himself in a low voice as he approached the living room.

"You, Olav!"

Maren was standing with her back turned, examining the dent on the refrigerator. He stopped without turning to face her.

11

"It was really good of you to help Kenneth with his bread. He's so small and vulnerable."

For a second the twelve-year-old new boy stood, hesitating, before turning around slowly.

"How old are you?"

"I'm twenty-six."

"Oh, right."

Olav went to bed hungry.

Raymond was snoring. Really snoring, like a grown man. The room was large, and in the faint light that entered through the darkened window Olav could discern a huge Rednex poster above his roommate's bed. In one corner there was a dismantled off-road bike, and Raymond's desktop was a chaotic jumble of textbooks, food wrappers, comics, and tools. His own desktop was completely bare.

The bedclothes were clean and starchy. They smelled strange but pleasant. Flowery, in some way. They were far nicer than the ones he had at home; they were adorned with Formula 1 racing cars and lots of bright colors. The pillowcase and quilt cover matched, and the bottom sheet was entirely blue, the same color as some of the cars. At home he never had any matching bedclothes.

The curtains stirred in the draft from the slightly open window. Raymond had decided that. He himself was used to a warm bedroom, and although he had new pajamas and a cozy quilt, he was shivering from the cold. He was hungry.

"Olav!"

It was the director. Or Agnes, as she liked to be called. She was whispering to him from the doorway.

"Are you sleeping?"

He turned over to face the wall and did not reply.

Go away, go away, said a voice inside his head, but it was no use. Now she was sitting on the edge of his bed.

"Don't touch me."

"I won't touch you, Olav. I just want to have a little chat. I heard you were angry at supper tonight."

Not a word.

"You have to understand that we can't have any of the children behaving like that. Imagine if all eight of you were to bounce sugar and jam off the walls all the time!"

She chuckled softly.

"That would never do!"

He still remained silent.

"I've brought you some food. Three slices. Cheese and sausage. And a glass of milk. I'm putting it down here beside the bed. If you want to eat it, then that's fine; if not we can agree that you'll throw it in the trash early tomorrow morning without any of us seeing it. Then no one will know whether you wanted it. Okay?"

Moving slightly, the boy turned around abruptly.

"Are you the one who decided I have to stay here?" he asked loudly and indignantly.

"Shhh," she hushed him. "You'll wake Raymond! No, you know perfectly well that I don't decide these things. My task is to take good care of you. With the other grown-ups. It's going to be fine. Although you're

13

most definitely going to miss your mother. But you'll be able to visit her often, you mustn't forget that."

Now he was sitting halfway up in the bed. He resembled a fat demon in the faint light — the outlandish raven-black hair, the wide mouth that even in the night darkness glowed bloodred. Involuntarily, she dropped her gaze. The hands on the quilt belonged to a young child. They were sizable, but the skin was like a baby's, and they were helplessly clutching two cars on the quilt cover.

My God, she thought. *This monster is only twelve years old. Twelve years!*

"Actually," he said, staring directly at her. "Actually you're my prison guard. This is a fucking prison!"

At that moment the director of the Spring Sunshine Foster Home, the sole institution in Oslo for children and young people, saw something she had never, in the course of her twenty-three years of employment in child welfare services, seen before. Beneath the boy's black, slender eyebrows she recognized an expression that so many despairing adults had, people whose children had been taken from them and who tarred her with the same brush as the rest of the official bureaucracy pursuing them. But Agnes Vestavik had never seen it in a child.

Hatred.

They sent me home from the clinic with renewed assurances. Everything was absolutely fine. He was just a bit voracious. And that was simply because he was a big, healthy boy. They sent me home after three days to an empty apartment. At the

14

social services office I had been given money for a cot, a bouncing cradle, and some baby clothes. A lady had paid a visit two or three times, and I noticed her stealing glances into corners and then lying about looking for the toilet. Just to check whether my house was clean. As though that had ever been a problem. I scrub and scrub. There's a constant reek of liquid detergent here.

He filled the apartment right away. I don't quite know, but it seemed as though from the very first evening he considered that this was his own place, his apartment, his mum. His nights. He did not cry. He just made a noise. Others might have called it crying, but it wasn't that. There were seldom any tears. The few times he really cried, it was actually easy to comfort him. Then he was hungry. I pushed my nipple into his mouth, and at that he shut up. Otherwise he just made a racket. A screaming, protesting noise while he waved his arms about, kicking off the quilt and wriggling out of his clothes. He filled the apartment to the bursting point so that I sometimes simply had to leave. I placed him in the bathroom, where the insulation is best, and tied him firmly to the bouncing cradle. For safety's sake, I surrounded him with cushions on all sides. He was only a few months old, so it was impossible for him to free himself from the chair. Then I went out. To the center, where I had a cup of coffee, read a magazine, visited some stores. Occasionally I had a cigarette. I had managed to stop when I was pregnant and realized I shouldn't smoke as long as I was breast-feeding. But one cigarette now and again couldn't do any harm. All the same, I had a guilty conscience afterward.

My outings came to an abrupt halt when he was five months. I hadn't been away long. Two hours, perhaps.

Maximum. When I arrived back home, it was eerily silent. I wrenched open the bathroom door, and there he lay, lifeless, halfway out of the chair with the seat belt around his neck. It must have taken a number of seconds for me to gather myself and unfasten him. He coughed and rasped and was completely blue in the face. I cried my eyes out and shook him, and eventually his face returned to normal. Except that he was silent.

I cuddled him close to me and for the first time felt that I loved him. My child was five months old. And I hadn't felt anything for him until then. Everything had been abnormal right from the start.

It was late. The new boy was worse than she had anticipated. She leafed through the psychologist's report despite not being in the right frame of mind to digest much of it. She knew the vocabulary. It was the same for all the children, with only a few variations in terminology, different combinations. "Major deficiencies in care over a lengthy period of time"; "Mother unable to protect the boy from bullying"; "The boy is easily led"; "The boy is an underachiever at school"; "Extensive, grave problems in setting boundaries"; "The boy alternates between unrestrained, aggressive behavior and a parenthetical, overreaching, and almost chivalrous demeanor toward his mother and other adults, something clearly symptomatic of the hypothesis of serious developmental disorder as a result of neglect"; "The boy's lack of impulse control may soon become an immediate danger to his environs, if he is not brought into an appropriate care setting, where he *is provided with the consistency, security, and predictability he so greatly needs"; "The boy treats other children with an adult attitude that frightens them, is ostracized, and degenerates into aggressive, antisocial conduct."*

Only the very worst cases landed up here. In Norway, children who for one reason or another were unable to grow up with their biological parents were expected to be placed in individual foster homes. That was the system. It was easy to find such homes for babies. Fairly straightforward as far as toddlers were concerned, up until about school-age. Then it suddenly became far more difficult. As a rule, however, they managed it. Except for the very worst cases. The ones that were so demanding, so damaged, so broken by their lives and their useless parents that no ordinary family could be expected to cope with the responsibility. These ended up with Agnes.

Smothering a yawn, she massaged the fleshy small of her back. Olav would probably get used to it. She had yet to give up on a child. Besides, strictly speaking, he was not the most difficult problem she had to deal with at the moment. Attempting in vain to find a more comfortable sitting position, she shoved Olav's file down into a drawer and opened up another one, a folder with a cardboard cover containing five sheets of paper. She sat staring at it. In the end she packed them away too, taking a deep breath, and locking the drawer carefully. The key was somewhat sticky, but she managed finally to release it from the keyhole. Stiff and sore, she stood up, lifted a potted plant from the built-in bookcase beside the window, and returned the key to its place. For a few moments she stood there, looking out.

The garden always seemed more extensive at night. The moonlight cast frosty blue shadows across the remnants of snow. Down toward the road, beside a low wire-mesh fence, she spotted Glenn's bicycle. With a sigh, she made up her mind to get tough with him this time. No bikes on icy, slippery roads. Two days previously, Christian had been instructed to lock it in the basement. Either he hadn't done so, or else Glenn had broken into the storeroom and retrieved it. She did not quite know which was worse, a slapdash employee or a totally disobedient youngster.

There was a draft from the old, rickety window. They had to prioritize, and the upper floor, where the children spent most of their waking hours, had been fitted with new windows first. God only knew when her office would reach further up the list of priorities. She sighed softly and crossed over to the door. Although it was by no means tempting to go home, the way things stood between her and her husband, her body longed for sleep. If she were lucky, he would have already retired for the night.

Before she left, she looked in on Olav again. A quarter century's experience with children told her at once that he was sleeping, although she could make out only the outline of his heavy shape in the bed. His breathing was quiet and even, and she took some time to tuck the quilt around him before closing the door quietly behind her. By then she had already smiled a little over the disappearance of the food and milk. Keeping to their bargain, she let the crockery remain.

In the dayroom, Christian was sitting with his feet up on the table, half asleep. Maren sat with her feet tucked beneath her in a winged armchair, reading a crime novel. As the director entered the room, Christian banged his feet down onto the floor in a reflex action. He should have been long gone, as his shift had finished an hour earlier. But he was too lazy.

"Honestly, it's difficult enough teaching the youngsters to have manners without you lacking them entirely as well," she said, directing herself to the young student who was employed part time on evening and night shifts. "What's more, I thought we had agreed that Glenn's bicycle was to be locked indoors!"

"Oh, bloody hell. I forgot it."

He looked shamefaced as he fiddled with a huge pimple on the left side of his nose.

"Listen, Christian," the director said, sitting down beside him, her back straight and knees clamped firmly together. "This is an institution run by the Salvation Army. We do what we can to clean up the children's dreadful speech habits. Why is it so difficult for you to respect my demand to avoid all that swearing? Do you not understand that you really offend me every time you utter all those words? Children are children. You're a grown man who ought to have learned to show consideration. Don't you see that?"

"Sorry, sorry," he mumbled submissively, and suddenly the pimple burst. Yellow pus ran out, and he stared in fascination at his finger.

19

"Heavens above," Agnes groaned, getting to her feet and making a move to leave.

As she put on her coat, she turned toward Maren, who, oblivious of the minor altercation, had continued to turn the pages of her book.

"I need to have a meeting with you soon, just the two of us," she said, and with a glance at Christian who was still looking incredulous at how much pus there was space for in a pimple, she added, "We must discuss the staffing roster for February and March. Can you draw up a proposal?"

"Mmm," Maren agreed, glancing up from her novel for a second. "Okay."

"It would be good if you could get it done tonight. Then we can discuss it tomorrow afternoon."

Glancing up again, Maren smiled and nodded. "That's fine, Agnes. It'll be ready tomorrow afternoon. Perfectly okay. Good night!"

"Good night to you both."

CHAPTER
TWO

It was a beautiful villa. Although the funds for renovation had not extended to a more reverential restoration — they had simply replaced the original eight-paned windows by H Windows with crossbars attached — the house and its spires towered imposingly over nearly four acres of ground. The brick walls were painted beige, but with decorative timber in green, in the Swiss style. Two entire large floors had been divided five years previously, with two living rooms, a conference room, kitchen, bathroom, laundry room, and a room they named the library, though in fact it was a kind of records room, on the ground floor. On the upper floor there were six bedrooms for the children, but several of them were double rooms and a couple of the single rooms were now pressed into service as homework rooms and common rooms. In addition, there was a staff bedroom. At the end of the corridor, to the right of the staircase, lay the director's office. Immediately across the hall was an enormous bathroom with a bathtub, as well as a smaller one with a shower and toilet. In addition to the good use of space on these two floors, there was an entire basement and a spacious, high-ceilinged attic. Following a fire inspection a few years earlier, ladders were installed at the windows at either end of the corridor, and there was a fire rope in every bedroom.

The youngsters loved fire drills. All except Kenneth. And now Olav. The former sat in the middle of the corridor, crying and clinging to the wall-mounted fire extinguisher. Olav stood with his legs apart, truculent, with his bottom lip more prominent than ever.

"No fuckin' way," he said petulantly. "No fuckin' way am I going down that rope."

"The ladder, then, Olav," Maren offered. "The ladder's not so scary. Also, you must get rid of that swearing very soon. You've been here for three weeks already, and your entire allowance is disappearing because of that!"

"Well then, go on, Olav."

It was Terje who was prodding him in the back. Terje was in his thirties and, on paper at least, the assistant director.

"I'll go right in front of you. Underneath you, in a way. So if you fall, I'll be there to catch you. Okay?"

"Not fuckin' likely," Olav said, taking a step back.

"Ten kroner says the idiot doesn't dare," Glenn shouted from outside the window, having already climbed up and down four times.

"What will you do if the place starts to burn down?" Terje asked. "Are you going to burn to death?"

Olav stared at him maliciously.

"You couldn't care less about that! Mum lives in a concrete apartment block. I could just move there, for instance."

Shaking his head, Terje gave up and let Maren take over with the stubborn child.

"What is it you're frightened of?" she asked quietly, indicating they should move into Olav's room.

He reluctantly shuffled after her.

"I'm not frightened."

He flopped onto the bed so it groaned audibly, and Maren found herself checking the solidity of the furniture before sitting down beside him.

"If you're not scared, then what's holding you back?"

"I just can't be bothered. I'm not scared."

From the corridor they could hear Kenneth sobbing bitterly through the excited yelling and Tarzan howls of the other youngsters as they swung on the ropes.

She was no saint. The dumbest things she knew were expressions such as "I'm so fond of children." Children were like adults: some were enchanting, some were charming, others were scumbags. As a professional foster worker, she thought that no one could identify when she did not like a child. She did not treat individuals alike, as individuals were not alike, but she was fair and did not have favorites. There was a subtle balance there she was proud of, but Olav *did* something to her.

No one had managed to break through to him since he arrived. All the same, there was something about his expression as he sat there, like a dressed Buddha trying to appear angry but actually only being sad; there was something about his entire macabre figure that drew her to him. In defiance of the ban on making physical contact, she calmly stroked his hair, and he allowed her to do so.

"What is it with you, little Olav?" she said quietly, caressing him again.

"I'm not exactly little, you know," he responded, but she sensed the hint of a smile in his voice.

"Just a bit," she said, laughing. "Sometimes, anyway."

"Do you like working here?" he asked suddenly, pushing her hand away from his head.

"Yes. I like it very, very much. I couldn't imagine working anywhere else in the whole wide world."

"How long have you been here?"

"About three years . . ."

Hesitating, she added, "Since I left college. School of Social Work. Almost four years. And I'm going to be here for many, many years to come."

"Why don't you go and have some children of your own instead?"

"I might well do that someday as well. But that's not why I work here, of course. Because I don't have children of my own, I mean. Most people who work here do have children of their own."

"How many pages are there in the Bible?" he asked abruptly.

"The Bible?"

"Yes, how many pages has it got? There must be fuckin' lots! Look how thick it is!"

He grabbed the Bible that was lying on the bedside table, as on every bedside table, and slapped it over and over again against his thigh before handing it to her.

Maren began to flick through it.

"You can have a look at the last page," he suggested. "You don't need to count them, you know."

"One thousand two hundred and seventy-one pages," she concluded. "Plus a few pages of maps. And you ... I mean what I said about that swearing of yours. Shall we try the fire ladder now?"

He stood up, and the bed sighed in relief.

"Now I'm going down. The stairs."

There was nothing further to discuss.

I made contact with children's services. Yes, when he was two years old. I was scared to death. I needed help. Someone had to look after him for a bit. Just a few hours a day. I had decided to phone several months earlier but kept putting it off for fear of what action they would take. They can't take him away from me. There were only the two of us. I was still breast-feeding him, although he now weighed nineteen kilos and devoured five meals a day. He ate everything. I don't know why I let him go on so long. For the ten minutes he was suckling, he was at least quiet. I was in control. It became like small pockets of peace. When he began to lose interest, I was the one who was beaten. Not him.

They were friendly. After being at home with me a few times, two or three, perhaps, they granted him a kindergarten place. From quarter past eight to five o'clock. They said I shouldn't leave him there so long, since I was a stay-at-home mum and could allow him to have slightly shorter days. It would be tiring for him, they said.

The boy was delivered at quarter past eight every morning. I never collected him before five. But never too late either.

I got a place at kindergarten, and survived.

Olav longed for home. It was like a craving in his body, something he had never felt before. He had never been away for so long. He tried to shrink the hole in his stomach by breathing hard and fast, but that only made him dizzy. His entire body ached. Then he attempted to take deep breaths again, but the craving, the painful hole, returned. It was enough to make him cry.

He did not know if it was his mum or the apartment or the bed or his belongings that he missed. He did not think too deeply about it either. It was one big jumble of loss.

He wanted to go home but he was not permitted to leave. He had to stay there for two months before he would be allowed a home visit, they had told him. Instead, his mum came to visit him twice a week. As if his mum had anything to do with the foster home. He saw the other children staring at her and the twins laughing every time she appeared. Kenneth was the only one who spoke to her, but then he did not have a mum at all, poor soul, so he was probably envious. An ugly and horrible mum was better than none at all.

She was able to stay there for two hours each visit. For the first hour, everything went well. They chatted a little, perhaps went for a walk around the neighborhood. Twice they had gone to a café and eaten cakes. It was a long walk, however, so on that visit the excursion had consumed almost all their time. The one occasion they had returned half an hour late, Agnes had scolded his mum. He saw that his mum was sorry, although she did not say anything. So then he had vandalized his cloakroom peg, and Agnes had been furious with him as well.

When the first hour had passed, it was more difficult to think of anything. Agnes suggested his mum should help him with his homework, but that was something she had never done before, so he was not thrilled with that. Instead they spent most of the time sitting in his room, without saying very much at all.

He longed to go home.

He was hungry.

He was always, always hungry. It had become much more agonizing since he had arrived at the foster home, where they did not give him enough food. Yesterday he had wanted a third serving of meatballs with lashings of sauce. Agnes had said no, although there was plenty left in the pot. Kenneth had offered him his portion, but just as he was about to push it all over onto his plate, Agnes had snatched the food from him and handed him an apple instead. But he didn't want an apple, he wanted meatballs.

He was so *bloody* hungry.

At the moment, the other children were outside. At least it was peaceful in the enormous house. It was an in-service day at school, and that was probably why they had held the fire drill today. He hauled himself out of bed, shaking one of his legs, as it had gone to sleep; it was tingling and prickling, and although painful, it tickled a little as well.

His leg almost gave way when he put his weight on it and limped across to the stairs. He could hear some voices from below, but it had to be the grown-ups.

Padding over to the window at the near end of the corridor, he spied Kenneth and the twins sledding on the slope down to the road. A sissy slope. Far too short, and besides, you had to brake to avoid crashing into the fence. He didn't know what had become of the older children, but they were given free rein and allowed to do almost anything. Yesterday Raymond had even been to McDonald's with his girlfriend. He had brought back a little figure, which he had given to Olav. It was bloody childish, so he passed it on to Kenneth.

Trying to sneak down the stairs, he discovered that the treads creaked slightly. It dawned on him that if he placed his feet at the extreme outer edges of each step, it did not make a noise, and he managed to descend the stairs almost soundlessly.

"Hi, Olav!"

He nearly jumped out of his skin. It was Maren.

"Why aren't you outside? All the other children are!"

"I can't be bothered. I want to watch TV."

"No TV watching so early in the day, I'm afraid. You'll have to find something else to do."

She smiled at him. She was the only adult in the foster home that he could abide. She was *logical*, something almost nobody was. Not his mum either. And certainly not *Agnes*.

"I'm starving," he whispered.

"But it's only half an hour since we ate lunch!"

"I only had two slices of bread."

Looking around, Maren saw no one and, placing her forefinger over a smiling mouth, she crept toward the kitchen with exaggerated movements, all the while

28

humming the *Pink Panther* tune. A smiling Olav crept behind her even though he thought it fairly stupid.

In the kitchen she opened the fridge a tiny crack and they both thrust their faces toward the gap. The light blinked on and off because the door was not properly open, so they had to swing it open a little wider.

"What do you want?" Maren whispered.

"The meatballs," Olav whispered back, pointing at the leftover food from the previous day.

"You can't have that. But you can have some yogurt."

He wasn't particularly pleased, but it was better than nothing.

"Can I put muesli on top?"

"Okay."

Picking up an economy carton of yogurt, Maren poured some of the contents into a small, deep dish. Olav had brought out the muesli packet from the pantry and was in the process of sprinkling a third scoop over the bowl when Agnes appeared at the door.

"What's going on here?"

Both of them froze for a second, before Maren grabbed the bowl of food and positioned herself in front of the boy.

"Olav's so hungry. A little yogurt can't do any harm."

Agnes did not utter a word as she circumnavigated the massive dining table to relieve Maren of the bowl. Still without a word, she produced a roll of plastic wrap from a drawer and, using it to cover the food, she pushed the two sinners away from the refrigerator and placed the bowl inside before closing the door.

"So. We do *not* eat between meals in this house. You both know that."

She did not even glance at Olav. But she stared hard at Maren as she spoke. Maren shrugged her shoulders in embarrassment and planted her hand on Olav's shoulder. After his initial astonishment, Olav pulled himself together.

"Fucking cow."

Agnes, about to leave the room, froze in midmovement and then turned around slowly.

"What did you say?"

Maren squeezed the boy's shoulder in an attempt to warn him.

"Fucking cow, bitch from hell!"

Now the boy was screaming.

Agnes Vestavik set upon him faster than anyone would have thought possible. Grabbing hold of his chin, she forced his face up against her own. He displayed his protest by narrowing his eyes.

"Expressions like that are *not* used here," she snarled, and Maren could have sworn that her left hand was raised as though for a stinging slap. If so, it would have been the first time in history that Agnes Vestavik had ever laid her hand on a child. After a moment's hesitation, she lowered her hand but continued her grip around the boy's face.

"Look at me!"

He screwed up his eyes even more tightly.

"Olav! Open your eyes and look at me!"

Olav's face was crimson, contrasting starkly with the livid marks around the director's fingers.

"I'll take care of him, allow me," Maren suggested in a muted voice, "I'll speak to him."

"Speak! We're not going to do any speaking here! We're not going —"

"Tramp cunt," Olav muttered through gritted teeth.

The director was now deathly pale. She lifted her left hand once more, and once again let it fall after a few seconds. Her grip around the boy's face became even more ferocious. Then she swallowed twice and slowly released her grasp. Nevertheless, the boy did not open his eyes and remained standing there with his face turned upward.

"I'll phone your mother and tell her she doesn't need to come here for a fortnight, do you understand? That will be a suitable punishment."

Maren opened her mouth to object, but closed it when she caught the director's eye. Instead she tried to place herself between the boy and Agnes, something that was rather difficult since Olav, on hearing the punishment, had opened both his eyes and his mouth, and was now ready to launch himself at the other woman. She, for her part, had turned away and was on her way out the door. Maren managed to stop the boy in his tracks by grabbing his arms and twisting them behind his back.

The boy roared. "I hate you! I hate that fucking cunt woman!"

Agnes slammed the door behind her and vanished.

"Mum," the boy yelled, trying to struggle free. "Mum!"

And then he deliberately bit his own tongue so it gushed with blood.

But he did not cry.

"Mum," he mumbled as the blood streamed out of his mouth.

Standing behind him, Maren suddenly noticed the boy was no longer attempting to tear himself free. Slowly she let him go and escorted him to a chair. Then she caught sight of the blood.

"Oh, my God, Olav," she said, terrified, grabbing some paper from a kitchen roll.

It rapidly became saturated with blood, and she used almost the entire roll before the flow was stanched sufficiently for her to inspect the injury more closely. Part of his tongue was almost torn off.

"Olav, there, there," she said, patting the paper towel on the wound.

At that, she realized there was not much more to be said. Apart from one thing.

"You must remember this, Olav, if you have a problem, if things are difficult, if the others are nasty to you, then you really must come to me. I'll always be able to help you. If you only hadn't got so angry just now, we could have sorted this out together. Can't you try to remember that another time? That I will always help you?"

She wasn't entirely certain, but she had a feeling the boy nodded, and she then stood up to phone for the family doctor.

His tongue had to be sewn with three stitches.

Only one member of staff was absent from the total of fourteen, and Agnes chaired the meeting. The staffing rosters for the next two months had been drafted, though they spent some time adjusting Maren's suggestions. Thereafter, they discussed the children, one by one.

"Raymond has been allocated a place on that course," Terje said. "He starts next week, so then he'll have three days of school and two days tinkering with motorbikes every week. He's looking forward to it."

Raymond was doing fine. He had lived at Spring Sunshine since the age of nine, and had been a hard nut for the first year. From then he had relaxed his shoulders, exhaled, and settled down, accepting that he could visit his mum only at weekends. His mother was fantastic. She had all the qualities a mother should have, considerate, stimulating, protective, and loving. When she was sober. For the first five years of his life things had gone well, and then she fell off the wagon again. At seven years of age, Raymond was placed in an individual foster home and all hell broke loose. He was so attached to his mother that it was impossible for anyone to assume the parental role, and after three pairs of foster parents had worn themselves out without his mother having managed to relinquish the bottle, he was transferred to Spring Sunshine, where things improved. His mother stayed dry from Friday morning, and opened her first bottle as soon as Raymond left on Sunday evening. Then she drank herself through the week to steel herself for the next forty-eight hours of sobriety. However, she was indisputably Raymond's mum and Raymond was doing fine.

There was not much to mention about the other residents, apart from Olav.

"We've really got our hands full with that one," sighed Cathrine, an anorexic day shift worker in her thirties. "Honestly, everybody, I'm actually scared of that boy! I haven't a chance when he refuses to budge!"

"Eat a bit more, then," Terje muttered, but was ignored.

"It was pretty melodramatic when his mother was leaving on Thursday," remarked Eirik, who had been on duty then. "He hung on to her legs, and she just stood there stock-still, staring at me, without even attempting to bring him to his senses. When I crouched down to try, I got this for my trouble!"

Leaning forward over the table, he tilted his head to one side, and everybody could see a bluish-yellow ring surrounding his left eye.

"The boy's downright dangerous! And his mother is creepy, for sure!"

"He never attacks the other children," Maren objected. "Quite the opposite, for he can actually be helpful. He has good habits and polite manners when he wants to show them. We mustn't exaggerate. As far as his mother's concerned, she's just desperate."

"Exaggerate! Is it not melodramatic when he kicks me in the eye, threatens to kill me, and then rips up all the other children's drawings into a thousand pieces?"

"As long as it's you and the drawings that suffer, then we have to take it in our stride," Agnes concluded, without even mentioning that morning's dramatic episode and indicating the meeting was over by packing her papers together. While chairs scraped the floor as the others stood up, she made a restraining motion with her hand and added, "I'd like to have an interview with each and every one of you," she said, without looking at any of them. "A kind of appraisal interview."

"Appraisal interview?"

Cathrine pointed out it was not normal to conduct reviews now, without warning and two months in advance of the due date.

"We're having them now. They'll be fairly brief. Terje, you first. We'll go up to my office."

In reality if not by name, Maren Kalsvik functioned as a kind of deputy director at Spring Sunshine, and she scrutinized her boss now. Agnes seemed exhausted. Her hair was lifeless, and the features of her usually round, smooth face had become sharper. Unbecoming shadows were visible underneath her eyes, and she occasionally appeared almost uninterested in the children. It had to be her marriage. Maren and Agnes weren't exactly friends, but they worked closely together and sometimes chatted about this and that when they were alone. Her marriage had been ailing in the past few months, that much she knew, and perhaps it was more serious than Agnes had confided. The punishment she had dished out for Olav's outburst was troubling. Had Agnes gone stark raving mad? Maren would use the interview to probe her boss's psychological state. She would ensure that Olav's punishment was overturned, and rightfully so. Punishing children by denying them the company of their parents was not only uneducational, it was also totally illegal.

"Can I be number two?" she asked. "I have a dentist's appointment later today."

Agnes did not complete the interviews with her colleagues until almost four hours had elapsed, despite the final two interviews lasting only ten minutes.

The house seemed to be breathing. Deeply and quietly. A safe, snug fortress for eight sleeping children.

At least they're having a good rest, Eirik thought contentedly as he switched off the TV.

The hour had drawn on until half past midnight, but, unusually for him, he did not feel tired. Could he have been asleep without noticing? He lifted a deck of playing cards and started a game of solitaire, normally a good sleeping pill, and after cheating a couple of times, it drifted over him. It would be just as well to use the bed that was made on the upper floor. On the way upstairs, he noticed Agnes had not left for home yet, or at least he had not observed her departure. It was unlikely that Agnes would leave without popping her head in the door of the TV room to say good night. Come to think of it, he did not understand why she had returned earlier that evening at around ten o'clock. All the reports were up-to-date, as that had been undertaken during the meeting earlier that day, and now she had been in her office for quite some time. He glanced again at the clock. Almost one. Stepping warily, he took a left turn in the corridor on the first floor and slowly depressed the door handle of the twins' bedroom. They were both lying in Kim-André's bed, looking like little angels with their arms around each other and small, open mouths breathing lightly and regularly. Eirik cautiously took hold of Roy-Morgan and lifted him over to his own bed, where the boy mumbled sleepy protests before rolling onto his stomach, sighing, and returning to his slumbers. As usual, the boys had left their light on. Leaving it like that, Eirik continued on his rounds.

They were all asleep. Raymond was snoring, his mouth open and head upturned, lying on his back with arms and legs spread-eagled, falling halfway off the narrow bed with his quilt reposing on the floor. Picking it up, the night attendant returned the long boyish legs to their rightful place without disturbing the occupant and stuffed the edge of the quilt down between the mattress and the edge of the bed in the forlorn hope that it would not slide off again.

He glanced across at Olav's bed, and froze. The bed was empty. That did not add up. Although he had been watching television, he would have noticed if the boy had gone out, as the door to the dayroom had been open. Or had it been? He felt hot under the collar.

Youngsters had run off before. It was easy to avoid coming home from school, or from a visit to the city or whatever. But this was his fault, and it was the middle of the night. And Olav was only twelve years old.

The window was open. The fire rope, fastened to a hook under the windowsill, hung out. Pushing the window wide open, Eirik stared down at the ground five meters below. But the boy had not dared to go near the ropes!

Without any thought about waking the sleeping children, he rushed out into the corridor, past the staff bedroom, shouting when he had reached almost two meters from the director's office inside the corridor at the right of the stairs, "Agnes! Agnes! Olav's run away!"

Storming into the office, he came to a halt, totally thunderstruck.

Behind her mahogany writing desk, purchased at a flea market for three hundred kroner, with a potted plant, telephone, cheap plastic writing surface, and red cup containing four pens and a pencil arrayed in front of her, Agnes Vestavik was sitting perfectly still. Her stare penetrated right through him with an expression of surprise and her mouth half open, a little rivulet of coagulated blood running down from one corner of her mouth. Though it was no longer running.

After standing rooted to the spot for half a minute, Eirik shuffled slowly and stiffly around the desk, as if showing respect for the dead. For she was as dead as she could be: thirteen centimeters of a knife shaft protruded from her back, at about the height of her heart.

Clasping his hands in front of his face, Eirik burst into tears.

CHAPTER
THREE

"That I solemnly swear."

She let her right hand fall. There were few things Chief Inspector Hanne Wilhelmsen liked less than being a witness in court. It was true that police officers — in contrast with other witnesses — were allowed to a large extent to attend by appointment, with the prosecutor phoning half an hour before they were due to appear in the witness box. Nevertheless, something always happened to cause a delay. Besides, it took time to bring to mind something that had occurred eighteen months, perhaps two years, earlier. Simply locating the case documents consumed enough time. The simplest solution would be to receive a copy of the prosecutor's documents a couple of days in advance, but Hanne Wilhelmsen knew, in common with the other fifteen hundred police officers at Oslo Police Station, that this was accomplished only in one of ten instances. The police attorneys proffered assurances and promises, but the papers never arrived, and as a rule one ended up rummaging through an archive that was more or less homemade.

Her court appearance concerned a triviality. Sitting with somber expressions, the gown-clad prosecutors were spending their working day investigating whether a twenty-one-year-old girl had bitten a police officer in the leg and spat in his ear during a demonstration.

Slurping on chewing gum, the young woman tugged at her lilac-colored hair and looked daggers at the chief inspector as she assumed her place in the witness box, dressed in full uniform. Hanne Wilhelmsen did not hear the word, but judging by the lip movements she could swear the accused formed the word "pig" before leaning back with an exaggerated sigh and casting her eyes to the ceiling, with her defense counsel making no move to ask her to behave more decorously.

The questioning this time was swiftly over and done with. Hanne Wilhelmsen had in fact seen what had taken place. In her off-duty hours she had happened to pass the square at Stortorget as a small group of people, pretty accurately known by the name of Blitz Youth, was furiously screaming about the bar they were standing outside being a fascist den. In fact, their description was spot on, as the police had known for a long time that it was the haunt of right-wing extremist groups. At the moment Hanne Wilhelmsen was walking past, the girl with the lilac hair was being hauled out and handcuffed by two officers, without offering much resistance. Chief Inspector Hanne Wilhelmsen had stopped and was standing only three or four meters away when the Blitzer asked one of the police officers if she could tell him a secret. Before he had time to answer, she had leaned toward his ear and dispatched a substantial lump of chewing gum and spittle. The enraged police officer had dropped her to the ground, whereupon the girl sank her teeth into his boot, just above the ankle. There must have been considerably greater strain on the accused's teeth and jaw than the shoe leather, especially since the bad-tempered police officer tried to shake her off. Eventually letting go, she had started to laugh, and at that was yanked onto her feet and packed into a waiting police van.

"Did you see clearly that she bit the policeman in the leg?"

It was the prosecutor posing the question, a small assistant police attorney of tender years, with red roses on his beardless cheeks. Wilhelmsen knew that this was his very first case.

"Well, to the extent that boots form a part of your leg, yes," responded the chief inspector, gazing at the judge.

He looked as though he might die of boredom at any moment.

"There is no doubt that she bit him?"

The prosecutor was insistent.

"She bit the police officer's leather boot. The court will have to decide whether that is biting him in the leg."

"Did you see that she had spat first?"

Hanne Wilhelmsen tried not to smile.

"Yes, she spat a large splodge of chewing gum right in his ear. It looked unpleasant."

The red-cheeked lawyer was satisfied, and the defense counsel did not have many questions either. Wilhelmsen was allowed to leave.

The girl would probably be behind bars for thirty days. Violence toward a public servant. Not good. As the chief inspector emerged from the new Oslo Courthouse onto the open space of C. J. Hambros plass, she stood still for a second, gently shaking her head.

"We spend our time and money on a lot of bizarre things," she muttered before flagging down a passing police car and being transported back to Grønlandsleiret 44, Oslo Police Station.

Her new office was twice as spacious as the old one and accompanied her job as chief inspector. Having been named to the post barely six months prior, Hanne was still unsure if she was actually comfortable with it. Administrative duties were no fun and at times deathly tedious. On the other hand, it was challenging to lead others in what she did best: investigation. She personally played a more active part in police work than was usual for chief inspectors, and she knew it was a topic of discussion, not all positive. With increasing clarity she realized that on the whole the position she had enjoyed for many years of being everyone's heroine, fortunately spared criticism and conflict, was over. Whereas previously she had constructively but noncommittally suggested rational solutions that others had implemented and taken the rap for, she now had the power and accountability to bear the brunt herself. As an ordinary detective she had withdrawn from every personal antagonism, every hint of intrigue, performing her job and discharging her duties splendidly, and then returned home with admiring glances following in her wake. Now she was right in the thick of it, with no escape route, her responsibilities making it necessary to mediate, make decisions, and control other people. Perhaps this ran counter to her internal instincts. So much of her life had been spent building a bulkhead between herself and others, a barrier she depended upon in order to hide behind. Whenever.

Hanne Wilhelmsen was not at all sure she was comfortable.

"Hanne, my turtledove, my sweetheart!"

A bronzed giant filled the doorway, wearing faded jeans without a belt, with a heavy gold chain attached to one belt loop and ending at the watch pocket on his right hip. His T-shirt was a fiery shade of red and emblazoned with a black instruction to FUCK OFF! above his broad chest. On his feet he had black boots with huge genuine spurs at the heels. His head was covered in half-a-centimeter-long blond, bristling hair. The beard was far longer, and to make matters worse, it was copper red.

"Billy T.! You've grown your hair!"

Chief Inspector Hanne Wilhelmsen stood up and was immediately subjected to an energetic display of affection from her burly visitor, who swept her off her feet and swung her around so vigorously that her coffee cup spilled over and the wastepaper basket was hurtled several meters across the floor. Finally he deposited her on the floor again, giving her a big smacking kiss on the chops, and then flopped down on a chair that appeared to be four sizes too small.

They had known each other since Police College, and in contrast to most of her other male friends, he had never ever come on to her. On the contrary, he had helped her out of embarrassing situations several times by being some kind of knight in shining armor, and she knew that at one time rumors had circulated about them. After he had acquired children here and there, none of them hers, fresh and entirely different rumors had circulated about her and he could not save her from that, but he had never, not for a moment, withdrawn from her. Quite the opposite: one beautiful night nine months earlier, during the legendary hot spring when they had all been on the verge of drowning in a crashing wave of criminality, he had forced her to face up to herself in a way that made her begin to think seriously, deep within herself, about the way she lived her life. But only deep within herself.

"I've just had a bloody wonderful time," he declared, beating her to it. "I've had a marvelous time, the boys have had a brilliant time, and to top it all I've met a bloody fantastic woman."

A fortnight in the Canary Islands. She wished it had been her.

"And now you're well rested and ready for work. With me. For me."

Her voice smooth as silk, she leaned toward him across the desk.

"To think I'm going to experience that. Being Billy T.'s boss. Every boss's nightmare. I'm looking forward to it!"

44

He contentedly stretched out his six-and-a-half-foot-tall body, folding his hands at the back of his neck.

"If I could ever adapt to having a boss, then it would have to be a lovely lady. And if I could ever adapt to a lovely lady, then it would have to be you. This will go well."

Billy T. had become a detective again. After many years as a cop in denims in Oslo Police Station's drug intervention unit, he had allowed himself to be persuaded by Hanne Wilhelmsen, who had even written his transfer application for him. It had cost her many bottles of red wine and a pricey dinner before he had signed up, at two o'clock one Saturday night. At nine o'clock the next morning he had phoned her in desperation, attempting to have the application form ripped to shreds, but she had laughed. It was out of the question. Now he was sitting here, obviously looking forward to it himself too.

"And the first thing you have to tackle is this."

She handed him three green folders, not too voluminous. A knife attack from the previous Saturday, a suspicious infant death that probably was a case of sudden infant death syndrome, and another death at the other end of the life span that would quite possibly turn out to be alcohol poisoning.

"These are child's play," she said.

Then she produced another folder.

"And this is the real work. A murder. Old-fashioned stabbing, right out of a cheap thriller. In a foster home! It happened last night. Talk to the crime scene team. Good luck. I'd prefer to have a load of people on the case, but with this double murder in Smestad last week, this is how it has to be. Four detectives max. Anyway, you'll be the lead investigator."

"Fuck, is that already decided?"

"Yes." She smiled ingratiatingly. "You'll work with Erik and Tone-Marit in the meantime."

Billy T. stood up and gathered his belongings with a heavy sigh.

"I should've been down there," he groaned.

"I'm glad you're not." Hanne Wilhelmsen's smile was saccharine sweet as she added, "T-shirts like that won't do here. Go and change it at once! And at the very least before you set off for the foster home!"

"We'll see about that," he muttered, deciding to wear the same shirt all week, before trudging out the door with spurs clinking.

Billy T. had changed his T-shirt all the same. On further reflection he had decided that the message was not suitable for children in a foster home, and now he was wearing a neutral white button-down shirt beneath an enormous well-worn sheepskin coat. He bumped his head on the doorframe as he clambered out of the undersized unmarked police car, making a futile attempt to rub away the pain on his way up the garden path. It was cold after a period of mild weather, and the gravel, dry and frosty, crunched under his pointed boots. Hanne Wilhelmsen had accompanied him. Billy T.'s strides were so long that she was forced to jog beside him.

"I ought to have danger money for driving these cars," Billy T. commented bitterly. "Am I bleeding?"

Bending over, he turned the crown of his head toward his colleague. The scalp was visible under the stubble of hair, with cuts and scars from a multitude of earlier collisions, but he was not bleeding.

"Wimp," Hanne Wilhelmsen said, kissing it better and opening a blue entrance door on which a half-moon-shaped window was divided into three at face height. A little flowery curtain prevented them from seeing inside.

They entered a porch, with cloakroom hooks along the wall on one side and a three-shelf wooden shoe rack on the other. A cheerful chaos of shoes in sizes from 32 to 44 was piled both on and around the shelves, but before Hanne Wilhelmsen had made up her mind whether to remove her footwear, Billy T. had already headed through the next door, and she followed after him with her shoes on. To their right, a staircase led to another floor, and the room facing them was a kind of sitting room. The place was deserted and silent.

"Cozy, really," Billy T. mumbled to himself as he lowered his head to avoid a mobile made of colorful cardboard witches decorated with crepe paper and dead birch rods. "This isn't quite how I had envisioned it."

"Did you picture it more like something out of Dickens? Or what did you imagine?" Hanne Wilhelmsen asked, standing still and listening. "It's so incredibly quiet here!"

In answer, a woman came running down the stairs. Somewhere in her late twenties, with long blonde hair in a French braid, she wore an embroidered quilted vest and flared denim jeans that were either bang up-to-date or heirlooms from the seventies.

"Sorry," she said breathlessly. "I was on the phone! Maren Kalsvik."

Her handshake was firm, but her eyes were red ringed and bloodshot. Her face was bare, with no hint of makeup, but her eyelashes were dark and unusually long. It must be her hair that was bleached, although it did not appear to be.

"All the youngsters have been transferred elsewhere. Just for the next twenty-four hours. It was the police . . ."

She stopped, somewhat bewildered.

"That is to say, the ones who were here during the night and early this morning, your colleagues . . . They were the ones who said so. That the children shouldn't be here while they were inspecting the place. The crime scene, I mean."

Running a slim hand with short nails over her fringe, she appeared even more exhausted.

"You'll probably want to see it as well."

Without waiting for a reply, she turned on her heel and walked upstairs again, the two police officers following her. The corridor they reached had a window at either end; the gable walls of the house and the corridor itself probably were about two meters wide, with doors on either side. They turned right, obviously heading for the room that lay farthest in, on the

48

left-hand side. Maren Kalsvik paused at the doorway and drew back, her eyelashes glittering with tears.

"We've been told not to go inside."

That did not apply to Hanne Wilhelmsen, who crept underneath the red-and-white plastic tape draped across with a warning not to enter the room. Pulling the tape down, Billy T. stepped across.

"She was sitting there," Hanne said, nodding in the direction of a desk chair upholstered in red woolen fabric while she leafed through a folder she had produced from a large shoulder bag. "With her back to the window. Facing the door."

For a moment she stood staring at the desk as Billy T. approached the window.

"Odd position, as a matter of fact," she added, directing herself to Maren Kalsvik, who was still standing at a respectful distance from the doorway. "Desks are usually placed facing a wall."

"It was her way of saying that everybody was welcome to come in," Maren replied. "She would never sit with her back turned."

Billy T. opened the window and cold, fresh air blasted into the room. Maren Kalsvik came closer to the plastic tape but jumped back when she discovered it was about to loosen at one end.

"The window was locked from inside," she informed them. "At least that's what the police said this morning. The catches were closed."

Billy T. tugged at a substantial spiral hook screwed into the wall right beside the windowsill.

"Fire rope fastener?"

He did not wait for a response but instead leaned out and peered downward. The ground below the window was covered by a thin layer of old snow, with no prints. As he let his eye run over the house wall, he noticed an obvious trail underneath the other four large windows on the upper floor. The snow had been trampled away entirely, and dozens of footprints crisscrossed the earth. Pulling his head back inside, he rubbed his earlobes.

"Where does that door lead?" he asked, pointing to a narrow door on the side wall.

"That's the staff bedroom. We sometimes use it as an office as well. That's where I was sitting speaking on the phone when you arrived."

"Is it eight children who live here?"

"Yes, we've actually got room for nine; we have a spare bed at present."

"Are all the bedrooms here on the first floor?"

She nodded. "They're situated along the corridor here. On both sides. I can show you them."

"Yes. Shortly," Hanne Wilhelmsen said. "Has anything been reported stolen?"

"No, not as far as we can see. We don't know, of course, what might have been in the drawers, but . . . the drawers are locked. They haven't been broken open."

"Where's the key?"

When she posed the question, Hanne Wilhelmsen was standing half turned away from Maren Kalsvik but nevertheless thought she noticed a hint of confusion cross the woman's face as she turned and made eye contact. Just a touch. Perhaps it was simply a figment of her imagination.

"It's under the plant pot," Maren Kalsvik answered. "On the bookshelf over there."

"Aha," Billy T. said as he lifted the decorative pot.

No key.

Maren Kalsvik seemed genuinely surprised.

"It's usually there. Perhaps the police have taken it?"

"Maybe."

The police officers exchanged a look, and Hanne Wilhelmsen jotted something in a spiral notebook before stuffing the papers back in her bag and indicating that they wanted to see the bedrooms.

Olav and Raymond shared a room. So did Glenn and Kenneth, while Anita and Jeanette had the room farthest away at the other end of the corridor. The twins stayed on the opposite side of the corridor. Two rooms were unoccupied.

"Why do some have to share when there are two empty bedrooms?"

"For social reasons. Kenneth is scared to be on his own. The twins want to be together. Olav . . ."

She stopped abruptly and repeated her continual hand movement across her fringe. "Olav is the one who disappeared. Agnes thought . . ."

Now she was clearly on the verge of tears. She took a couple of convulsive breaths before pulling herself together.

"Agnes thought Raymond would be a good influence on Olav. He's tough and big and actually quite good with the younger ones. Although he protested about

51

having a new roommate. From purely social, or educational reasons, if you will. The empty rooms are used for doing homework and that kind of thing."

"Have you still not heard from the runaway?"

"No. We're dreadfully worried. He hasn't gone home, but that's not particularly odd. He had no money, as far as we know, and it's a terrible distance to walk."

Billy T. strode along the corridor, counting out the meters under his breath. Back at the director's office, he had to raise his voice so the others could hear him.

"This window here, it doesn't usually remain open?"

He could see from the faint lilac-colored dust along the ledges that the technicians had been searching for prints.

"No," Maren called back. "It's always closed at this time of year. But we had a fire drill yesterday. The youngsters were flying up and down the ropes and ladders for an hour."

He could see that. The window had become warped and opened only very stiffly, but he banged it open with brute force. Below, he saw the same jumble of footprints that he had spotted underneath the windows on the other wall of the house. The emergency ladder could slide along the wall so that it could not be accessed from the ground. It was broad and sturdy, with rough, scuffed rungs. He tentatively released the lock on either side, and the lower part tumbled to the ground on well-greased runners. A solid piece of machinery. He pulled on a wire that looped over a smaller runner at the side of the window, and the lower part of the ladder returned obediently. When it was all the way up, it clicked decisively, and Billy T. folded the locking mechanism back into place before closing the window, quickly ascertaining that the rooms opposite the director's office were two bathrooms, one large and one small, and approached the two women again without uttering a word.

"We must interview all of you," Hanne Wilhelmsen was saying, almost apologetically. "You'll be called in turn. It would be a fantastic help if you could take the trouble to compile a list of everyone who lives here, and even more important, everyone who works here. Their names and dates of birth, of course, but also their background, residence, family situation, how long they have worked here, and so on. As speedily as possible."

The woman nodded.

The two police officers returned to the ground floor with Maren Kalsvik at their heels. They inspected the remainder of the house in silence, making a few notes. The woman with the French braid closed the door behind them around an hour after their arrival.

Without further instructions, Billy T. jumped over a low-growing hedge dividing the gravel path from the grassy lawn. Turning up his jacket lapels, he buttoned up in front with the two remaining buttons that had not yet been torn off and thrust his hands into his pockets. Then he scurried around the corner, stopping below the only gable window on the first floor, around six meters above the ground. Understanding what he was up to, Hanne Wilhelmsen followed close behind.

A week of mild weather had soaked the terrain to such an extent that numerous footprints, small and large, were outlined on the brown earth. Frost had set in that morning, and the area now looked like a miniature lunar landscape, with shallow valleys and sharp little mountains crisscrossing, lacking any structure and utterly lacking any significance.

"That fire drill happened at a helluva convenient time," Billy T. commented glumly. "Even the most finicky crime scene technician would be at a loss here."

"But they have made an effort all the same," Hanne said, waving her finger toward tiny particles of plaster that almost merged into the patches of frost, and the red contrast spray in several of the prints. "If anyone walked here *after* the fire drill — and they would of course have had to do that if they were using this route into the house — then those footprints would be *on top.* Do we know when the frost set in?"

"Not until the early hours of the morning. In fact, it was still soft underfoot here when the police arrived at half past one."

The chief inspector picked her way carefully around the well-trodden area in the private hope that it still harbored a secret or two they might be able to wrest from it. She subsequently took up position immediately beside the wall and stretched up to reach the folded fire ladder. There was a gap of more than half a meter from her fingertips to the foot of the ladder.

"Can you manage it?"

Tentatively they exchanged places, but even Billy T., six foot seven in his stocking feet and with arms like a gorilla, had some distance to go to reach the bottom rung of the ladder.

"An umbrella or something with a hook at the end would be enough," Hanne Wilhelmsen said, blowing on her right hand.

"No, the catch prevents it from being pulled down from here. I checked it from the top. Solid machinery. This ladder here can only be operated from inside. Exactly as it should be. And it can also only be put back in place again from inside. If you pushed it up from here, you'd have to be fairly strong to replace it on its catch up there. And you haven't a chance of locking it."

"But then," Hanne Wilhelmsen said, "we've the following choice: either this isn't the way the murderer entered the building, or else we have a very limited list of suspects."

Although Billy T.'s expression revealed he was fully aware of her reasoning, she added quietly, "Because if the ladder was used, then it was used by someone who had access in order to lower it earlier in the evening, so it was standing ready for use, *and* had the opportunity to lock it again afterward. From inside. Realistically, that means one of the staff."

"Or one of the youngsters," Billy T. muttered, shivering.

The temperature continued to drop.

The hunger was worse, even though he was freezing as well. Really he should have put on more clothes. Long underpants, for example, would have been useful. Luckily he had kept an outdoor jacket in his room, though his leather jacket that was hanging downstairs on a hook in the porch with his name in cheerful flowery lettering above it would have been better. But he hadn't thought. Or he hadn't taken the chance. Anyway, his sneakers weren't particularly suitable for this time of year. And his tongue was stinging like fuck.

The fire rope had been bloody easy. Glenn and Terje had said he didn't dare, but it was just that he couldn't be bothered. Not then. He couldn't be bothered with anything when someone was dishing out orders. But it had gone really well when there was a point to it. Even with the rucksack on his back.

How far he had walked since he had left the foster home was impossible to calculate, but it felt like many kilometers.

"I'm probably still in Oslo," he said under his breath in an attempt to convince himself, as he peered from the garage at the million twinkling lights of the city underneath a pink haze down the hillside below him.

It was stupid that he didn't have any money. He hadn't thought about that either. Inside a sock, tucked deep in the third shelf of the closet in the room he shared with Raymond, he had stashed a hundred and fifty kroner. Mum had given it to him. A hundred and fifty kroner was a lot of money, maybe even enough money for a taxi all the way home. He had a feeling, somewhere deep down inside, that this was exactly the reason he had been given precisely that sum of money. A hundred kroner or two hundred kroner would have been more logical.

"Logical means that something is easy to understand."

His teeth were chattering, and he pressed his hands against his stomach as it emitted a long, low growl for food.

"I'm starving to death," he continued quietly as his teeth set off on an uncontrollable merry dance. "Either I'll freeze to death, or I'll starve to death."

The house to which the garage he was sitting in belonged lay in darkness, although his Swatch showed it was ten past nine in the evening. At five o'clock he had expected that someone would arrive home, but no one came. There was no car there either, despite the colossal size of the garage. Perhaps they were away, the people who lived here. It was probably a family. Outside the entrance steps there was a handsome sledge, the kind with skis underneath and a steering wheel. At Christmas he had been so sure he would receive one like that, but then he was given a paint box instead. Mum had looked sorry. But he knew she was hard up. He had been given a Power Ranger as well, and at least that was something he had wanted. But Mum didn't remember it was the red one he had yearned for. The red one was the boss. He had got the green one. Just like the time two years ago when he'd got the Michelangelo turtle when he had wanted only Raphael.

Maybe he had slept for a while. At least he was surprised to see the time was now past midnight. The middle of the night. It was a long time since he had been awake so late. The house was still deserted. His hunger was so great that he felt dizzy when he stood up. Without really making a decision about it, he approached the outer door. Of course it was locked. With an ordinary lock and padlock.

He stood on the concrete stair, his hand resting indecisively on the wrought-iron railing. For ages. Then he peered over the edge, down at a fairly large basement window reaching all the way to the ground. He trudged down the four steps, and before thinking about it any further, had used the sledge as a battering ram to smash the window. It dawned on him there might not be enough room for him to slide through the window frame, but it went smoothly. He threw his rucksack down first. On the inside, there was a long counter only a meter from the window, so it wasn't even creepy making his way inside. Because he was quite afraid of the dark, he managed to locate a light switch, and a considerable number of seconds went by before it struck him it was obviously pretty stupid to have the light on. Holding the door handle tightly, he darkened the room and stepped out into a little corridor where a staircase leading to the ground floor was visible in the very faint light entering from outside, through the broken window. Fortunately, the door to the ground floor was not fitted with a lock.

There wasn't much food in the refrigerator. There was no milk, for example. He also couldn't find any bread, although he looked high and low. But there were a few eggs in a drawer in the fridge door, and Olav knew how to cook eggs. First you had to boil the water, and then wait for seven minutes. Although he hadn't eaten eggs with fish cakes before, it tasted delicious now. He was so hungry. It was slightly difficult to eat without touching the wound on his tongue, and the stitches constantly grated on everything, but it was okay. And the entire pantry was full of canned food.

It was two o'clock before he fell asleep, in a darkened kitchen with no cover other than a long lady's coat he found in the hallway. Totally exhausted, he didn't even have the energy to think about what he would do the next day. That didn't matter. Now he just wanted to sleep.

He was only three years old the first time he injured me. Really it wasn't his fault. He was just a burly three-year-old. Although he picked up such a horrendous amount, and the kindergarten boasted that he was so smart (maybe they were just trying to comfort me), he still had only about ten words to say. Mummy was not one of them. He must have been the only child in the history of the world who couldn't say Mummy. His kindergarten teacher reassured me by saying that all children were different. She had a brother who was a professor, she said, and he hadn't spoken a single word until he was four. As though that would be any concern of mine.

I had made the dinner. He was sitting in his Tripp Trapp chair that I'd been given money by social services to buy. There was only just enough room for him behind the safety rail, but I couldn't really take that off, as he wasn't old enough yet. He was extra grumpy. I had accidentally burned his fish fingers; I had suddenly suffered from an upset stomach and spent ages in the toilet. The charred pieces were inedible, but fortunately I had more in the freezer. He began to get impatient. I was becoming dreadfully nervous because of all his screaming. Noisy, tearless, and disruptive screaming.

The neighbors gave me meaningful looks if I fumbled slightly too long with the lock on the garbage chute and was unlucky enough to encounter one of them, so they must have heard him.

I didn't have anything other than a packet of licorice boats to give him to pacify his impatience. It disappeared fast. When I was finally able to shovel five fish fingers over from the frying pan to his plate decorated with Karius and Baktus, I thought he was satisfied. After putting the frying pan back on the cooker to cool down, I sat myself directly across from him and peeled two potatoes. He looked contented, with his mouth full of fish. I smiled at him, he was so sweet and angelic as he sat there, so quiet and happy. I reached out for his hand.

Without any kind of warning, he stabbed his fork into the back of my hand. It was only a child's fork, luckily, the kind with only three tines, almost like a cake fork. But it broke through my skin with a strength that no one would believe came from a three-year-old child, and blood spurted out. I was so gobsmacked that I couldn't do anything. He tore the fork loose and put all his strength behind another lunge. The pain was indescribable. But the worst thing of all was that I was so scared. I sat with a three-year-old facing me, and I was more afraid of him than I had ever been of his drunken father.

My God, I was scared of my three-year-old son!

Terje Welby had been lying awake for three hours, the adrenaline coursing suddenly and undesirably through him every time he was anywhere near the verge of sleep. The sheet was already damp from his exertions. He hauled himself around, moaning; his back was bothering him. Placing the pillow over his head, he muttered to himself, "I *must* sleep. I simply *must* sleep."

The telephone rang.

He battered his hand on the bedside light and the glass shade scudded to the floor, smashing into a thousand pieces. He sat up, sucking the blood from his fingers and staring in dismay at the telephone.

It did not give up, and it seemed as though the noise jangled more and more. All of a sudden he grabbed the receiver.

"Hello!"

"Hi, Terje, it's Maren here. Sorry for phoning in the middle of the night."

"It doesn't matter," he rushed to say, noticing on the bedside clock that the day was only three hours old.

"Terje, I need to know."

"Know what?"

"You know what I mean."

He sat up against the headboard, pulling at his clammy T-shirt.

"No, honestly, I don't!"

Silence fell.

"Had Agnes found out about it?" she asked at last.

He swallowed so loudly she could hear it over the phone.

"No. She hadn't found out."

If nothing else, he was pleased she could not see him.

"Terje, don't be angry."

"I'm not angry."

"Tell me."

"Tell you what?"

"Was it you who killed her?"

"No, Maren, it wasn't me. I did not kill her." His back was more painful than ever.

CHAPTER
FOUR

"Look at them out there. Look at them!"

Charging into the sparsely equipped chief inspector's office without knocking, Billy T. gesticulated out toward Åkebergveien, where two men in coats were scuffling wildly. A Volvo was sitting there with its snout impertinently far up the backside of the latest model Toyota Corolla.

"There was a bang, and then the guy in front flew out and hauled the other guy from his car without as much as a hello! I bet ya a hundred that the Volvo'll win."

"Who is the owner of the Volvo?" Hanne asked without showing much interest but at least standing up and moving over to the window where Billy T. was now positioned, in brilliant good humor.

"The guy with the lighter coat. The tall one."

"I'm not betting against him," Hanne said, as the man in question dealt a perfect right hook to the Toyota owner, who stumbled backward, losing his footing and falling to the ground.

"Self-defense, pure and simple," Billy T. roared. "It was the Toyota who started it!"

As the man struck down was attempting to clamber back to his feet, two uniformed police officers came running. With no caps or jackets, they had probably seen the incident from some window or other as well.

"Typical Torvald," Billy T. commented irritably. "Spoiling everything."

He remained standing for a minute to see how things turned out, but of course the two combatants stopped fighting as soon as they clapped eyes on the pair in uniform. They obviously smoothed it over and were surprisingly quickly absorbed in completing an insurance claim form.

"Life offers pleasures large and small," Billy T. said as he sat down to face his boss. "Though it hasn't decided to give us particularly much in the way of pleasures in this foster home case."

"Oh?"

"Forensic traces: millions. Usable: zilch."

An enormous fist covered the cigarette packet lying on Hanne Wilhelmsen's desk.

"I've told you that you need to stop that," he interrupted himself. "You're killing yourself, darling."

"You know, I get enough of that at home. I can't bear having the same song and dance here too," she retorted with an unexpected note of irritation in her voice.

Billy T. was not so easily frightened off.

"Cecilie's the chick to tell you. She knows what's good for her girlfriend. A physician and all that."

Her expression darkening, Hanne Wilhelmsen swiftly rose to her feet and closed the half-open door to the corridor beyond. Billy T. made use of the opportunity to crumple the packet in his hand, with at least ten cigarettes inside, and throw the whole lot in the wastepaper bin.

"So. One packet fewer coffin nails," he declared in satisfaction.

She became angrier than he had anticipated.

"Listen here, Billy T. You're my friend. You put up with a lot from your friends. But I demand one thing: respect. *Both* for my insistence that I don't want talk about my private life when others can overhear, *and* for my belongings. Nag me if you like about my smoking, I know you do that with the best of intentions. *But leave my bloody things alone!*"

Furious, she leaned over the wastepaper basket and fished out the crumpled pack of cigarettes from among the paper and apple cores. A couple of the cigarettes had survived, although they were bent. Lighting one, she took several deep puffs.

"So. Where were we?"

Billy T. lowered his hands, left flailing in midair after his outburst.

"Apologies, apologies, Hanne. I really didn't mean to —"

"Okay," she truncated his remarks with a faint smile. "Forensic evidence."

"Loads," Billy T. mumbled, shamefaced and still taken aback by her violent reaction. "Fingerprints all over the shop, except where we want them. On the knife. It's entirely lacking in traces of the person who used it. A pretty ordinary knife. Bought at Ikea, of all places. That's the one place in the whole world where

65

it's totally impossible to find out anything about who purchased such an item. They sell millions of knives. As far as the footprints are concerned . . ."

He shifted position in his seat.

". . . they're unclear and of minimal value. You saw for yourself what it was like out there. But they're carrying out further work on checking them. Probably it'll turn out that they all originate from the children and adults at the home. In other words —"

Hanne interrupted him again. "In other words we're facing the most enjoyable and classical of all police work!"

She leaned forward, smiling. Billy T. did likewise, and with their faces only twenty centimeters apart, they chorused, "Tactical investigation!"

They laughed, and Hanne pushed a small bundle of typed papers toward him.

"This is the list of all the children and staff at the home. Maren Kalsvik compiled it."

"Then we have to take it for what it's worth, then, since she's also one of those under most suspicion."

"They all are," said Hanne curtly. "But look here."

The list contained a short CV of all the staff members. The youngest was Christian, who was twenty. The eldest was someone called Synnøve Danielsen, who had been there since the home opened in 1967. Like Christian, she had no professional qualifications, but in contrast to him, oceans of experience. Moreover, three of the staff were social workers, two were male nurses, three child welfare officers, one a kindergarten teacher, and one an auto mechanic. The final person on the list, Terje Welby, was a high school teacher with qualifications in history, education, and literature.

Spring Sunshine Foster Home was run by the Salvation Army, but the operational budget was predominantly met by the public purse. They had been allocated eleven and a half posts, filled by the fourteen members of staff, some part time.

"There are thirteen now," Billy T. commented laconically. "Who has taken over the director's post?"

"As far as I understand, it's Terje Welby, who is the assistant director, at least on paper. But he put his back out during the fire drill and was signed off sick today. Maren's probably running the show now."

"Hmm. Convenient."

"How so?"

"That sick leave."

"We'll have to check that out."

"That should be very simple. It'll be harder to find some motives among this lot here."

"There are always motives. The problem is just to find the person who has the strong enough motive. Besides, it could have been someone from outside, it could have been one of the children. Doesn't sound plausible, but we can't rule anything out. Have the children been interviewed?"

"Barely. It seems completely unlikely to me. The person on night duty had been on his rounds when he found the body, and he ought to have training to know whether children are really sleeping or just playacting. He swears they were all sleeping like logs. You would have to be a bit of a devil to have murdered your foster-carer and then fallen into a deep dreamless sleep."

He rubbed his hands over his face.

"No, the only possibility is of course the one who disappeared. He's a hard nut, apparently. Brand-new, only been there for three weeks. Bloody strange and difficult too."

Hanne Wilhelmsen leafed through the papers.

"A twelve-year-old? A twelve-year-old would hardly be able to stab with such force that the knife goes right through skin and bone to pierce the heart of a well-built woman!"

She stubbed out her cigarette determinedly in a tasteless brown glass ashtray.

"Well, he's said to be big, you know," Billy T. insisted. "Really abnormally large."

"In any case, it's a bad opening move to concentrate our efforts on a twelve-year-old boy. Leave that open for the moment."

Then she added, "Though it's imperative we find him, of course. For many reasons. He may have seen something. But in the meantime we need to rummage around in these people's private lives as thoroughly as possible. Look for everything. Expenditure, lovers, sexual inclinations, . . ."

A slight blush spread beneath the dark blue eyes, and she lit the last serviceable cigarette in order to deflect attention.

". . . family quarrels. Everything. What's more, we need to investigate the victim's life and lifestyle. Get things started."

"In that case I'll go for another visit to the home and see if there are any alternative routes for our murderer to arrive or leave," Billy T. said as he stood up.

It was half past two. Hanne Wilhelmsen paused for a moment's thought, calculating that she could be home by five.

"I'm coming too," she declared, scurrying after him across the blue linoleum in the corridor on the way to the elevator.

"You're not fucking suited to be a chief inspector, Hanne." He guffawed. "There's far too much curiosity in that skull of yours!"

"What a mouth you've got," she answered with mock severity.

As the massive metal doors guarding the entrance floodgates of Oslo Police Station closed hostilely behind them, she gripped his arm for a second and he came to a halt.

"You need to know one thing. You should be glad I can get so angry at you."

Then she marched on. He didn't understand a thing but was really keen to believe her.

All the children had returned now, and two identical boys of eight or nine years opened the door, staring in alarm at the tall bearded man.

"Hi there, boys, I'm Billy T. I'm a policeman. Are there any grown-ups here?"

The two boys seemed somewhat reassured as they withdrew, whispering. Billy T. and Hanne Wilhelmsen followed them. The last time they had visited, they had been struck by the silence. Now it seemed all the youngsters were exerting themselves to recover lost ground.

An almost adult boy was sitting in the middle of the floor tinkering with a bicycle. By his side sat a little sparrow of a lad, looking elated every time he was allowed to hold a tool. The older boy was talking to the younger one in a low, friendly voice, almost lost in the shouts from a fourteen-year-old who was running about triumphantly waving a bra with his outstretched arm and a hot-tempered girl chasing after him.

"Anita thinks she's got boobs!"

"Throw it here, Glenn! Here!"

The two eight-year-olds jumped around him, before one clambered up on an enormous worktable, waving his arms and continuing to yell, "Glenn, Glenn! Here!"

"Anita thinks she's got boobs," Glenn repeated, so tall that even if he had stopped now, the two-year-elder girl would not have been able to reach the embarrassing garment she so desperately wanted to retrieve and that he was now waving with his arm extended while standing on tiptoe.

"Jeanette, help me," Anita said plaintively.

"Give over, Glenn," was the only help she received from a plump young girl sitting totally unconcerned at the table, drawing. "Roy-Morgan! Don't step on my drawing!"

She reached out a clenched fist, causing the boy to cry out in pain and start to cry.

"Good heavens, children! Glenn, give over with that. Let Anita have her bra back. At once! And you!"

70

The eight-year-old who was standing on one leg up on the table, rubbing his other leg, leaped down to the floor before Maren Kalsvik managed to say anything further.

Then she caught sight of the two visitors in the doorway.

"Oh, sorry," she said in confusion. "I didn't know there was anybody here!"

"Anybody here?"

Billy T. grinned so broadly his teeth shone through his bushy beard.

"You've got a house full, so you have, woman!"

The two boys had continued fiddling with the bike on the floor directly in front of them.

"I've told you before, Raymond," Maren said with a resigned hand gesture. "You can do that down in the basement. This is not a workshop!"

"It's so cold down there," he protested.

She gave up, and the boy looked up at her in surprise.

"Is it okay, then, or . . ." he asked, taken aback.

Shrugging her shoulders, she redirected her attention to the two police officers. The last thirty-six hours had taken their toll. She had pulled her hair back with a simple rubber band rather than braiding it. Several strands had loosened, and together with the sunken shoulders and her baggy clothes, it gave her an almost slovenly look. Her eyes were still red-rimmed.

"Did you not get the lists?"

"Oh, yes," Hanne Wilhelmsen responded. "Thanks very much. They're a great help."

A brief nod in the direction of the children indicated to Maren Kalsvik that the police officers wanted to talk to her in a different location.

"We can go in here," she said, opening the door to a bright, attractive room with four beanbags, a sofa, and two armchairs in front of a twenty-eight-inch television in the left-hand corner beside the outer wall. The two women each sat in an armchair while Billy T. plumped down on a beanbag. He ended up almost flat on the floor, but Maren Kalsvik did not seem to notice.

"The guy who was on night duty, is he here now?" Hanne Wilhelmsen was speaking.

"No, he's on sick leave."

"Him too? Is there an epidemic here, or what?" Billy T. grumbled from his position near the floor.

"Terje hurt his back during the fire drill. Slipped disc, or something like that. He seemed fine when we finished, but the pains started during the course of the evening, he says. As far as Eirik is concerned, he's just about in shock. It can't have been very pleasant, finding her. He was totally unhinged when he phoned. At first I thought someone was playing a joke on me, and in fact I was about to put down the phone when I realized it was deadly serious. He was completely hysterical."

"Do you know where he was sitting?"

"Sitting?"

"Yes, was it not in this room that he was sitting for most of the evening?"

"Oh, I see, yes."

Running her hand through her hair was obviously a bad habit of hers.

72

"No, I'm not sure about that. But all the adults usually sit in one of the armchairs."

She looked at Billy T., blinking.

"He probably sat in this chair. It's the one nearest the TV. It's not usually on very loud."

Struggling to his feet, Billy T. stepped over to the door and swung it open.

"Do you keep the door open when you're sitting here?"

"There isn't any rule about it. But I usually do, at least. In case any of the children should call out. Or come down. Kenneth has walked in his sleep now and again."

"But you can't see out into the living room from that position!"

Maren Kalsvik turned around to face the policeman.

"That's not really necessary. The most important thing is to hear the children. They know that we usually sit here in the evenings. Some of us also sleep here, in fact, although there's a bed on the upper floor. The outside door always has to be kept locked."

"Does it sometimes happen that it's not?"

"Of course it might well happ —"

The little mechanic's assistant came in, crying, and hesitated for a moment before rushing past Billy T. in the doorway and catapulting himself onto Maren's lap.

"Glenn says that I killed Agnes," he sobbed.

"Kenneth, it's okay," she said into his ear. "What nonsense. There's nobody who thinks you killed Agnes. You were so fond of her. And you are so kind."

73

"But he says I did it. And he says the police have come to get me."

He was in floods of tears and gasped for breath as he clung to the woman. She tentatively held the little arms around her neck and loosened their grip in order to make eye contact.

"Dear little Kenneth. He's only teasing you. You know that Glenn loves to tease. You mustn't take it seriously. Ask that man there if they've come to get you. He's the policeman."

The boy seemed to shrink smaller and smaller. He had retained a premature appearance, with large, slightly protruding eyes and a narrow, almost pinched face ending in a sharp chin. Now he was looking at Billy T., frightened out of his wits, while convulsively clutching Maren Kalsvik's hand.

The officer hunkered down in front of the boy, smiling. "Kenneth. Is that your name?"

The boy nodded imperceptibly.

"My name's Billy T. Sometimes people call me Billy Coffee."

There was a glimmer in the tear-stained eyes.

"See, you've got a sense of humor too." He grinned and rumpled the boy's hair gently. "I'll tell you one thing, Kenneth. We don't think any of the children can have done this. And the thing we are one hundred percent, totally and completely, sure of, is that you haven't done anything wrong at all. Here . . ."

He extended his fist and took hold of the tiny child's hand that now had released Maren's.

"I'll shake your hand on one thing: you're not going to be taken away by any policemen. Because we know you haven't done anything wrong. I can see it in you. A handsome, honest guy. And I've had loads of training in seeing these things."

Now Kenneth was smiling, if not entirely convincingly.

"Quite sure?"

"Quite sure." Billy T. crossed his heart.

"Can you tell that to Glenn?" the boy whispered.

"Of course."

He stood up and discovered that Raymond, the bicycle repairer, was standing at the door, leaning on the doorframe with his arms crossed. They stared into each other's eyes for a fleeting moment, and then the boy started to speak, in a muted, almost monotonous voice. "Of course it's not Kenneth. It's no' me either. But I wouldn't be so sure that it can't be one of us. That Olav was a foulmouthed character. He's nearly as strong as a grown-up. And he's the most violent kid I've ever come across. What's more, he told me he was going to kill Agnes."

Silence descended, even the children in the other room were standing behind the boy in the doorway to hear the exchange. Hanne Wilhelmsen felt a strong impulse to put an end to it all by taking the boy to another room without spectators, but Billy T., realizing what she was about to say, made a dismissive gesture.

"He said that a few times. When we were going to bed, for instance. I didn't bother to answer, the new

75

ones are always so angry about everything and everybody."

Now he was smiling for the first time. Beneath his wispy hair and scarred face, he was actually good-looking, with even, white teeth and dark eyes.

"I was like that too, in the beginning. But with Olav it seemed kinda worse. He seemed absolutely deadly serious. He even told me how he was going to do it. He was going to use a knife, he said. I remember that well, because I thought it was so strange he wasn't going to use a shotgun or a machine gun, like I used to talk about. Of course, a knife's easier to get hold of. There's piles of them lying in the kitchen. So if I was a cop, I wouldn't look any further than that boy. He ran off too, you know."

He had obviously said his piece. Yawning, he made to turn and retreat to the living room. However, Billy T. stopped him.

"But the knife that was used to kill Agnes wasn't from here," he said quietly. "You don't buy your knives from Ikea."

Clearly totally uninterested, the boy shrugged his shoulders and continued on his way out the door. "Whatever you say," he muttered, almost inaudibly. "But I'd bet a hundred note on Olav."

Olav was extremely bored with canned food. Moreover, his thumb was painfully swollen. They didn't have an ordinary can opener there, at least not like the one his mum used. The one he had finally found was much smaller, and using it hurt his hand. Mostly he had eaten the canned food cold, and he was fed up with that. Struggling to half open the lid on a can of meatballs, he cut himself.

"Fucking hell!"

He stuck his finger in his mouth to suck the blood and whimpered when his thumb touched the wound on his tongue. Some of the blood had ended up in the sauce, creating a red filigree pattern in the pale brown gravy.

"Bloody lid."

Pouring the contents into an oversized saucepan, he gingerly turned one of the knobs on the cooker. The numbers and symbols showing which burner they belonged to were completely worn away, but he guessed right this time too. After a few minutes, the food began to bubble, and he stirred energetically a couple of times, scraping the base of the pan. Before the food was properly cooked through, he put the whole shebang down on the tabletop and ate from the saucepan.

By now he had spent one night and one day here, without leaving the kitchen. He slept there and ate there. The remainder of the time he sat on the floor, thinking. Once he had peered into the living room but became frightened by the huge curtainless panorama windows with their view over the entire city. For a moment he had considered moving the television set carefully into the kitchen but quickly discovered that the aerial cable would not reach.

Agnes was dead. That was something at least he was quite certain about, although he had never seen anyone dead before. She had such a strange expression on her face, and her eyes were open. He had always imagined that people closed their eyes when they died.

If only he could phone Mum ... There was a telephone in the hallway, secure and with no windows in sight. It even had a dial tone, for he had checked it out. But Mum's house was probably crawling with policemen. On the television it always showed them going to people's homes when they had done something wrong. They lurked in the bushes and then *bang!* they pounced when the person arrived. They were probably tapping the phone as well.

For a while he sat musing on where they had located the tape recorder they always used, with someone sitting wearing earphones listening in beside it. At the neighbor's house perhaps. She was a real cow. Or in the basement. Or maybe they even had one of those massive delivery trucks with no windows and lots of equipment installed inside.

Before he conceived of any reasonable answer to his puzzle, he fell fast asleep. Even though it was still early afternoon, despite being more alone than ever before, and very, very scared.

I was amazed at the child welfare service. They had visited me, so I must be located somewhere in their enormous filing cabinets. When the doorbell rang now and again — a salesman perhaps, or more likely a gang of hooligans who disappeared in a shower of yelling and screeching when I finally showed my face — I was paralyzed with fear. Most preferably I would sit as quiet as a mouse, pretending I was not here. But I knew they had their methods anyway, so I might as well open the door. It was never the child welfare service.

When the kindergarten called me to a private meeting one afternoon, I was nonetheless convinced. I wondered where I would go. That didn't take much time: I didn't have a single place to run to. My mother understood nothing, and all her fussing got on my nerves. Actually I believe she doesn't even like the child, just like everybody else. I had hardly seen anyone other than her since the boy was born. That was five years ago.

But the child welfare service wasn't present at the meeting either. It was only the director, and she had always treated me decently. Now she was serious and seemed angry that the boy was with me. But what on earth should I have done with him? I said nothing.

He had cut through the refrigerator cable that same day. It could have been dangerous for him. If it had been only the one time, then it might have been just a silly notion. A boyish prank. But she felt it was part of a destructive pattern, and he had become too demanding for them. He did not play with the other children. He spoiled everything for them. He knew no boundaries. He was hyperactive.

I said nothing. Inside my head was just a ghastly throbbing lump, and the only thing at all I managed to form a thought about was the fear of losing the kindergarten place. But I said nothing.

Perhaps she realized that, because suddenly she became friendlier. They had applied for support hours, she told me. Fifteen hours with an assistant per week. BUP and PPT and other abbreviations I had no idea about at that time, would be brought in. But she didn't say a word about children's services. Eventually I understood the most important point: my boy would be able to continue at kindergarten. My head cleared a little, and I began to breathe again. I felt a pain in my stomach.

The next day, at the social security office, I found a brochure. It was about MBD — minimal brain dysfunction. I was sitting beside the leaflets and flipped through them in boredom while trying not to make eye contact with the others sitting waiting there. But then something caught my eye. A checklist. A whole load of signs that children were suffering from brain damage, without anyone being to blame.

Everything fell into place! The restlessness, the energetic activity, the poor language skills when it was obvious he wasn't any more stupid than other children, the difficulties in playing with other children — it was as though I were reading about my own boy. There was something wrong with his brain. Something that nobody could have done anything about. Something that was nothing to do with me. I took three copies of the little leaflet with me and felt a glimmer of hope.

"It would obviously be a piece of cake to get past a sleepy night watchman sitting with his back turned, watching TV. Both up and down. As long as the door was open."

"Or if the murderer had a key. But that doesn't alter the fact of the person in question having to be familiar with the house. He or she must have known where the staff member on night duty was usually located, and also known the difference between all the similar doors on the first floor."

Billy T. had accompanied her home. They were now sitting at either end of a deep American sofa, while the pine table facing them was strewn with big feet. The room was not large, and it did not help matters that bookshelves covered one entire wall.

"And what's more," Hanne added, taking a gulp of her tea and realizing it was still too hot. "What's more, the person in question must have known that Agnes was there, on that very evening. She wasn't on duty, you know."

"No, but it's not at all certain that the murderer was there to kill anyone. It could have been something else he was after, and the knife may have been a security measure."

"What could anyone have been after in that office? The potted plant?"

"There were at least a few locked drawers, so there must have been something inside them. Though they hadn't been forced open. That key, though, do you remember that?"

Frowning, Hanne Wilhelmsen tilted her head slightly to one side.

"Yes," she exclaimed. "The key Maren Kalsvik said should be under the plant pot! She looked surprised when we didn't find it. Do you know where it is?"

"The crime scene technician had taken it. It's been examined for fingerprints. Nothing of any use."

"Had it been cleaned?"

"Not necessarily. On such a tiny key it only takes a little friction, quite naturally, for there be to be nothing to lift off. So we don't know anything about how far the murderer had ransacked the drawers. There were some papers there, several psychologists' reports and also the woman's own notes about totally trivial matters, purchases, memoranda, and so on."

"But *if* anyone was looking for something in the drawers, then it must be someone who knew where the key was to be found."

"Then we're looking first and foremost for someone who knew the home well," Billy T. concluded. "And who was at least prepared for Agnes to be there, and who either came to kill her or knew that he might have to do so in order to get hold of something in the director's office."

"That pretty much sums it up," Hanne said thoughtfully, as her partner, a blonde, slight woman appeared at the door.

"Billy T.! So good to see you! Are you staying for dinner? You're so taaaaned!"

Leaning over the man on the sofa, Cecilie Vibe kissed him on the cheek.

"Can't say no to dinner with the city's two nicest ladies, you know," he replied, grinning.

He did not leave for home until almost midnight.

CHAPTER
FIVE

Agnes Vestavik's husband was born on May 8, 1945, the day Norwegians were liberated from occupation by Nazi Germany. Nevertheless, he did not look happy or particularly peaceful. Billy T. knew he would have great difficulty remembering his facial features: a middle-sized mouth under a middle-sized nose under midblue eyes. His rather hostile countenance could of course be blamed on the unfortunate situation; the man's wife had been brutally murdered only two days previously, and now he was sitting here being questioned by the police. On the other hand, it could be a mannerism that had become fixed.

About five foot eleven, he obviously tolerated the family's eating habits better than his wife had done, as the guy was almost skinny. He was dressed as befitted the manager of a men's clothing store. Gray slacks in fine wool, a white shirt, and a discreet navy blue tie underneath a houndstooth suit jacket. His hairline was receding noticeably, but he still had an impressive head of hair.

"I understand this is distressing," Billy T. embarked on a lesson learned by heart. "But as you undoubtedly appreciate, there are a number of things we need to clarify."

His words had a strange resonance, the diction and phrasing contrasting sharply with the shorthaired, almost frightening figure dressed in flannel shirt and cowboy boots with spurs. However, the man appeared not to notice.

"I understand, I understand," he muttered impatiently while running a narrow hand with an even narrower wedding ring across his face. "Let's get it over with."

"How are the children coping?"

"Amanda doesn't understand much of it. The youngest. The two older ones are naturally very upset."

Now his eyes filled with tears. Perhaps it was for his own sake. Maybe it was at the thought of the grieving children. Opening his eyes wide in an effort to prevent his tears from spilling, he shook his head vigorously.

"I don't understand . . ."

"No, these things are fairly incomprehensible when they first occur."

Billy T. lifted his hands from the keyboard of the PC. At last the computer age had reached at least some parts of Oslo Police Station.

"We'll start with the easiest questions," he said, offering the man a cup of coffee. He refused politely.

"When did you meet?"

"I don't really remember. I have a younger sister who was one of Agnes's friends. But we didn't start seeing each other until she was grown up. In that way, I mean."

He looked slightly confused, but Billy T. smiled reassuringly.

"I understand. When did you get married?"

"In 1972. Agnes was twenty-two and had already started in child welfare services. She was already working with children. I was . . . twenty-seven. But we had been engaged for a while, a year. Then Petter was born in 1976, and Joachim in 1978. Amanda came along in February 1991."

"A real afterthought, then!"

"Yes, but very planned."

Now the man smiled for the first time, though faintly and without the smile reaching his eyes.

"Marriage problems?"

Billy T. felt uncomfortable but performed his duty efficiently. The man had obviously realized this would come up, because he sighed deeply and seemed to brace himself by sitting up straight in his chair.

"No more than other people, I would have thought. We've had our ups and downs. Everybody gets a bit fed up after a while, I think. But we had the children, we had the house and mutual friends and all that kind of thing. Recently it's been quite . . . slightly strained. She had problems at work, I think, though I don't know what they are. I suppose I haven't been very good at paying attention. I don't really know . . ."

Now the tears spilled over. Making a convulsive effort to pull himself together, his attempt forced out a sharp, almost snorting, sob. Billy T. allowed him time to produce a handkerchief: elegant, masculine, and freshly

85

ironed. He blew his nose noisily and dried both eyes by pressing the handkerchief on them one at a time.

"We didn't argue very much," he finally continued. "It was more that we didn't talk to each other. She became so distant, and dreadfully irritable. Some evenings it was so severe I thought she was going through menopause. Even though she was only forty-five."

He darted a look at the police officer, begging for understanding, and received an appropriate answer.

"Women can be difficult," Billy T. concurred sympathetically. "With or without menopause. Did she want a divorce?"

Something in the man's facial expression closed down. Folding his handkerchief neatly, he stuffed it into his breast pocket and then cleared his throat, shifted his position on the seat, and looked the policeman in the eye. From being a passive, gray-clad widower, he now seemed almost aggressive.

"Who has claimed that?"

Billy T. raised his arms defensively. "No one. No one has claimed that. I'm only asking."

"No, we weren't going to divorce."

"But was there talk of it? Did *she* talk about it?"

"No."

"No?"

"Yes. No."

"Did she never mention the possibility of divorce? She had never mentioned that possibility through more than twenty years of marriage with all its ups and downs?"

"No, she hadn't."

"Well."

Billy T. gave up and opened a desk drawer. It had already managed to become fairly chaotic, but he quickly found a sheet of paper that he placed on the desktop in front of him and pushed across to the man.

His complexion had been ashen, but Billy T. could swear that he noticeably turned a paler shade of gray.

"Where did you get that?" he asked curtly, pushing the offending paper back after seeing what it was.

"But Vestavik, you must appreciate that this information is in the public domain. Company registers, population registers, there are all kinds of publicly accessible sources of information."

He flung out his long arms.

"We are a public agency! We get hold of whatever we need."

The sheet of paper showed that Gregusson Men's Fashions, where Agnes Vestavik's husband was the general manager, was a family-owned and extremely solid business. Family owned in reality meant it was entirely owned by Agnes Vestavik, née Gregusson. She had no siblings, and when her father died in 1989, all the shares were transferred to Agnes. Although her father, as a right-minded and religious man, had not placed any conditions on his will, after friendly advice from the family lawyer, Agnes had taken out sole ownership and separation of marital property on the entire estate. One never knew. The shop provided a healthy annual dividend, but the salary of the general manager remained fixed for the past eight years, and it was not an impressive sum.

"Exactly. That there's never been a secret," Mr Vestavik commented tersely. "My job's secure regardless of whether we became divorced. We've got laws covering that sort of thing in this country."

"Your job, yes," Billy T. replied calmly. "But the house was also hers, of course. Her childhood home, isn't that so?"

Silence descended on the room. Faint shouts and laughter could be heard from the corridor outside, and from the window the barely audible sounds of a newly released detainee slinging his curses at all and sundry, and uniformed police officers in particular. The subdued hum of the PC seemed to increase in volume.

"So you think I'm the one who murdered her?" the widower blurted out at last, pointing an indignant forefinger at Billy T. "For the sake of a house I would kill my wife of twenty-three years, the mother of my children. For the sake of a house!"

Furious, he leaned across the desk and smacked his fist on its surface. He appeared confused about whether he should stand up or remain seated, and the result was that he perched on the edge of the chair, as though about to pounce.

"I don't think anything, Vestavik. I'm not alleging anything either. I'm only pointing out a number of circumstances that are sufficiently interesting that we can't afford to let them lie. It's not just the house. There's quite a significant income from the shop, and that's something Agnes had built up during the course

88

of your marriage. The truth actually is that you don't own as much as a nail in the wall. Or more correctly, you *didn't* own a nail in the wall. I assume you now retain undivided possession of the estate. We don't have any information about the existence of a will. Isn't that the case?"

Fishing out his handkerchief again, the man was far from meticulous in his use of it on this occasion. His knuckles whitened as he held the fabric.

"Of course there's no will. No one had planned for Agnes to die. What's more, we weren't about to split up."

Suddenly he was struck by the logic of his own point and launched into a tirade.

"Precisely! She hadn't written any will. That shows we hadn't fallen out. Nowhere near a divorce, at least. If she'd had plans of that nature, she would probably have made sure I wouldn't end up with everything. Besides, you're completely wrong."

He broke off and appeared to hesitate before throwing his trump card on the table.

"I have to share the estate with my children. You don't retain undivided possession of separate property funds."

"But your children won't eject you from the house, will they?" Billy T. said caustically, placing his palms on the desktop and leaning over toward the interviewee.

The outburst only partially concealed his annoyance at being mistaken.

There was loud and repeated rapping at the door, and the widower, startled, collapsed back onto his chair. Hanne Wilhelmsen entered, holding out her hand to the man and introducing herself.

"It was dreadful, what happened to your wife," she remarked soothingly. "We'll do our very best to find out what happened."

"Then you need to look somewhere other than the family," the man sullenly retorted, though obviously disarmed by the chief inspector's friendly manner.

"Oh, you know how it is," Hanne said with a note of regret in her voice. "Police work can be fairly ruthless. But we can't leave a single stone unturned in a case like this. I'm sure you understand that. It's only routine, and the faster we finish with you, the quicker you and your family can try to move on after this tragic event."

He seemed appeased. Hanne Wilhelmsen exchanged a few words with Billy T. before disappearing out the door.

The interview lasted for two more hours and proceeded in a reasonably amicable manner. Billy T. learned that the husband was relatively familiar with the foster home, as he had been there several times, naturally. Their own house was only a stone's throw away, and Agnes had worked there for twelve years. On the night of the murder she had told him at dinnertime that she had to go back later that evening. Neither of their two older children was at home: the eldest attended a folk high school, while Joachim at sixteen was at school camp with his classmates. Agnes herself had put Amanda to bed before returning to the foster home at around half past nine. She had asked him not to wait up, as she might be home late. He had watched some television and gone to bed at his usual time, about half past eleven. Amanda usually slept well at night, but on that evening she had been awakened by a nightmare and was so nervous he had allowed her to lie with him in the double bed. Neither of them had woken up until a minister was standing at the door at around four o'clock in the morning. He had neither made nor received any phone calls the entire evening. He couldn't quite recall off the top of his head what TV program he had watched, but after Billy T. had provided him with a television schedule for the evening in question, he was able to furnish a concise and accurate account of a film shown on TV3.

"Anything else?" Billy T. asked in conclusion.

"What do you mean?"

"Is there anything else you think might be of importance for the case?" Billy T. clarified impatiently.

"Well, yes. Perhaps one thing."

Pulling out his wallet, he searched for a piece of paper that was obviously not there. Then he thrust his hand back into his inside pocket, sighing. It seemed that he was considering whether he ought to inform him of what was on his mind.

"Some money's been taken out," he embarked hesitantly.

"Money?"

"From the account. I only know about it from the bank statement. I don't know where or by whom. But on the very same date, three checks were cashed, each for ten thousand kroner."

"Thirty thousand kroner?"

"Yes."

Tugging at his ear, Billy T. stared at the floor.

"From Agnes's personal account. You understand, we had a joint account, and then she had one of her own. But of course I opened her statement as well when it arrived yesterday."

The widower seemed bashful about interfering with his wife's mail. Billy T. assured him it was quite in order.

"Have you any idea what she could have used it for?"

Vestavik shook his head and sighed deeply.

"But it might be that she froze the account afterward. I haven't been able to investigate that yet. Maybe the checks were stolen?"

"Maybe so," Billy T. said pensively. "Can we have your permission to check that out, as a matter of routine?"

"Of course."

After the interview had been printed out and signed, Billy T. escorted him from the gray concrete building. He shook the widower's hand briefly before bounding up three flights of stairs and barging into Hanne Wilhelmsen's office without knocking on the door.

"Fucking hell, Hanne," he exclaimed with a scowl. "You should know better than to come charging in during an interview. What if I'd been in the middle of a confession!"

"But you weren't," she answered coolly. "I was listening at the door. The fact is that the two of you were about to really fall out with each other. So I had to come in, you know, and lower the temperature a little. Did it help?"

"Well, yes, I suppose so."

"So you see. Can he be eliminated?"

"No, not yet. He sounds pretty watertight. Besides, it takes a lot more to murder your old woman, he's right about that. They have a child who's barely four years old. And two big boys. I'm not so sure. But he definitely can't be eliminated yet."

"Wife murder is not so unusual," Hanne said, staring into thin air. "On the contrary. Murder usually occurs in close relationships between the perpetrator and victim."

"But in that case it would have had to be deliberate, Hanne. Then the guy would have to be fairly cold-blooded. He didn't appear to be like that, although the relationship between them must have been relatively frosty. It looks like the lady was swindled out of thirty thousand kroner after somebody got hold of her checkbook, and she hadn't said a peep to her husband about it."

"What are you saying?"

"You heard what I said. He opened the bank statement yesterday, and on the same date three checks for ten thousand kroner had been cashed. After that, nothing at all has been taken out."

They looked at each other for a long time.

"Has he done it himself and realized we would stumble upon it at some point? And then been farsighted enough to cough up right away?"

"Doubtful. He seemed bewildered himself. Almost quite disconcerted."

Rising to her feet, Hanne stubbed out her cigarette and tried in vain to stifle a yawn.

"We'll see. Find out what the others have discovered, will you? Ask Tone-Marit to pursue the money angle. And then you report to me again tomorrow. I'm off home."

Odd Vestavik felt clammy. He tugged at his collar and loosened his seat belt in an attempt to find a more comfortable sitting position, but it did not help in the slightest.

He had been knocked sideways by all that about the estate. He ought to have told them. On the other hand, it would be digging his own grave if he told them that only three weeks ago Agnes had rather surprisingly approached him with a new nuptial settlement. It determined that all of her separate property and funds should transfer to joint ownership in the event of her passing away. That was how it was expressed: "passing away." And "demise." He had taken issue because it seemed even lawyers were unable to employ the straightforward word "death." That was what Agnes was: dead.

He had forwarded it for official registration only two days before Agnes died. It had taken him aback that the police did not know about it. The document must still be lying in an in-box at the city registrar's office. How long did these things take?

They would get to know about it. Then it would be suspicious that he had not mentioned it.

He slowed down and was tooted angrily by a car behind him. He decided to turn around. He had lied to the police.

Then he speeded up again, continuing on his homeward journey. Perhaps they would never find out. Anyway, he was far, far too tired to make up his mind about it at the moment.

He would have to sleep on it.

But he was profoundly perturbed about the thirty thousand kroner.

Maren had assumed the management role entirely, something that had happened automatically. Both the staff and the children treated her as the new boss, without formalities or objections. Although Terje had returned from sick leave on a part-time basis, he did not voice any objections to her doing his job either. The children had fallen back into their daily routine remarkably quickly, playing and quarreling, doing their homework and eating their meals, and only Kenneth seemed anxious about a woman having been brutally stabbed to death only a few meters away from his bedroom. He checked and double-checked his room every night for murderers and robbers, under the bed, in the closets, and even inside a toy box that could not under any circumstances conceal anyone other than a tiny child. Or perhaps a little but extremely dangerous dragon. The staff members patiently allowed him to enact this ritual before lying beside him for an hour until he fell asleep.

Olav had been away for three whole days now. He had been reported missing to police forces throughout southeastern Norway, and a report would be passed to the media the following day. Even the police were deeply concerned.

"All the same, they don't seem to be connecting him with the murder," Maren Kalsvik said, drumming her pencil on the coffee table in the living room. "I actually find that pretty strange. It's a totally different set of police officers who're dealing with his disappearance from those who're working on the murder case."

Terje Welby sighed despondently.

"They probably realize a twelve-year-old doesn't kill people," he responded. "At least not like that. With a huge knife."

"If a child is going to kill someone, it's hardly going to be with a gun," she commented dryly, before standing up and crossing over to the large double wooden doors with a mirror that separated the "good" living room from what they called the dayroom.

Pulling the doors together in the middle until she heard a little click, she then returned to her seat on the sofa, lifting the pencil and putting it abstractedly into her mouth. After a couple of forcible bites, it broke in two.

"There's one thing I really wonder about, Terje," she said quietly, spitting splinters of wood. Setting the pencil down and spitting some more, she fixed her eyes on her colleague as she continued, "What happened to

96

those papers lying in the drawer that proved the whole situation?"

He reacted immediately by turning incredibly red in the face, with sweat trickling down over his tight lips.

"Papers? What papers?"

His words were spoken with a snarl, as he glanced apprehensively at the closed doors.

"The papers proving what you had done," Maren said. "The papers Agnes had drawn up concerning the matter."

"But she didn't know anything!"

His desperation etched white spots on all the crimson in his face. He looked ill. He made a sudden violent movement with his upper body and then a moaning sound.

"Bloody hell," he thundered, sitting back warily in his chair. "You have to believe me, Maren, she didn't know anything!"

"You're lying."

Her assertion was articulated as an incontrovertible truth, unshakable, with no room for discussion. She even smiled, a tired and joyless contortion containing both resignation and irritation.

"I know you're lying. Agnes had found out about the theft. Or thefts, I should perhaps say. I can give you all the details, but that's probably not necessary. She was extremely disappointed. And quite furious."

Previously he had been so incensed that she doubted whether higher levels existed in the man's emotional register, but she was wrong. Gasping and panting for breath, his vocal pitch now resembled that of a child when he managed to force out the words, "Did she *tell* that to *you*?"

Several agonizing seconds elapsed before she replied. She stared out the window, where fresh snow had started to fall, in enormous white flakes that would melt as soon as they reached the earth. Shaking her head gently, she turned to face Terje.

"No, actually she didn't. But I know it all the same. And I know she had collected evidence. It wouldn't be too difficult to find, if you simply began to scrutinize the accounts. The papers were lying in the drawer. The one that was locked. And the papers weren't there when the police arrived. If they had them, then you would have been hauled in long ago. And that hasn't happened. You haven't even been questioned."

The final sentence had the inflection of a question, and he shook his head in confirmation.

"Why haven't I been? Is it some form of psychological torture, or what?"

The white on his face had started to meet the fiery red halfway. Now he was pink and dripping wet. The beard on his cheeks was curling from the dampness, and three drops of sweat were running down in front of his left ear.

"But I'd put most of it back, Maren! I told you that, didn't I? My God, it's not as if we're talking about large sums of money!"

"To be honest, Terje, I don't think the police would be particularly bothered about the amounts."

Flinging out her arms in despair, she threw him a condescending look.

"But almost all of it was paid back! I'm *quite* sure that Agnes didn't know anything. She didn't have the foggiest suspicion! But she knew something else, Maren. She knew something else, something that . . ."

He did not continue.

Maren Kalsvik leaned back demonstratively in her chair. They could hear some children clattering through the dayroom, laughing boisterously, and there was a faint thumping sound from Raymond's stereo equipment on the floor above. Outside, the snow was falling more and more heavily, and it seemed as though there would be enough to form a blanket on the ground after all. The temperature had fluctuated wildly over the past two days, up and down, up and down.

Like a child caught in the act, she thought. Downright denials about something that was so blatantly obvious. Catching his eye, she held his gaze.

"Terje. I *know* that Agnes knew. You know that too. I *know* she had papers to prove it. You know that as well. I'm your friend, for God's sake!"

This last was spoken emphatically, and she underlined it further by striking the table.

"Those papers were there before Agnes died, and they were gone when the police turned up. There's only one possible explanation: you were there and removed them at some point during the evening or night. Don't you think you might as well admit it?"

He sat there, paralyzed, in the chair.

She stood up and turned away from him before suddenly whirling around again.

"I can help you, Terje! For God's sake, I *want* to help you! I don't want you to be arrested for something you haven't done! We've traipsed in and out of here every day, eaten meals together, chatted together, we've almost lived together, Terje! But if I have to take responsibility for this here . . ."

She gesticulated expressively with her arms, turning her eyes heavenward and muttering something he couldn't catch.

"Honestly. I'm holding something back from the police. I can't be answerable for that unless I know what happened. And what didn't happen. Don't you understand that? You mustn't go on lying! Not to me."

As though he were gathering his strength, he breathed in and out three times, deeply and rapidly.

"I was here," he whispered. "I was here around twelve o'clock. I was going to take the papers from the drawer. But only to see what she actually knew, Maren! When I saw her dead in the chair, I was totally shocked."

He cradled his head in his hands and rocked his body to and fro.

"You just *have to* believe me, Maren!"

"You can't have had enough of a shock to prevent you from finding the papers and taking them with you, then," Maren said calmly.

She had sat down again, and now her right hand was continually running through her hair.

"No, what should I have done? If the police had found them, I would be the most likely candidate to be the killer!"

Glenn burst in through the double doors. Startled, Terje kicked his foot against the table in front of him.

"Sh . . . sugar," he said through clenched teeth, turning abruptly toward the boy who was requesting money to go to the movies. "How many times have I told you to knock on doors before you go into a room? Eh? How many times have I told you?"

Enraged, he grabbed hold of the fourteen-year-old's arm and squeezed it tight. Glenn whimpered and tried to pull himself free.

"Let me go, you," he complained. "Have you gone crazy or what?"

"I'm so sick and tired of you doing whatever you want all over the place," Terje spluttered, releasing his grip on the boy and at the same time shoving him roughly against the wall. "Now you need to get a bloody grip!"

"Ten kroner deducted from your weekly pocket money," the youngster mumbled, rubbing his left upper arm. "I only wanted cinema money!"

Maren had witnessed these goings-on with an amazement that stunned her rigid. Now she pulled herself together and gave Terje a stern look before escorting Glenn out of the room and handing him a fifty-kroner note.

"Is he sick, or what?" Glenn asked.

"He's got a sore back," she said reassuringly. "He's upset too. About Agnes. We all are. What film are you going to see?"

"*The Client.*"

"Is there much violence in it?"

"No. It's just the usual kind of thriller, I think."

"Fine. Come straight home. Have a nice time."

The boy muttered all the way out into the hallway, vigorously rubbing his tender arm.

Maren returned, closing the doors again. After a moment's hesitation, she grabbed hold of an old black key hanging on a nail beside the doorframe, inserted it into the classical keyhole, and rotated it. There was a grinding of metal against metal, demonstrating that the key had hardly ever been used in many years. She sank into the winged armchair once more. Although she was clearly marked by the events of recent days, it was as though something had flared up in her weary eyes. A spark of vitality, an almost serene determination. Terje felt it rather than saw it and took heart.

"You won't say anything to the police?"

He was pathetic. Not only had he lied, both about having been at the home at a rather critical point in time, and also about Agnes not knowing about his embezzlement from the business accounts. As well as the somewhat significant point that he had appropriated the papers from the director's desk drawer. Now it looked as though he was ready to kneel down and beg for assistance.

"Why did you lie, Terje? Did you not trust me?"

His gaze flitted from her face and was about to fall to the floor. Then he caught himself and rested his eye instead on a point twenty centimeters above her head, remaining sitting like that, with his arms on the armrests and gripping the edges tenaciously with his

102

hands, almost as though he were at the dentist's. He did not answer.

"I need to know exactly what happened. Was it the shortfall that Agnes wanted to talk to you about earlier in the day? Was that why she embarked on a round of staff interviews? Did she show you the papers?"

"No," he eventually whispered. "No, she didn't show me any papers. She simply told me she had discovered certain irregularities, and she was extremely disappointed. She waved some papers about, and I understood that they concerned me. She asked me . . ."

Now, drawing his feet up onto the chair, he lowered his head, with an eye on each knee, like a child, or almost like a deformed fetus. When he continued, his voice was indistinct and difficult to understand.

"I was to make a written statement before anything would happen. I was to hand it in the next day. That is to say, the day after she . . . she died."

Suddenly he let his feet drop to the floor again. He did not cry, but his face was contorted into a kind of rictus Maren had never witnessed before. Fleeting tics crossed his mouth in lightning flashes, and his eyes almost looked as though they were about to disappear into his head. For a moment she was really frightened.

"Terje! Terje, pull yourself together!"

Standing up, she perched on the table between them. She attempted to hold his hand, but he would not relinquish his grasp of the armrest, so instead she placed her right hand on his thigh. He felt abnormally hot; the heat burned through his trouser leg and made the palm of her hand sweaty after only a few seconds.

"I won't say anything. But I need to know what happened. You must understand that. So I don't say anything wrong to the police."

His eyes had fallen back into place. He was breathing more quietly and she could see his knuckles were no longer quite so chalk white.

"I only wanted to know what she had found out. For all I knew, she might only have uncovered a tiny fraction. And most of it had been put back again, you see. I was only . . . She was smart, wanting to have my version first."

"Are you sure she was dead when you came on the scene?"

"Sure?"

Now his eyes were fixed on hers again, in disbelief.

"She had an enormous knife between her shoulder blades and wasn't making any sign of breathing. That's what I call dead."

"But did you check? Did you take her pulse, or did you consider the possibility of artificial respiration? Was she warm, for example?"

"I didn't touch her. Of course I didn't. I was in a state of total shock. The only thing I could think of when I managed to compose myself was to take those papers and get the hell out of there."

"Was the drawer open?"

"No, it was locked. But the key was where it usually is. Underneath the plant pot."

"Did you know that too?" She seemed slightly surprised.

104

"Yes, I found out about that a few years ago. I caught her by accident once. Idiotic hiding place. Just about the first place anyone would look. Did you know about it?"

She did not reply but instead stood up and stepped over to the window again. Darkness had settled like a viscous carpet over the garden, with an irregular pattern of wet white rags overlaying all the dark gray. As she pulled her vest tighter with a familiar movement demonstrating she virtually lived in that garment, it struck her that it was time for the children's television.

"The police wouldn't have believed you," she said to his reflection on the windowpane. "I have problems myself. The way you've lied about it."

"I appreciate that. I can't expect you to believe me. But it's true, Maren. I didn't kill her."

She let him have the last word but gave him a look he was unable to interpret as she left to keep Kenneth and the twins company in front of the TV screen.

"Oslo Police are searching for twelve-year-old Olav Håkonsen, who disappeared from his home on Tuesday evening. The boy was apparently wearing denim jeans, a navy blue jacket, and sneakers."

"Goodness, I thought the news program had stopped issuing that kind of missing person report," Cecilie Vibe exclaimed from her relaxed Friday pose on the sofa.

A vague, fairly worthless photograph of the boy accompanied the news report, delivered by a pale, oval, nondescript female face with a remarkably mellifluous voice.

105

"They make exceptions," Hanne mumbled, hushing her with an arm motion.

"The boy is about five foot two in height and strongly built. Information should be directed to the Oslo Police or your nearest police station."

The well-dressed woman then moved on to describe an allegedly two-headed cat that had been born in California.

"Strongly built, I suppose that's one way of putting it," Hanne said. "From what I understand, the boy is grossly overweight."

She zapped over to TV2, where a dark-haired lady was smiling repeatedly and talking about nothing at all. She zapped back to the weather forecast on NRK.

"Tickle my feet," she requested, propping her feet on Cecilie's lap.

"Where can the boy have gone?" Cecilie asked, absentmindedly stroking the soles of Hanne's feet with her fingers.

"We don't actually know. It's starting to seem a bit sinister. We were pretty sure he would go home to his mother by some means or other, but he hasn't managed to do that. Or had the opportunity to. Take off my socks!"

Cecilie pulled the white tube socks from her feet and continued her hand movements.

"Do you think something has happened to him?"

"Not sure. If it hadn't been for the boy running off by himself, and therefore probably trying to hide, we would be really scared. Another child abduction, possibly. But he's in hiding. He's twelve years old and can probably hold out for a while. We're assuming he ran away willingly. It's not likely that he's been exposed to any criminal activities. If we assume he didn't murder the lady at the foster home, and we do, then the disappearance has nothing to do with the murder at all. He's been threatening to run away since he arrived there. But obviously we're concerned. For instance, he might have seen or heard something. And we're very interested in *that*. But . . . a twelve-year-old on the run is not good under any circumstances. Don't stop!"

Cecilie resumed her tickling, still as uninspired as ever.

"What's it actually like at that kind of foster home? I didn't think we had institutions of that type any longer. And why did they say he had disappeared from 'his home'?"

"Probably don't want to stigmatize him too much, I would think . . . The foster home looks almost like an ordinary home, only much larger. Very nice, really. The youngsters looked as though they enjoyed being there. We certainly don't have many foster homes like that, with a group of children being looked after, any longer. Most children are placed in individual foster homes."

Cecilie began to invest more energy in her touch, allowing her featherlight fingers to glide up Hanne's leg, underneath the fabric of her trousers. An irreverent interpretation of Grieg's music blasting from the TV set announced the start of *Around Norway*. Hanne used the remote control to reduce the volume. Sitting up on the sofa without lowering her legs, she leaned toward her girlfriend and they kissed, warm, slow, and teasingly.

"Why don't we have children?" Cecilie whispered to Hanne's mouth.

"We can try to make one now, at once," Hanne said with a smile.

"Don't joke."

Cecilie drew back, pushing Hanne's feet down onto the floor.

Hanne inflated her cheeks and allowed the air to flow out through her lips in an exaggerated gesture of resignation.

"Not now, Cecilie. We're not going to discuss that now."

"When, then?"

They looked at each other, and an old, almost forgotten battle flared into a new skirmish.

"Never. We're finished with that. It's been decided."

"Honestly, Hanne, how many years have passed since we made up our minds? Back then I was quite clear — it was for the time being. Now we're almost thirty-six, and I can hear my biological clock ticking louder and louder."

"You? Biological clock? Huh!"

Hanne caressed Cecilie's face, smooth, soft, and with no more than a tiny network of fine laugh lines at the corner of each eye. She wasn't only pretty, she was wearing incredibly well. People who had not known them for a long time were convinced Hanne was several years older than her partner. In fact, she was sixteen days younger. Her hand slid down toward Cecilie's breasts.

"Don't do that," Cecilie said in annoyance, pushing away the unwelcome hand. "If we're going to have children, we have to make a decision soon. Tonight's as good as any other night."

"No, it's not, think about it."

Hanne grabbed the beer bottle sitting between them and refilled her own glass. Her movement was so abrupt that the liquid spilled over profusely, running over the tabletop and menacingly threatening to overflow the edge onto the carpet. She swore and rushed out with angry stride to fetch a cloth. The beer had already formed a dark stain on the yellow carpet by the time she returned, and it took her several minutes to set things straight. Cecilie made not the slightest sign of helping. Instead, with feigned interest, she watched a story about a man who had taken a doctorate in Latin at the age of ninety-three and in addition woodcarving as a hobby.

"Tonight's *not* just as good as any other night," Hanne growled. "I've had an exhausting week, I've missed you, I've been looking forward to an enjoyable evening at home, I've been looking forward to spending time with you, I can't bear to quarrel, and what's more, it's true that we decided not to have children years ago."

She slapped the wet cloth down, causing the drops of beer to spatter across the table.

"*You* have decided for us," Cecilie said quietly.

109

Hanne realized the battle was lost. They had to go through this, as they did at irregular but fortunately increasingly lengthy intervals, reiterating the fundamental conditions for the difficult lifestyle they had embarked on when they found each other one spring day a hundred years ago, when they were both just finishing high school and discovering the realities of life. Hanne hated these discussions.

"You hate talking about anything difficult," her mind reader commented. "If only you had *some* idea of how hopeless that makes things for me. I have to steel myself for weeks in advance when I want to bring up something that's not just about the joys of spring."

"Okay. Talk away. Everything's my fault. I've spoiled your whole life. Are we finished now?"

Hanne threw out her arms, then crossed them. She stared at the TV screen, where a blonde woman was now standing, clad in a traditional Norwegian cardigan, at the top of the Holmen-kollen ski jump, talking about an eleven-year-old girl who was a rising star in the sport.

"Hanne," Cecilie ventured before pausing for a moment. "Of course we won't have children if you don't want to. We must agree in that case. One hundred percent. I'll give in if you say no. But is it so strange, really, that I'd like to talk about it?"

Her voice was no longer angry or dismissive. But that was not enough. Hanne continued to sit motionless, her eyes stiffly fixed on the little ski jumper hovering sixty meters above the landing slope.

110

Now it was Cecilie who grabbed the remote control. The sound vanished and the screen flickered to black with a tiny dot that continued to diminish before being swallowed up by all the darkness.

"I was watching that program," Hanne said, her gaze still fastened on the spot where the white dot had disappeared. "I can in fact manage to do two things at the one time."

She was startled as Cecilie burst into tears. Cecilie hardly ever cried. She, Hanne, was the one who resorted to tears at all hours of the day and night. Cecilie was the one who put things right, who was calm and logical, who had insight and courage and could face the world with unwavering rationality. Kneeling on the floor in front of Cecilie, she attempted to lift her hands away from her face, but it could not be done.

"Cecilie, darling, I'm so sorry. I didn't mean to be a grouch. Of course we can talk about it."

The slender figure reacted by withdrawing even further into herself, and when Hanne tried to stroke her back, she trembled, as though in aversion. Hanne retracted her hand and stared at it as if it might conceal something frightful.

"Cecilie," she whispered, terror stricken. "What's wrong with you?"

The woman on the sofa continued to weep, but now at least she was trying to say something. At first it was totally incomprehensible, but eventually she calmed down a little. Finally she moved her hands from her face and looked directly at Hanne.

111

"I get so completely worn out, Hanne. I'm so tired of
. . . I've often thought . . . The New Testament. Peter
who denied Jesus and all that stuff, at Eastertime. Do
you know why there's so much emphasis on that? It's
because . . ."

Her violent sobbing seemed almost abnormal, she
was gasping for breath and becoming blue in the face.
Hanne didn't dare to move a muscle.

"It's because," Cecilie continued once she had
regained her breath, "it's the worst thing you can do to
anyone. To deny another person. You have denied me
for almost seventeen years, are you aware of that?"

Hanne fought a determined battle against all the
defenses snapping into place inside her head. She
clenched her teeth and rubbed her hands over her face.

"But, Cecilie, that's not what we're talking about just
now," she said slightly hesitantly, for fear of setting the
convulsive sobbing into motion again.

"Yes it is, in a way it is," Cecilie insisted. "Everything
hangs together. Your defensive walls in every direction
and that excruciating routine of yours that appears just
as surely as *amen* in church every time I raise any
important issue. *Bang, bang, bang* it goes, and then
you're like an impregnable fortress. Don't you
appreciate how dangerous that is?"

Hanne felt the fear that clutched at her like claws on
her spine on the few occasions she understood Cecilie
was seriously questioning their relationship. She ground
her teeth as she battled against her own reactions and
managed to hold them somewhat in check.

"If we're going to continue to live together you *must* pull yourself together, Hanne."

It wasn't even a threat. It was simply the truth. They both knew it. Hanne probably knew it better.

"I will pull myself together, Cecilie," she promised swiftly and breathlessly. "I'll pull myself together wonderfully. I swear. Not from tomorrow or from next week. From right now. We can have heaps of children. We can invite the entire police station here. I can place an announcement in . . . We'll have a civil partnership!"

She leaped up with energetic enthusiasm.

"We'll get married! I'll invite all my family, and everyone at work and . . ."

Cecilie stared at her and started to laugh. A peculiar, unfamiliar mixture of laughter and tears, while she shook her head in despair.

"That's not what I'm asking for. That's all nonsense, Hanne. I don't need all that stuff all at once. I just need to have the feeling we're moving forward. It was lovely that at long last you allowed Billy T. to enter our lives. Was that really so awful, do you think?"

Without waiting for an answer, she grabbed a cushion from the sofa and hugged it to herself as she continued, "Billy T.'s enough for the moment. But only for the moment. Soon I have to meet your family. At least your brothers and sisters. And as far as this about children is concerned . . . Sit down now, please."

She replaced the cushion and cautiously patted the seat beside her.

Hanne stood like a statue, white as a ghost, adopting a terrified pose. Giving herself a shake, she sat down at the far edge of the sofa. Her thighs bounced up and down in a nervous rhythm, and she clenched her fists so ferociously that her nails dug into the palms of her hands.

"Take it easy, my friend."

Cecilie had almost regained control over herself and the situation. She drew her girlfriend toward her and could feel how much Hanne was shaking. They remained sitting in silence for a considerable time before they were both able to breathe easily, calmly.

"Do you think it's odd that I want to know why you don't want to have children?" Cecilie whispered into Hanne's ear.

"No. But it's so difficult to talk about it. I know you'd like to have children. It's exactly as if I'm stealing something from you whenever I say no. It's just as if I'm stealing something from you all the time by being your girlfriend. I feel so small. So . . . nasty."

Cecilie smiled. But she didn't utter a word.

"It's just that I . . ." Hanne began, sitting up straight. "I feel it would be wrong for the child."

Cecilie protested. "Wrong for the child? Think about what the two of us can offer a child! It's more than the majority of children in Norway receive: intelligent parents, financial security, at least one pair of grandparents . . ."

They both smiled fleetingly.

"Yes, that's right," Hanne replied. "We could offer a great deal. But then I think that if I can't quite dare to accept myself, then it's bloody unfair to make life difficult for a child. Think of all the shit the youngster would have to put up with. At school. On the street. All the questions. Besides, I really believe all children ought to have a dad."

"But it could have a dad! Claus has said he's willing to take on that role, he's said that for years now!"

"Honestly, Cecilie. Should the youngster have two mothers here and two fathers at Claus and Petter's house? Great fun at end-of-term parties!"

Cecilie did not protest further, but not because she was in agreement. She disagreed fundamentally, deep within herself. Claus and Petter were good-looking, well-educated, kind, sensible, and stable men. She and Hanne had been quarreling and making love through thick and thin for almost seventeen years now. They would probably go on doing so until the day they died. There was plenty of room for a child in their relationship. There was a lot she wanted to say, but she kept her mouth shut. She had no idea why.

"I really believe a child should come into being through a mother and a father loving each other," Hanne continued in low tones, leaning closer toward Cecilie. "Okay, so that's not always the way it is. Okay, so there are loads of children who come into this world by accident, through carelessness, outside marriage, without love. Many of them get on well, and they're all equally precious."

Taking a deep breath, she sat up to take a gulp of beer and then remained sitting there, turning the glass around and around on its axis while shaking her head listlessly.

115

"I know all of that, of course. But I don't think it should be like that if I have the choice! I want the very best for my child, and *I can't give it that*! Don't you understand that, sweetheart?"

Cecilie did not. But she realized that Hanne for once in her life had opened her innermost recesses, at least a tiny crack. In itself that was such an earth-shattering event that for the moment she required no more. Smiling, she stroked Hanne's back.

"No, I don't understand it. But it's great you're telling me about it."

The silence was broken only by the sound of the glass being rotated.

"Adopting would be a different matter," Hanne said suddenly, standing up just as abruptly. "There are all those children waiting in a queue out there. All the ones nobody wants. Then a well-established lesbian couple in Oslo would be an alternative that's a thousand times better. Than a street in Brazil, for example."

"Adoption," Cecilie mumbled weakly. "You know that's not legal."

They stared at each other yet again.

"No," Hanne said. "It's not legal. It ought to be. It will be."

"We'll be too old by then."

Neither of them dropped eye contact.

"I don't want us to create our own child, Cecilie. I'll never want that. Never."

There was no more to say on the matter.

Hanne felt herself beaten black and blue. And had a thumping headache. An inexplicable sense of relief filled her without entirely being able to alleviate the ever-present hidden pain of guilt that always tormented her. At certain times strongly, at other times only as an extremely feeble murmur.

Cecilie stood up also and remained standing, facing Hanne for a few seconds before letting her hand slide slowly over her face.

"Are we going to eat, or what?"

Hanne switched on the TV set in order to resume the Friday evening ambience. On NRK, the presenter Petter Nome was chatting as though nothing at all had happened.

The wallpaper on one wall was now completely destroyed, apart from an occasional mountain-shaped fragment he had not been able to tear loose. Large and small curls of paper surrounded him on the floor, almost like a carpenter's workshop. He wanted to strip that wall entirely before making a start on the next one. It was an amusing way to pass the time, and once or twice he had managed to rip off huge sheets measuring almost a meter in length.

Although still more canned food remained, he was starting to take a gloomy view of the prospect of lingering there. He could not quite remember what day it was, but it struck him as fairly certain that the residents would not absent themselves forever. He ought to find somewhere else. What's more, he was stinking. He had already removed one stitch from his tongue, but it had bled so fucking badly he had let the other two stay put.

The temptation of the telephone persisted. Inside his stomach sat a tender lump of homesickness. Perhaps the police had given up. Then he thrust the thought aside.

However, it didn't let itself be chased off so easily. At home he had a bed, a lovely blue Stompa bed, and he could get decent food. Pork chops. He wanted to go to his mum. He really wanted to go home.

Gingerly, he lifted the telephone receiver but dropped it as soon as he heard the dial tone and started on the other wall. This was more difficult, because someone had painted on top of the wallpaper so it adhered more firmly. The strips were smaller here, some as minuscule as locks of hair. Giving up halfway through, he padded out to the corridor again. Outside it was dark, and the only faint illumination there came from the lamp in a little windowless toilet that he had left switched on the entire time.

Now he did not hesitate. Tapping in the familiar number, he let it ring. It took ages, and he was just on the point of giving up, intrigued about where on earth his mum could be. It was evening. She was always at home. Then she answered.

"Hello?"

He said nothing.

"Hello?"

"Mum."

"Olav!"

"Mum."

"Where . . . . where are you?"

"I don't know. I want to come home."

118

Unexpectedly, he started crying, shocking him more than it did his mother. Gulping slightly, he tasted his own tears that contained a faint memory of early childhood. Homesickness overwhelmed him, and he repeated, "I want to come home, Mum."

"Olav, listen to me. You have to find out where you are."

"Are the police with you?"

"No. Are you in Oslo?"

"They'll send me back to that fucking home. Or to jail."

"No children are ever put in prison, Olav. You have to tell me what it looks like where you are."

He tried to explain. What the kitchen looked like, what the house looked like. He described the thousand twinkling lights outside the dark windowpane in the living room and the pale pink haze lying like a heavy cloud over the city below him.

He's in Oslo. My God, he's in Oslo, she thought.

"You need to sneak outside and search for the street sign, Olav. I have to know more exactly where you are."

When she heard scraping sounds emanating from the phone, she rushed to give him a helpful warning. "Don't put down the handset! Just leave it lying at the side of the phone until you come back in again. Do it now. Go out. There's usually a street sign at the intersections. Look for an intersection. The nearest one."

He followed her instructions, returning six or seven minutes later, now able to furnish her with two street names.

"Now stay there for a while. Half an hour or so. Do you have your watch with you?"

"Yes."

"When exactly half an hour has passed, go down to that intersection and wait for me. You must *not* be impatient. I'm coming, but it might take me some time to find my way."

"I want to go home, Mum."

Now he burst into tears again.

"I'll come for you, Olav. I'll come for you right away."

Then he heard the click at the other end.

She had to gain access to a car, and her mother was the only possibility. Her heart sank, and for a second she weighed the possibility of a taxi but decided that was too risky. Now that the boy had been reported missing on television and all that, it was far too hazardous to involve other people. So it would have to be her mother's car.

In fact the plan went more smoothly than she had feared. She gave the excuse of having an appointment with the police, and her mother was too drunk to consider how unlikely it was that the police would want to talk to her late on a Friday evening. Three-quarters of an hour after the boy had phoned, she arrived at an intersection in the Grefsen district. The development was filled with detached houses from the immediate postwar period, with the occasional seventies house built in parents' gardens, all of them enclosed by low fences. The intersection was brightly lit, but the boy had been smart enough to retreat slightly, and he stood

120

underneath hanging lilac bushes, in their black winter guise, beside one of the gardens, where he clung to a gate, shrinking into the shadows. All the same, she spotted him at once, but then she was on the lookout for him, of course.

He obviously recognized his grandmother's car immediately, because he sidled out from the bushes before she had a chance to stop the vehicle. Heavy and clumsy, he scurried around the front to open the passenger-side door. Wheezing, he flopped down on the seat without removing his rucksack, swinging his legs around and slamming the door with far too much force.

They said nothing. He was no longer crying. An hour later, he was standing in the shower, and then ate heartily before falling fast asleep. They had hardly exchanged a word.

My God, what'll I do? It's true I was able to sneak him into the apartment without being seen; for safety's sake we came through the basement entrance at the back of the building and encountered no one on the stairs. But what now?

The police phone me every day, though that's not a problem. They've said I have to be interviewed one more time. Next week, probably. That doesn't matter anyway, for they won't come here. But of course he can't be kept hidden forever.

He's afraid now. He hates that foster home, and that gives me some control over him, at least for a while.

Just like that time he demolished the building in the children's playground. It happened when we were living in Skedsmokorset. Or was it Skårer? No, it must have been

Skedsmo, because he was only six years old. Just for a second, some road workers had left a steamroller sitting, unsupervised, with its motor switched on. Somehow he managed to climb up into the huge monster, and it started to move forward. I saw it with my own eyes, from the window. He had just returned home from kindergarten and wanted to go outside. I stood there, paralyzed, watching the steamroller, situated only ten or twelve meters away from the little blue-painted building. He didn't even have a chance to steer it away. They told me that afterward. The steering wheel is far too heavy for a small child, they said. I think he wanted to. The steamroller was positioned on a slight incline and had picked up some speed by the time it hit the wall. I heard the noise of the massive machine as it nudged against the little house before it gave way. At the same time the road workers discovered what was about to happen, and they came running but were too late to stop it. The impact was a deafening racket. Thank God it was that time of day. The children's playground had been closed for several hours. If there had been people inside the house, God only knows what the outcome would have been.

The road workers were courteous about it. It was their fault, they said. They shouldn't have been so remiss that there was a chance of a child using the steamroller. But everyone in the street knew he was to blame, and we had to move house again.

For some reason, though, the incident scared him. For a few days he was so amenable that it almost alarmed me. Now I might experience the same thing again. He seems dreadfully frightened.

But what will I do when he no longer is?

122

CHAPTER
SIX

Outside, blizzard conditions and ten degrees Celsius below freezing; inside, a sweaty Monday morning and Billy T. trying fruitlessly to identify a comfortable sitting position on the cramped chair in Hanne Wilhelmsen's office. With the rest of the Homicide Section working tenaciously on a double murder case in the upmarket West End and the media swarming all over it, there were now only the two of them, assisted by Erik Henriksen and Tone-Marit Steen, left toiling on the knife murder of an unfortunate foster home worker.

"At least we'll be left well alone by the press," Billy T. remarked. "Every cloud has a silver lining."

The crime scene report was lying on the chief inspector's desk. One day ahead of schedule, just six days since the killing, but it did not reveal anything they did not already know. The most critical information would be contained in the forensic report — ready in four months. The best-case scenario.

"But I've found out a great deal."

Billy T. stretched out his legs.

"We're left with only known fingerprints. On the window-sills, in the director's office, on the doors. All the prints naturally correspond to the places they were found. That bloody fire drill destroyed a lot. The footprints are a mess, but the team is still working on checking them against the footwear belonging to the children and staff. We probably won't find anything significant there either. As far as fibers, hairs, and suchlike are concerned, we don't have anything to go on in the meantime. The folk in the crime scene team are discouraged, to say the least."

"What about the body?" Hanne asked, attempting to feign interest.

"The postmortem shows the knife hit the bull's-eye. Between two ribs, the third and fourth, I believe."

He rustled his notes.

"The murderer either got lucky or has a thorough knowledge of anatomy. The knife went straight through the aorta, into the left atrium and ended up in the left ventricle. A considerable amount of force had to be used. Apart from that, the lady was slightly overweight, had some kidney stones and a benign little cyst on one ovary. Plus a punctured lung beside her heart. And a tiny cut on her right forefinger covered by a Band-Aid. In other words, she died from the stab wound."

"Who's been questioned so far?"

The question was directed at Erik Henriksen, a broad-shouldered, boyish, red-haired police officer who was clever and suffered from a major crush on Hanne Wilhelmsen, now of a somewhat resigned nature. They had worked together for a couple of years, and he was overjoyed at her promotion to chief inspector.

124

"Thirteen in total," he said, placing the interview reports in front of her. "Eleven members of staff, her husband, and her eldest son."

"Why not all the staff? Who's missing?"

"We haven't reached Terje Welby yet. Or Eirik Vassbunn, who was on night duty. The one who found the body. Or, to be more specific, I've talked to him but only enough to write a second-hand account. He's in total shock. Can't see the point of stressing him out any further."

Hanne Wilhelmsen refrained from expressing her opinion of that judgment and remained sitting, deep in thought. Clasping her hands together, she raised them to her face as though in silent prayer. No one spoke for twenty seconds, until Billy T. gave a loud, lingering yawn.

"Have we found anyone with a motive, boys and girls?" the chief inspector asked, once her prayer was concluded.

"Her widower has a kind of motive, yes," Billy T. said. "But I still don't think he did it. As far as the others go, I don't see much at all. No one profits from the lady's sudden passing. No one we can see, at least. She was pretty well liked by the staff, and very well liked by the children."

"Except Olav, as far as I understand," Tone-Marit muttered, embarrassed at having to speak up.

"That's right, but he more or less hated everybody and everything. With the exception of Maren Kalsvik. She was the only one he listened to."

Lighting up a cigarette, Hanne Wilhelmsen ignored Tone-Marit's disapproving coughing.

"Let's begin at the other end, then," she said, leaning her head back to send a perfect smoke ring into the room. "What kind of motives could anyone think of for killing a little lady who owns a little shop and runs a little foster home and who's employed by the Salvation Army?"

Billy T. grinned.

"A bit of a stumper, boss! Homicides are usually about sex, money, or pure and simple hatred. We can ignore sex in this case . . ."

"Now you're showing your damn prejudices, Billy T.," Hanne protested. "For all we know, she could have a jilted boyfriend somewhere."

"Or girlfriend." Billy T. grinned again, disregarding her immediate glare. "Okay. We'll have to search for this forty-five-year-old, overweight little dame's passionate and bloodthirsty former lover. Or else we can concentrate on the money angle."

"Who's responsible for the accounts in a place like that?" Hanne suddenly inquired.

"Agnes. But this Terje Welby also had access to all the business accounts. He's the assistant director, at least on paper. Maren Kalsvik, who has filled the deputy director role, doesn't have any involvement in financial affairs."

"Are we talking about large sums of money here?"

Her increasing interest was obvious.

"Well, yes, I would think so. Think about what it must cost to run a house like that! With loads of staff!

And eight youngsters! I'm skinned alive by my four . . ."

When his own financial responsibilities crossed his mind, he sat there in gloomy silence.

"Check that more closely, Tone-Marit. Have a look at the accounts and see if there's anything in that. It could well be . . ."

Propping her feet up on the desktop, Hanne took a deep drag of her cigarette.

"Killing to cover up another crime is a familiar motive as well."

"But then it's all about sex or money all the same," Billy T. broke in, tearing himself away from his ruminations about his financial worries.

"True enough, but investigate it anyway. And one more thing: What about the children's parents? Is there anything to investigate there?"

"Most of them are entirely out of the picture. But we'll have a closer look at that, of course. The one who looks most interesting is the mother of the boy who's run off."

Tone-Marit paged through a neat loose-leaf binder perched on her knee.

"Birgitte Håkonsen," she read aloud. "The boy had only been living there for three weeks, but she had already managed to scare the pants off most of the staff. Not that she said very much. She just stood there, apparently, an enormous silent figure with a strange look in her eyes."

"Humph," Hanne Wilhelmsen muttered.

"What?"

"Forget it. Was the boy placed there voluntarily?"

"No, far from it. The mother has fought the child welfare service with tooth and claw. And that in itself is quite curious. All the other children are voluntary placements. Only Olav was forced to go there."

"Have we interviewed her?"

"Honestly, Hanne," Billy T. protested. "Do you think the mother of a boy, three weeks after his being placed there, is going to sneak into a foster home and kill somebody?"

"Certainly not. But we do have to talk to her."

"We've actually done that already," Erik Henriksen said. "That is to say, the guy who's dealing with the boy's disappearance has spoken to her. Several times. A proper interview, and he's been checking in with her every day to find out if she's heard anything from him."

"All right. Get me copies of those interviews. And the boy's still missing?"

"Yes. They're now starting to think that something may have happened to him. How long can a twelve-year-old remain in hiding?"

"Hanne, are you serious?" Billy T. said in annoyance. "Are we really going to waste time on this woman?"

"One thing's for sure," Hanne Wilhelmsen responded. "And that is, as far as *children* are concerned, passionate emotions are brought into play."

Billy T. shrugged his shoulders, and the other two tried not to look at either of them. They all realized the meeting was over.

Before leaving, Billy T. pointed out the possibility of finding something of interest in the telephone directory sitting on the cheap desk belonging to the foster home director. Having decided to check that out, his most striking discovery was two yellow Post-it notes recently attached to the metal directory. One had turned out to be the number for Diakonhjemmet University College's School of Social Work, the other he had quite simply not yet managed to check. But there might be something of significance there.

"I doubt it," Hanne said indifferently. She remained lost in her own confused thoughts long after the door slammed shut behind her three ill-tempered police officers.

He was smirking again only two hours later. As usual, he burst into her office without knocking, and as usual, she jumped out of her skin. However, there was no point in reprimanding him. He leaned toward her with outstretched arms, resting his hands on the desktop, and inclining his head toward hers. His scalp shone, but he jerked it away before Hanne Wilhelmsen could admire her reflection.

"Good old hairstyle," he declared, sounding satisfied. "Feel it!"

She stroked his crown, warm, clean, and pleasurable against the palm of her hand.

"Like silk, isn't it?"

Gratified, he straightened up to his full height and assured himself with his own hands that his scalp was still baby soft.

"Finest skull in the station. In the whole of Oslo! But I have to shave it twice a day. Twice a day!"

129

Hanne smiled, shaking her head.

"Sometimes your ego gets totally out of hand," she said. "Have you come here to show me that? Besides, I thought you were suited to having some hair on your head. Not quite so desperately macho, somehow."

He remained standing, a look of triumph in his intense eyes, as though her comments about his macho image were construed as a compliment rather than criticism. She was never going to understand him entirely. His towering figure was both terrifying and attractive. His proportions were so well balanced it took some of the edge off his awe-inspiring size. Stripped of his jewelry — an inverse cross on one ear, a chunky, long gold chain around his neck, and a broad bracelet of hammered metal encircling his left wrist — he could be clad in an SS uniform and present the perfect prototype of Goebbels's PR machine at the end of the thirties. His straight, well-shaped nose, his narrow but nevertheless sensual lips, his coloring, his fierce blue eyes — everything accorded with Hitler's distorted caricature of the authentic Aryan. Billy T. was kind. But first and foremost, he was incredibly loyal and possessed an instinct she never once considered to be surpassed by her own.

"Have you come here to praise yourself, or to tell me something important?"

"Something important," he roared. "A man's appearance is important, you know!"

"You wouldn't think so to look at you," she said, waving her hands in a gesture indicating he ought to come to the point.

130

"Our boy has apparently been in Grefsen for a few days," he said, perching himself on the edge of her desk. "Olav, that is. The runaway boy."

"What? Has he been found?"

"No. But a family who had been on holiday in Austria got a fairly unpleasant surprise when they returned home. Someone had been there eating their porridge, so to speak. Half their store of canned food has gone, all their toilet paper used up, the wallpaper's been torn off half the kitchen walls, but the house is almost undisturbed."

Hanne stubbed out her cigarette in a shower of ash.

"Grefsen? That must be more than ten kilometers from the foster home, isn't it?"

"Sixteen, to be precise. He has walked all the way on those thick legs of his, if they're not mistaken about him having no money on him. Although a taxi driver would have alerted us by now, with all those news reports and such. The worst thing is he's gone in totally the wrong direction if he was attempting to make his way home."

Hanne noticed a faint smell of aftershave lotion, just a tiny whiff under her nose. Did he use aftershave on his head?

"Well," Billy T. concluded as he stood up to leave, "he has at least set off on another stage of his journey, and his mother hasn't heard a peep, she says. But it sounds fairly definite that he's the one who's been there; they're checking out fingerprints as we speak. It'll be easy to sort out the boy's prints at the foster home, so we've had a bit of luck there."

Stretching himself, he touched the ceiling with the palms of his hands. A moment later, he dropped them, and Hanne could see two faint impressions of his hands on the pale gray painted surface.

When he left, she sat there staring at the marks with a sense of enjoyment she could not for the life of her explain.

Terje Welby was sweating in the stuffy and clammy little two-room apartment he had moved into a year earlier, after a divorce that had cost him two children, a terraced house, and two and a half thousand kroner a month. He had backed the wrong horse when Eva, a snazzy young summer worker at the foster home, had taken him by storm. She was only nineteen years old and looked Finnish. At least the way he imagined Finnish women to look. She laughed constantly and appealed to the best and worst in him. His astonishment that she had allowed herself to be seduced so easily had progressed all too quickly into an exaggerated belief in his own merit. She promised him nothing, but he had taken it for granted that they would become a couple. Six hectic, fantastic months afterward, he was in the process of moving in with her when he was supplanted by a broad-shouldered twenty-one-year-old suffering from acne. With his tail between his legs, Terje had begged his wife, a woman of his own age, for a second chance. However, she had used those six months to emerge from a catastrophe into a contented belief in an existence without the tomcat who had caused her so much pain. He now saw

132

his sons every other weekend, but they seemed increasingly uninterested, complaining about having to share a room with their father.

Financial problems had increased his depression. He performed his job, drank a few beers at the neighborhood bar every Saturday and Wednesday, and discovered to his chagrin that his wife had appropriated all their mutual friends.

Now his hands were shaking, and the papers confronting him rustled threateningly every time he touched them. Igniting a lighter, he drew the flickering flame over to the corner of the first sheet and held it in his outstretched arm over the kitchen sink, where it burst into flames more rapidly than he had expected. He burned his fingers and issued a timid oath before placing his hand underneath the cold running water. A short time later, all the papers had been reduced to a mess of ashes and water.

Opening the window did not help. The room became chilly, but he was still sweating.

Hanne Wilhelmsen did not quite know where she was heading, though she had an address on a yellow Post-it note attached to the air bag on her steering wheel. Birgitte Håkonsen's address. Olav's mother. But for some time Hanne Wilhelmsen was driving in the opposite direction.

She lingered at the interchange beside the Postgiro building, and after circumnavigating three times to the accompaniment of increasingly loud honking from irritated fellow motorists, she allowed the vehicle to choose its own route.

Twenty-five minutes later she was in one of Oslo's oldest suburbs, a monument to misguided housing policy that gave her the shivers. Low-rise gray apartment blocks stood like diffuse, haphazard, discolored building bricks adorned with sad little curtains from the Hansen & Dysvik store, lending the houses the appearance of lying prostrate with their eyes closed. The occasional jungle gym had been erected at some time in the distant past, with no thought of any need for future maintenance. Every surface that could possibly be reached by adolescent boys was covered in tags, illegible, bold lettering — a cryptic code only those under the age of twenty could understand. Trash cans, the few green ones graciously bestowed upon them by the council, were sitting askew with their open mouths stuffed with dog-shit bags. A gray and muggy haze hung over this area of the city.

A shopping center was located slap-bang in the middle. A huge Lego brick that had perhaps once been white but now more or less blended into its surroundings. It had obviously been built on the principle of the greatest possible floor space for the least possible financial outlay. Inside this enormous brick you could trudge from an argument with the child welfare service to collect money from the social services office and then travel on to spend it in a dirty, smoky café on the ground floor. It must be where everybody was hanging out, since the neighborhood outside was deserted.

The chief inspector parked her car, bringing the yellow sticky with her. Double-checking that the vehicle was locked, she strode across the parking lot onto a little walkway marked with a square sign showing the well-known pictogram of adult and child walking hand in hand, barely visible beneath all the tags. It was askew and dog-eared. The walkway was asphalted and strewn with gravel.

Apartment 14b, first floor.

Hanne Wilhelmsen's head was a tumult of noise: all her alarm bells were ringing, since this action of hers was highly irregular. In order to muffle the racket, she struggled to think whether she had ever done anything similar in the past. Visiting a witness for an interview outside the police station.

Never.

It didn't make matters any better that she was entirely on her own.

For a second she considered the possibility of simply not presenting her police ID. Making it a private visit, a visit from one woman to another. Insane. She was from the police.

Some attempt had been made to protect the entrance door with a small roof constructed from tar paper with a little gutter running along the edge, to no great effect. The door was worn and unpainted, decorated with the ubiquitous initials in red and black, and the doorbells were situated on the right-hand side of the door, though no one had bothered to insert their nameplates underneath the glass. A few names were stuck on with Scotch tape, while others had used masking tape without even going to the effort of trimming the corners. Four doorbells were blank.

B. Håkonsen had at least tried to do it properly. A card adorned with her name written in clear, elegant script was neatly taped in place. Just before Hanne Wilhelmsen pressed the doorbell, she took several steps back, beyond the little roof, staring up at the building's façade.

The apartment block was four stories high and there seemed to be two apartments on each floor. She tried to guess which side belonged to the Håkonsens, but it was impossible to judge. She made up her mind to return home. Then, stepping resolutely forward, she placed her finger on the button.

Since it was remarkably peaceful in the neighborhood — the only sound to be heard was the distant drone of motorway traffic and a monotonous *dunk-dunk* from a building site nearby — she could actually hear the bell chiming somewhere inside the building. Extremely faintly, but all the same a distinct ringing. She felt relieved when no one responded and was just about to admit defeat when a voice crackled from the loudspeaker.

"Hello?"

"Hello, it's . . . My name's Hanne Wilhelmsen. I'm from the police. Could I come in?"

"Hello?"

Hanne leaned closer to the gray metal plate that functioned as both loudspeaker and microphone.

"My name is Hanne Wilhelmsen," she shouted in an exaggeratedly distinct voice. "I'm from the police. Could I . . ."

A click inside the wall startled Hanne Wilhelmsen, but the sound was not accompanied by a buzz from the door-release mechanism. Fairly irritated now, she rang the doorbell one more time.

This time nobody answered, and after a minute, she pressed the button again, holding it down for ten seconds, angrily and tenaciously.

Still no voice materialized, but before she could jab the button once more, the door release sounded. Tentatively grabbing hold of the cold metal door handle, she wrenched the door toward her. It was open.

No welcome committee waiting to greet her here. The usual apartment block odor in the entrance hall, a conglomeration of all sorts of dinners and washing powders mixed with a faint smell of garbage. As she traversed the ground floor, she recognized the stink of babies' diapers from a securely tied plastic bag sitting on the doormat. She walked up the stairs to the first floor.

Looking around, she saw a little floral-edged card with handwriting identical to that next to the bell downstairs. Sighing, she rang the doorbell, and the door immediately opened.

The woman standing in the doorway was a sorry sight, wearing an enormous jogging suit that nevertheless failed to disguise her peculiar body shape. She was almost as broad in the hips as she was tall, and on her feet the little pair of sealskin slippers provided more than an indication that the size of her feet bore no relation to the bulk of her body. Her black, straight hair framed a round face with a dark red mouth.

Oddest of all, however, were her eyes. They appeared tiny but so deeply set that they were difficult to distinguish, with long eyelashes curling almost a centimeter around her pudgy eye sockets and looking as though they had sprouted from two narrow, empty slits in her head.

She did nothing, said nothing. Hanne Wilhelmsen took a step forward, hoping the woman would move aside, but it was to no avail.

"Could I come in for a moment? Is it convenient?"

Instead of answering, the woman turned her back and padded through the hallway. Since she had left the door open, Hanne interpreted this as some kind of permission to enter and hesitantly followed her inside. The oblong hallway was dim, making the off-white rectangle of the living room door looming at one end difficult to see. She nearly stumbled on a slippery rag rug.

The sparsely furnished living room was tidy, and the windows shone, smelling freshly cleaned. The most striking aspect of the room was all the light. Above a small dining table with a flowery centerpiece fashioned from fabric and paper hung a pendant reminiscent of a carpenter's workshop lamp but with a more attractive shade. Its bulb had to be at least two hundred watts. On the longest wall, there were no fewer than six wall lamps, each with two lights. In addition, the room contained four standard lamps and three long,

138

unshaded fluorescent tubes along the window. It was a dazzling array.

The old sofa was upholstered in blue check material and appeared to have been well used at one end, where one cushion was lower than the others and where Hanne noticed that even the frame had begun to sag. A coffee table of varnished pine was adorned with several issues of the *Se og Hør* gossip magazine. Apart from those, there was no reading material in the entire room, except a few brochures on a dark shelf. Hanne could not ascertain what they were about.

Sitting down in her usual seat, the woman signaled Hanne toward an armchair from the sixties, covered in red nubbly fabric with oval teak inserts on each of the armrests. Hanne Wilhelmsen accepted the invitation.

"Can I offer you some coffee?"

Her voice was unexpectedly deep, with a lovely singsong intonation that might indicate some kind of hidden dialect. Since fetching coffee would necessitate the woman going to the bother of standing up and leaving the room, Hanne declined, but when she sensed disappointment on the otherwise impassive face, she changed her mind.

"As a matter of fact, yes. Perhaps a small cup."

Despite her unwieldy body shape, she moved smoothly, almost gracefully, walking like a cat, the sealskin slippers soundless on the linoleum on her way to the kitchen. She soon returned carrying a red metal enameled tray, with two coffee cups, a plate of plain biscuits, and a thermos jug. Pouring the coffee, she then pushed the biscuits invitingly across to Hanne's side of the table.

"Go ahead, help yourself," she encouraged her, taking a sip of her own coffee.

"You must be wondering why I'm here," Hanne said, at a loss for a conversation starter.

The woman did not reply but continued to sit, staring at her with a blank face.

"I've really come to talk to you about your boy, Olav."

Still not a twitch on the face.

"At least now we know nothing serious has happened to him," she added in an optimistic tone. "In all probability he's been staying at a house in Grefsen and has had food and shelter."

"Yes, so I've heard," the woman finally said. "They phoned me earlier today."

"Have you heard from him at all?"

"No."

"Have you any idea where he can have gone? Does he have any family — grandparents, for example?"

"No. Well, yes, but nobody he would visit."

This was not particularly edifying. Hanne drank a little of the coffee, finding it good, and scalding hot. Her alarm bells had subsided slightly, but she was still wondering why she had come here at all. She put down her cup. A trickle of coffee had spilled onto the saucer, and she momentarily looked around for a napkin. Her hostess kept a poker face.

"It must have been tough. Just being the two of you, I mean. Because the boy's father, he . . ."

"He's dead."

The woman spoke without bitterness, without sorrow, in the same melodic tone. Neutral and pleasant, like a radio announcer.

"I don't have children myself, so I don't really know how exhausting it is," Hanne said, wondering whether she would be allowed to smoke here. No ashtray was in evidence, but she dared to ask regardless, and the woman smiled for the first time, though without revealing her teeth. Standing up again, this time she returned with an ashtray the size of a dinner plate.

"I stopped years ago," she said. "But maybe I could have one of yours?"

Hanne leaned forward to light the cigarette she had passed to her. When Birgitte Håkonsen touched her hand, it struck Hanne how soft her skin was. Soft, dry, and warm. The woman inhaled her first drag like a habitual heavy smoker.

"No, neither did I know how exhausting it was," she said slowly, the smoke oozing out through her nose and mouth. "But as far as Olav is concerned, he has MBD, so it's not my fault he's so special."

"No, I suppose not," Hanne agreed, hoping to hear more.

"I asked for help early on. Even at the hospital when he was born I knew he wasn't like all the others. But they didn't believe me. When they finally . . ."

Now the vacant, expressionless face burst into life.

". . . When I finally managed to convince them there was something wrong, they wanted to take him from me. After I had struggled with him for nearly eleven years. I didn't want him to go to any foster home, you see. I just wanted some help. There are medications. Ritalin. I asked for a support contact. Perhaps a temporary foster placement."

Hanne was not certain, but it seemed as though the deep holes where eyes should be filled up with water. The woman blinked energetically.

"But that's not of interest to you, I shouldn't think," she said quietly.

"Yes, it is, actually. I'm trying to build up a picture of the boy. I've never seen him, of course. Only a photograph. He looks like you."

"Yes, what a fate that is, to tell the truth."

She stubbed out her cigarette with a practiced motion. Hanne offered her another, and she looked as though she would like to accept but shook her head all the same, waving her hand dismissively.

"He looks like me from the outside, but he's completely different inside. He thinks up the most unbelievable things. It's something to do with the way he perceives things. Just as if he . . . He sees something good where others see something bad, and bad where others see good. When someone tries to be kind to him, he thinks they're being nasty. When he tries to be polite and pleasant, other children become afraid. And then he does look fairly frightening. It's exactly as though he's . . . the opposite of all the others. An inside-out child, so to speak."

The woman drew her feet up underneath her body, stroking her hair away from her face with an unexpectedly feminine gesture.

142

"When all the children are looking forward to Christmas, he dreads it because it only lasts a few days. When it's summertime and all the children want to go out and swim, he sits inside eating, saying he's too fat to go outside. When an ordinary child would cry and be unhappy, he smiles and doesn't want me to comfort him. Have you read *The Snow Queen*?"

Hanne shook her head.

"Hans Christian Andersen. It's about a mirror that distorts everything. It breaks into a thousand pieces, and people who get a splinter in their eye see everything crooked and crazy, everything bad and ugly. If you get one in your heart, then you become cold as ice."

She leaned forward, perhaps wondering whether it was possible to change her mind about that cigarette. Before Hanne had got as far as asking her, the woman continued.

"Olav has a good heart. He just wants to be kind. But he's got a splinter of that troll mirror in his eye."

Chief Inspector Hanne Wilhelmsen was at a loss. She blushed in shame, but fortunately the steam from the hot coffee helped her to conceal it. Without thinking more closely about it, she rubbed her right eye.

"We all have a little splinter that keeps us from seeing things the way they really are. You too."

Now she smiled properly. Her teeth were uneven, but white and well cared for.

"You thought I was stupid, didn't you? A social services client who loses her child to the child welfare service! Who doesn't have a job or a family, and who hasn't got a single book on her bookshelf!"

"No, no, not at all," Hanne lied.

"Yes, you did," insisted the woman. "And in many ways I am like that. I was an idiot to marry his father. I was weak and stupid and didn't . . ."

Now the tears came flowing out of the little wells in her face and she used the chubby, smooth back of her hand to dry her cheeks. Then she pulled herself together and went back to the beginning, her feet sliding down to the floor again and her face falling into a blank, dead expression.

"What do you want from me, anyway?"

"To be honest, I don't really know. We're burning the candle at both ends with this case, and I feel there's something about Olav that we ought to know."

"He didn't do it."

Now her voice was no longer pleasant. It had risen half an octave, becoming almost shrill.

Hanne raised her hand in defense.

"No, no, that's not what we think. But he might have seen something. Or heard something. We're really very anxious to speak to him. But I don't suppose it'll be long until he reappears."

"I *know* he didn't do it. And he hasn't seen or heard anything either. You can just keep away from my boy! It's bad enough that the child welfare . . ."

Her eyes came into view. Perhaps because the pressure from inside was so great, they almost popped out. Or maybe it was only because she opened them up as far as they would go. Amazingly enough, they were bright blue.

"Mrs Håkonsen," Hanne ventured.

"Don't 'Mrs Håkonsen' me," the woman interjected. "You know *nothing* about Olav. You've not the foggiest idea how he is and how he experiences the world. When he ran away, it was because he hated being there. He wanted to come home! *Home*, do you understand! Here! It may not seem like much of a home to you, but I'm the only person in the whole world who loves Olav. *The only person in the whole world!* But do you pay any attention to that? No, not at all, you take the boy away like a parcel and expect me to cooperate! 'You have to understand, Mrs Håkonsen, that Olav needs help with the conflicting loyalties he will feel at moving, and it's important you cooperate.'"

She spat out the quote, a distorted rictus deforming her face.

"Understand? Cooperate? When they take from me the only thing I live for? And as far as that *Agnes* is concerned . . ."

She used the same unpleasant tone.

". . . I'm not sorry for a single second about her death. Going about thinking she can be some kind of mother to every Tom, Dick, and Harry. *Olav's already got a mother! Me!* Do you know what she did before my boy ran away? She punished him by saying I couldn't visit him for a fortnight. A fortnight! It's not even legal to do that! Olav phoned me and . . ."

She sank back onto the sofa, falling silent.

Clearing her throat, Hanne lifted her cup from the saucer. The bottom was wet with coffee, and she held her hand underneath in an attempt to prevent it from causing a stain. It was no use, though, and a large drip fell onto the cream-colored carpet.

"I don't know anything about the case at the child welfare service, Mrs Håkonsen," was the only comment she managed to make.

The woman appeared to be preparing to continue her outburst, then changed her mind. Perhaps all her strength had drained away. She subsided onto the sofa and remained sitting there in complete silence.

"I didn't mean to upset you," Hanne apologized. "That really wasn't my intention."

The woman did not answer, and Hanne realized she ought to leave. Getting to her feet, she thanked her for the coffee and apologized once again for disturbing her. When she entered the hallway, she was almost sure she heard something through a closed door that she assumed led into the bedroom. She considered asking if there was anybody there, but let it drop. She had already stretched the limits far enough with this woman who did not have especially friendly feelings toward public servants. On a shelf beside the coat closet lay a pile of books with protective library covers. They were the last items she noticed before the door slammed behind her.

As she stepped down the concrete stairs, observing that no one had yet been bothered to put the diapers down the garbage chute, it struck her once again how graceful the woman's movements had been. Birgitte

Håkonsen was totally different from how she had pictured her.

It was still gray, wet, and deserted outside, but fortunately her car was not vandalized. Not even as much as the tiniest little tag.

Surprisingly enough, he managed to keep quiet. It just shows how frightened he is. The policewoman was here for at least half an hour. I can't remember him ever staying so quiet for as long as that before.

Once, long ago, he was probably about eight, we had moved to Oslo for the first time, and he sat in his room for as long as that. I think. When I hadn't heard a sound for over an hour, I went in to give him some food. The apartment was on the ground floor, and sunlight never reached inside. In the gloom I wondered whether he had fallen asleep. But he had vanished. I was terrified, and didn't know what to do. So I just sat there, on his bed, and waited. Just before midnight, the police came to the door and brought him back. The boy was smiling from ear to ear and stinking of alcohol. He staggered into his room while the polite police officer told me he had been lured into drinking by some older boys. It would be best if I were to get a physician to have a look at him, the man thought. It wasn't at all clear how much alcohol he had consumed.

I didn't phone for a doctor. But I sat in his room all night. He puked like a pig and was sober in two days. In fact he let me help him with a few things, and was very quiet. Eight years old and dead drunk. But then he's inherited those genes, I suppose.

They say they don't think he did it. Murdered Agnes. But that's just something they say. Although the policewoman seemed nice enough, I know what to expect from that sort. They prattle on and on and then end up doing something quite different.

I know he didn't do it. I know I need to keep him hidden. But how long can I manage that?

CHAPTER
SEVEN

"How many times do I have to say that this is a routine interview?"

Billy T. was clearly annoyed. Across the desk from him sat a strong, beefy man of fifty-three, behaving like a little brat.

"This is your phone number, is it not?"

He waved a yellow note enclosed in a zipped plastic pocket.

The man still did not respond.

"For God's sake, man, do I have to resort to a judicial examination or what? Do you think that would be in your best interests? I know this is your number. Can't you just answer the question? It surely can't be so dangerous to answer something we already know?"

"Why are you asking when you already know the answer?" the man muttered brusquely. "I don't need to give you any more than my name and address. I can't understand why I'm here anyway."

Billy T. felt it was time for a break. His patience was about to run out, and from bitter experience he knew it paid to count to one hundred. Somewhere else entirely. Instructing the man to remain seated, he rapidly scanned the room to satisfy himself there was nothing lying there that other eyes should not see. He stuffed two folders into the drawer, locked it, and disappeared out the door.

"Fuck, Hanne, that lover boy'll be the death of me. He won't answer any questions at all. Talk about making yourself suspicious!"

Flopping down on Hanne's desktop, he rubbed his hands over his skull and tugged at his nose.

"Strictly speaking, do we know for sure they had a relationship?"

"Let me spell this out," Billy T. said, counting on his fingers. "Number one, he's talked about a new lady friend to his workmates. He's a car salesman. Number two, he's told the same folk that he's screwing his way to some money. Number three, he had just moved house. That meant he had changed his number, and so she had written it down. Number four, his number was the very last phone number in her life that Agnes rang."

"How do you know that?"

"Quite simple, I hit the repeat button on her phone. Last number. To that *idiot*."

He punched his fist on the desk by his side.

"And number five, her husband talked about how distant and irritable she had been these last few months."

"That's not exactly decisive evidence you've got there," Hanne said.

"No, I agree. But that blockhead might have told me what was going on, and I could stop building castles in the sky! I'm willing to listen to anything at all; it's difficult enough to think about Agnes Vestavik sitting on his lap, a fat, bald car salesman. She was supposed to be conventional and Christian!"

"Prejudice and presumption again, Billy T. Religious people have the same urges as you and me. You'll have to try to find a chink in his armor."

She used both hands to shove his back off her desk.

"Off you go, I've got work to do. What's more, if they were lovers, why in the world would he kill her? Wouldn't that be biting the hand that was feeding him?"

"Sure," Billy T. mumbled, trudging back to the obstinate car salesman.

"Have you reconsidered? Willing to be a bit more cooperative, perhaps?"

"That's what you say," the man exclaimed, furious. "The police are going about poking their noses in at my workplace, asking questions and making life difficult for me, dragging me in for an interview in the middle of the working day and accusing me of killing and murder and even worse than that!"

Billy T. did not even crack a smile.

"Have I for a single second accused you of murder?"

The man stared at his shoes. Now Billy T. could discern a touch of uncertainty in his broad masculine face.

"Listen here," he continued, his voice almost friendly now. "I'm accusing you of only one thing in the meantime, and that is that you were having an affair with Agnes Vestavik. That's certainly not a crime. When we 'poke our noses in' to that, it's not to punish you. It's in order to construct the most complete picture

151

possible of what her life was like. What she did, whom she knew, and how she lived. To be quite honest, we're really stuck. It's not so easy to come up with a motive for killing a neat and proper foster home worker with a neat and proper life. When we discover it's not so neat and proper after all, then obviously we're going to be interested. That doesn't mean, though, that we think you've killed your lady friend."

Bingo. That was a far better tactic. Appealing to his better nature.

Leaning forward, the man put his head in his hands and sat there, without moving a muscle. Billy T. allowed him whatever time he needed.

Eventually he lifted his head, stroking the bristles on his cheek as he took a deep breath.

"We had a relationship. A kind of relationship. I mean, we didn't have sex. But she was . . . We were . . . in love."

It seemed as though he had never used the word before and thought it too beautiful for his coarse, wide mouth. He appreciated it himself.

"We were involved with each other," he corrected himself. "We met to chat, to be together. We went for walks. She was . . ."

He did not manage to explain what she was, for he was now fighting tears and emerged victorious. But it took several minutes.

"You have to understand I could never have murdered Agnes! My God, she was the best thing that had happened to me for years!"

"How did you meet?"

152

"How do you think? She came to buy a car, of course. She came with her husband, a nondescript fool. Didn't even know the difference between cylinder capacity and horsepower. It was obvious Agnes was the one who held the purse strings, and she was the one who subsequently followed the matter up. We got on well, and so . . . well, so it just continued."

"What about your talk at work? About screwing your way into some money?"

"Oh, that . . . just boys' talk."

He did not even seem embarrassed. Billy T. felt tempted to comment that boys over sixteen should not tell lies about that type of thing, but he let it be.

"What were you talking about on the evening she was killed?"

"Talking? I didn't see her that evening!"

He stared in alarm at Billy T. and gripped the armrests tightly.

"Take it easy. I mean the phone conversation you had. She phoned you from her office. At some time or other that evening."

The man looked genuinely taken aback.

"No, she didn't," he said explicitly, shaking his head vigorously. "I was in Drøbak with a car and didn't get back until after midnight. Met an old pal and had a few cups of coffee in a café before driving back. I can prove it too!"

Billy T. made a face and stared the other man directly in the eye without uttering a word. The car salesman lost the tussle and dropped his gaze.

"Well," Billy T. said, "didn't she know you wouldn't be at home?"

"I don't remember, but *I* knew at least that she would be working. She had problems at work. Something about someone having let her down. She didn't say very much about it, but she was extremely disappointed."

"Someone? Male or female?"

"No idea. She was very particular about professional confidentiality. Said very little about the youngsters there as well, even though they took up all her days and nights."

Billy T. fetched a cup of burned coffee for the man and started to write. Within half an hour there was nothing more to be heard in the little office apart from Billy T.'s bulky fingers battering the computer keyboard. When he considered himself finished, he had only one question remaining.

"Was there to be something more between you? Was she talking about a divorce?"

The expression on the man's face was impossible to decipher.

"I don't know if anything would have come of it. But she told me she had made up her mind long ago, and that she had told her husband so."

"Did she say that quite clearly?"

"Yes."

"Straight out: 'I've told my husband that I want a divorce,' not 'My husband doesn't want a divorce' or 'He'll be upset if we get divorced'?"

"Yes, straight out. Several times. At least . . ."

154

He cast his eyes to the ceiling, considering carefully. "At least she said it on two occasions."

"Okay," Billy T. said curtly and obtained the witness's signature on the interview report before bringing the session to a close.

"Stick around in Oslo, won't you?" he added as he opened to door to the corridor.

"Where else would I be?" the man replied as he vanished out of sight.

Tone-Marit was nobody's fool. She had been with the police for four years and nine months and had only three months to go until she could call herself sergeant and add another stripe to the one she already possessed on the uniform she seldom or never wore. Although she hadn't been in the section for more than a year, Hanne was already impressed by the twenty-six-year-old. She was thorough rather than innovative, and conscientious rather than actually smart, but thoroughness and conscientiousness had shaped many exceptional investigators.

Now she was stuck. She didn't have a great grasp of book-keeping and sat with three thick loose-leaf binders facing her, terms like "current assets" and "fixed assets," "operating profit" and "balance sheet" swirling in her head for two hours.

Something had come to her attention in the meantime. An unusual number of receipts had been authorized by Terje Welby. As far as she had understood, his role as assistant director had largely been overtaken by Maren Kalsvik. True enough, *she* didn't have the power to authorize payments, but it would then have been natural for Agnes Vestavik to assume most of the economic responsibility.

"Ask the boys in Accounts," Billy T. advised her after leafing through the folders at random. "For the moment, I'll give this Terje Welby a little shake."

He grinned broadly in anticipation, and Tone-Marit gratefully packed up the binders to do as he said.

"Have you found out anything more about the missing thirty thousand from Agnes's bank account?"

Placing her hands on the folders, Tone-Marit nodded.

"Only that they were withdrawn in three different locations around the city. And that the account was blocked two days later. The same day that Agnes was killed. I've asked the banks to look for the actual checks, so we can see what's going on. But that can take time; everything not on the data system takes an age of course."

"So does everything that's on the data system," Billy T. muttered.

It was only a week since Agnes Vestavik's murder, and Hanne felt it had been an eternity. Little response was forthcoming from the superintendent, who was normally a considerate man with great sensitivity to the problems of his subordinates. Today he had brushed her off. The double murder in Smestad occupied all his resources: a shipowner and his somewhat dipsomaniac, decrepit wife had been found with their heads blown off in what seemed to be the most grotesque robbery and murder in Norwegian criminal history. The newspapers were gorging themselves in the borderland between social pornography and gossip column, mixing smoothly with the usual smear campaign against incompetent police officers, and the police commissioner was impatient, to put it mildly. Agnes Vestavik's fate had aroused a scintilla of interest on the first day, but now it was ancient history. For everyone except the small band of four still fumbling around hunting for motive and opportunity.

"My God," Hanne muttered. "Times have changed. Ten years ago, a murder such as this would have turned the department upside down. We would have been given twenty men and all the resources we needed."

Erik Henriksen did not know how to take the outburst. Did she mean he was a lightweight? He chose to keep his mouth shut.

"But . . ." She suddenly smiled, as though she had only just realized he was sitting there. "What have you found out?"

"The Lover," the young officer began. "He's had severe financial problems."

Financial problems. Who on earth doesn't have financial problems? Hanne Wilhelmsen thought, refraining from lighting the cigarette she so longed for.

"People don't go around killing other people even if they have financial problems." She sighed. "Every other person would probably say they have problems of that nature if we asked them. We have to find out something more! Something more . . . passionate! Hatred, contempt, fear, something in that direction. The guy

157

was besotted with the woman. They weren't married, so he didn't have any financial interest in her."

"But the boys at work say he had been very quiet recently. The past couple of weeks or so. Seemed almost depressed, they said."

"So what?" Hanne challenged as she formed a tent shape with her fingers. "What does that imply? If Agnes had broken up with him, or whatever we should say to describe ending a platonic relationship, then he still doesn't have any grounds for killing the woman! With a knife! And what's more, it would be remarkable if nobody noticed or heard a distressing argument between two former lovers ending in murder."

She shook her head, discouraged, and sat up straight in her office chair.

"No, now I'm being unfair, Erik."

She smiled.

"I don't mean to take it out on you. But isn't this a strange case? No one's bothered. The superintendent can hardly take the trouble to speak to me. The newspapers are completely uninterested. The foster home continues as though nothing has happened. The youngsters shout and play, her husband remains living where he has always lived, the world goes on spinning on its axis, and a week after Agnes Vestavik was dispatched, it's almost as if I'm not bothering either. In a month's time, hardly anyone will remember the case. Do you know one thing —"

She interrupted herself by digging out an edition of *Arbeider-bladet* from a pile of newspapers on the floor.

158

"Here," she said, leafing through to a headline. "There are now more homicides committed in Oslo in real life than in crime novels! For the first time in history. Heavens above!"

She slapped the palm of her hand against her forehead.

"Novelists can't even keep up with us! A murder here, a homicide there, who cares? Now there have to be two at once in order to gain any recognition. Or else the corpse has to be desecrated or the victim wealthy. Or a prostitute. Or a footballer or a celebrity or a politician. Or even better: the *perpetrator* is rich or a celebrity. An anonymous woman who doesn't have any special qualities other than a quiet life with a 'sort of' lover, and nobody's going to get excited about it. Are you bothered by this?"

The final interrogative was said as Hanne leaned across the desktop, staring him directly in the eyes.

Erik Henriksen swallowed audibly.

"Of course I'm bothered about it," he mumbled, swallowing again. "It's my job to be."

"Exactly! We bother about it because it's our job. But the superintendent's not bothered, he's quite happy to push it all over onto our plates. The newspapers aren't bothered, because they haven't found enough gossip in the case. And we don't bother ourselves either, since we're able to go home with glad hearts every evening and eat our meatballs and gravy without a single thought for a four-year-old somewhere who has lost her mother in a way that it's actually part of our task to prevent. *Prevent!* That's our foremost task, you know!

159

To prevent crime. When did you last prevent a crime, Erik?"

He was tempted to explain how he had prevented a friend from drunk driving last Saturday night but sensibly let it drop.

The phone rang, startling Erik Henriksen. Hanne Wilhelmsen allowed it to ring four times before answering.

"Wilhelmsen," she said brusquely into the receiver.

"Is that Hanne Wilhelmsen?"

"Yes. Who am I speaking to?"

"It's Maren Kalsvik. From the Spring Sunshine Home."

"Oh yes."

"I'm phoning because I'm worried about Terje Welby. You know, the assistant director. The one with the bad back."

"Why is that?"

Hanne Wilhelmsen placed a finger on her lips as a sign Erik should remain silent, pointing to the door and making a gesture asking him to close it. He misunderstood and was on his way out the door when Hanne placed a hand over the receiver and whispered, "No, no, Erik, come in and close the door. But keep quiet."

Then she carefully pressed the loudspeaker button on the handset.

"He's on part-time sick leave and finished early today. But he was supposed to drop by to accompany one of the youngsters to a motorcycle class. He should have been here two hours ago. I've phoned him several times. Finally I went to his house, as he stays not far from here, but the door was locked. But only with the one lock. The security lock hadn't been used, and that usually means he's at home."

Hanne Wilhelmsen was not in the mood to worry about a grown man who had been missing for only two hours.

"He might have forgotten about it," she said wearily. "He could have had something else to do. Perhaps he's at the doctor's, for all I know. Going missing for two hours in the case of a person over three years old isn't a police matter."

It went quiet at the other end of the line, and then Hanne could hear sounds that told her the woman was crying. Very softly.

"Everything's probably okay," said Hanne, trying to reassure her, in a slightly less dismissive tone. "He'll probably turn up soon."

"But you see," the woman began again, before tears got the better of her. It took quite awhile before she was able to pull herself together.

"There's so much more to it," the woman ventured once more. "I can't explain it over the phone, but there really *is* cause to be alarmed. He . . . I just can't bring myself to talk about it now. But couldn't you *please* come over here and see if everything's okay? Please!"

Erik Henriksen had drawn closer to the desk and telephone and was sitting with his arms folded, elbows leaning on the desktop. She glimpsed his watch, a cheap imitation Rolex Oyster.

161

"I'll be with you in half an hour," she said, wrapping up the conversation.

Erik looked quizzically at her, and she nodded. He might just as well accompany her.

"My God."

Hanne halted and looked dejectedly at the young officer.

"Here I sit, berating you because nobody's bothering any longer, and yet I try to dismiss someone who is doing exactly that. Bothering."

They had a stroke of luck and had to wait only ten minutes for a service vehicle. That was close to a record.

The entrance door was locked, exactly as Maren Kalsvik had said. In the minuscule gap between doorplate and frame, she could see the security lock had not been used, confirming Maren's account. Thrusting her hand into her pocket, Hanne Wilhelmsen fished out a couple of tissues and attempted to pull the door handle down without touching it too much. Erik Henriksen looked at her in surprise.

"Just a safety measure," she assured him.

They were confronted with a locked door and a grown man who had been missing for barely three hours. Not exactly grounds for a legal forced entry. If her dependable colleague, Police Attorney Håkon Sand, hadn't been so damn modern as to take an entire year's paternity leave, she could have sorted something out. At the moment Hanne had no idea who was on attorney duty and she needed a lawyer's permission to break into the apartment.

She had to get inside. The information Maren Kalsvik, convulsed with sobs and in a dreadful state, had spent half an hour relating was so alarming that they were approaching a decision to arrest him. However, explaining to a lawyer that a terrific motive had cropped up and that a suspect had in fact been at the scene of Agnes Vestavik's tragic demise at an extremely critical point in time was not a conversation one ideally had over the phone. On the other hand, it could be a matter of life or death.

Instructing Erik to stand his ground but not to touch anything, she trotted back to the car and after a great deal of hassle succeeded in contacting the duty lawyer on her cell phone. She was in luck. The attorney was an old — if rather weary — cunning fox. Noting the points, he gave her the green light and transferred her to the crime desk. They promised her backup within half an hour.

Actually they took three-quarters of an hour to arrive, but it was worth the wait. Two silent types, who knew what they were doing, without any further ado positioned themselves outside the door with a substantial battering ram consisting of a heavy square iron plate attached to a long shaft with hand grips for four pairs of hands. Hanne and Erik posted themselves at the rear.

"One, two, and THREE," called the first officer as they swung the battering ram to and fro at one and two, allowing it to crash through the door at three.

163

The timber did not have a chance. The door split open, helplessly releasing its hold on the frame struggling in vain to stay firmly attached, and fell back inside the room. It remained lying at an angle, but the upper part was leaning toward the wall of the hallway, only a meter and a half across. Elbowing her way in front of the two assisting officers, Hanne Wilhelmsen rushed into the apartment.

The hallway was empty, and there was no one in the living room either. She stood still for a second, scanning what appeared to be a typical bachelor's pad: furnishings were cobbled together, one window lacked curtains, and no attempt had been made to make it attractive or comfortable. No pictures on the walls, not a single potted plant. The kitchen sink was full of dirty glasses.

"Hanne, come here," she heard from the hallway.

Three male backs were blocking the bathroom doorway. She placed a hand on the nearest pair of shoulders, and they all drew back.

She whistled under her breath.

Terje Welby was sitting on the toilet seat. Or more correctly, his mortal remains were sitting there. He had kept his shoes on, and apart from those, he was wearing jeans with no belt and a T-shirt. His head had fallen onto his chest, and his arms were hanging limply at his sides. Viewed like this, he might appear to be a man who had collapsed after having too much to drink, if his feet had not been planted in an enormous pool of blood and both of his wrists slashed.

164

Hanne slowly stepped into the room, where there was hardly space for two people. Without touching either the body or any other item, she leaned toward each of his hands, confirming it was only on the left side that he had reached as far as the main artery. But there he had certainly done a good job. A ten-centimeter-long cut ripped through the bottom part of his lower arm, and despite all the blood, she could discern the white of sinew and bone.

An empty whisky bottle had been discarded in the basin. On the floor lay a large carpet knife, with the blade fully extended and covered in blood.

She cautiously placed two fingers on his neck, but he was already quite cold, and there was no sign of life.

"He's dead all right," she said softly, backing out of the bathroom. "Send for Forensics."

The final comment was directed at one of the assisting officers.

"Crime scene technicians? For an obvious case of suicide?"

"Call them in," Hanne insisted, hunkering down at the bathroom door without taking time to explain her decision to the random policeman sent to assist her.

For his part, he shrugged his shoulders, sending a meaningful glance to his colleague, and sloped off to carry out her order. A chief inspector was a chief inspector, after all.

First they took photographs. Hanne Wilhelmsen, who had to vacate the area to give the technician elbowroom, was impressed by how lithely he moved around in the tiny space without ever coming into contact with the body, the blood, or the walls. He exited the room a couple of times in order to change his film, but did not speak. When the bathroom had been comprehensively photographed, two men began to make precise measurements of the position of the corpse in relation to the ceiling, the basin, and all four walls. They exchanged the occasional comment, and one of them jotted down notes in a spiral notebook once the distances had been ascertained. Hanne noticed that they operated within a millimeter's accuracy.

Thereafter, they set to work to obtain prints. It dawned on Hanne that it had been a long time since she had been present at a crime scene examination, because instead of using only the black or white powder she was used to, they sometimes made use of some kind of spray that deposited an indefinable color at certain points.

Two hours later, their efforts were concluded. The body was carefully placed on a stretcher and driven to the hospital, where it would shortly lie on an icy metal bench in a yellow room to be picked clean.

"Clear case of suicide, if you ask me," one of the technicians remarked as he packed his case. "Do you want us to seal the apartment?"

"Yes, but then we really need to put the door back again," Hanne replied.

Not long afterward, the door was more or less in place, and two eyelet screws were fastened to the frame and doorplate. A fine metal wire was laced through them and the ends joined together with a little seal of lead in the center.

"Thanks very much, boys," Hanne said in a lackluster voice as she sent Erik off in the technicians' vehicle.

"I'm going home. Tell them I'm keeping the car until tomorrow morning."

She was deeply, heartily sorry.

Erik Henriksen fortunately had the foresight to call a minister. He himself did not feel quite mature enough to break the news to an ex-wife and two little boys that their daddy was dead. The clergyman had promised to attend to it at once. That had been an hour and a half earlier, so he assumed it had all been taken care of. It dawned on him that Maren Kalsvik ought to be told that her anxiety had been well founded. It was not exactly something one did by phone, so he dropped by the foster home on his way home.

It was dinnertime, and from the kitchen the sounds of eating could be heard: the clinking of glass, scraping of cutlery on china, and lots of voices, big and small. As usual, it was Maren Kalsvik who greeted him, and she stiffened when she caught sight of him.

"What's the matter?" she asked, sounding scared. "Has something happened?"

"Could we go somewhere private?" the police officer said awkwardly, avoiding eye contact with the woman.

She escorted him to a kind of conference room that obviously was adjacent to the kitchen, with a door leading from the day-room. Flopping down on an office chair, she tugged at her fringe.

"What's the matter?" she repeated.

"You were right," he launched into an explanation but caught himself. "I mean, there *were* grounds for concern. He had . . ."

Now he looked around, walking over to the door to ensure it was properly closed.

"He's dead," he said softly, after sitting down at the opposite side of the massive conference table.

"Dead? How is he dead?"

"Well, dead," the officer said, somewhat discouraged. "He had taken his own life. I'd rather not go into details."

"My God," Maren whispered, her face turning more ashen than ever.

She closed her eyes and swayed violently in the chair, which did not have armrests. Quick as a flash, Erik Henriksen dashed around to catch hold of her before she fell to the floor. She blinked her eyes and moaned softly.

"It's all my fault," she said, breaking down in wild sobs. "Everything's just my fault."

Then she leaned close to the bewildered officer who was not especially well trained to cope with what was going on. But he held her in his arms for a spell.

"For fuck's sake," Christian whispered excitedly as he tumbled out of the archive room into the adjoining office. Erik Henriksen had led Maren Kalsvik from the conference room upstairs to the first floor.

168

"This is starting to get spooky! *Fucking spooky!*"

He adjusted his clothes and rubbed his neck where, from previous experience, he knew a hickey was shortly about to bloom.

Cathrine, the skinny therapist, twentysomething going on thirty, followed after him. They had been sneaking into the archive room while they thought all the others were eating their meal and had been so wrapped up in their own bodies they had not heard the doorbell ring. When Maren and the police officer entered the neighboring room, they were trapped.

They had heard all of it.

"Taken his own life! My God!"

Cathrine was shaken, but not so much so that she refrained from taking the opportunity to lean toward a mirror beside the window to check her makeup. She made an openmouthed grimace as she ran a forefinger under each eye.

"Does that mean he's the one who whacked Agnes, or what?"

"Probably," Christian said with steadily increasing delight, grinning broadly.

"Look at you," she said, rebuking him gently and stroking her hand over his mouth. "Wipe off that grin. This is awful!"

Taking hold of her wrist, he shoved her down onto a chair and sat on the edge of the table beside her.

"I really would never have believed it," he said.

"Who did you think it was, then?"

Pushing himself farther onto the tabletop, he parked his feet on the seat of a chair. Then he propped his elbows on his knees and cupped his hands to support his face. His smile had vanished, and he looked deep in thought.

"Who did *you* think it was?" he parried.

Cathrine shrugged her shoulders, hemming and hawing.

"Well, that depends, I didn't really believe it was anyone in particular, I don't think."

"But *somebody* must have done it," Christian insisted.

"What about Olav?"

"Hah!"

"Don't be so high and mighty, of course it could have been him! He ran away and everything!"

"You surely haven't gone around thinking that boy could have done something like that? He's only twelve, you know."

"Well, who did *you* think it was?" she insisted once again.

"I thought it was Maren."

"Maren?"

She blinked quickly, thinking for a moment of confusion that she had misheard him. Could Maren, kind, clever, efficient, and almost self-effacing Maren, have killed Agnes? Christian was sweet, but he couldn't be quite right in the head.

"What in the world made you think that?"

"Look," he said eagerly, taking her hands in his, "who gains most from Agnes's death? To start with . . ."

Releasing his grasp, he tapped the tip of her nose lightly with his forefinger.

170

". . . it's Agnes who puts a stop to things every time Maren thinks something or other should be changed. All the time. Do you remember she supported the children when they wanted their bedtime to be put back by half an hour? Agnes said it was out of the question. And the time we were able to get a trip abroad for all the kids for the same price as it cost to hire that bloody awful cabin on the south coast? Agnes put her foot down."

Before she managed to protest the suggestion that bedtimes and quashed foreign excursions could be a motive for murder, he tapped her on the nose one more time.

"Second, it was Maren who became the boss here when Agnes went. You saw how she just took over straightaway. Terje's only a fool with fancy papers, everybody knows that."

"Was," Cathrine corrected him, immediately feeling somewhat queasy.

The excitement about the scandalous news began to recede in the face of the stark fact of Terje's death.

"Besides, he wasn't a fool," she added.

"Third . . ."

Now she managed to protect her nose from a fresh onslaught.

". . . Terje was a weakling and a wimp and I could never in my life believe he could work up the courage to kill anybody at all."

With his arms raised above his head and in the midst of an enormous yawn, he continued. "But I was wrong, darling. It must have been Terje. Why would he commit suicide otherwise? And only a few days after the murder. Case solved."

Jumping down to the floor, he retreated behind the chair where Cathrine was sitting and squeezed her thin frame.

"Why do we have to be so bloody secretive?" he whispered into her neck.

Wrenching herself out of his embrace, she answered despondently, "You are nineteen years old, Christian. Only nineteen."

Shaking his head and momentarily annoyed, he let her go. Then he recovered his equanimity and disappeared from the room to check if the news of the suicide was official.

Cathrine remained sitting with a vague sense of missing something. Only now did she notice the window was slightly ajar. The curtains were fluttering gently, admitting a brisk gust of air that seemed colder than it actually was, an obscure scent of wet earth and grimy snow and rotting vegetation. She stood up to close it but caught the curtain in the gap between window frame and ledge. As she succeeded in pushing open the tricky window to rescue the cloth, she had a feeling there was something significant that had slipped her memory. It was exactly as if a thought had rushed so swiftly past her mind that she had not quite caught sight of it, had not grasped it properly, and she stood there for a long time struggling to retrieve it. She even closed her eyes in an effort to concentrate. Was there something she had seen? Heard? Overheard, perhaps?

"Cathrine, can you help me wash my hair?"

Jeanette was standing in the doorway tugging at her straggly locks that did look rather greasy.

The thought had vanished. But it was important, and Cathrine hoped it would return another time. She fixed the floral curtain before going upstairs to the bathroom with the chubby eleven-year-old.

"Have you ever been in love with a boy?" Hanne Wilhelmsen asked in the dark as it was approaching midnight and they had just come to bed.

Cecilie chuckled, a surprised, rolling laugh.

"What on earth kind of question is that?" she inquired, twisting around on her side so she was face-to-face with Hanne. "I've never been in love with anyone except for you!"

"Don't joke! Of course you have. You just haven't done anything about it. At seventeen it was obvious you'd fallen a little bit in love. I remember that teacher of yours, for example. I was bloody jealous."

In the gloom, Cecilie could see Hanne's profile outlined on the blue striped wallpaper, and she let her finger run along her forehead and nose until she stopped and was rewarded with a kiss.

"Does that mean *you* have been in love at some time?"

"We're talking about *you* at the moment," Hanne insisted. "Have you ever been in love with a boy? A man?"

Cecilie sat up in bed, wrapping herself tightly in her quilt.

"Honestly, what's this all about?"

173

"Nothing serious. I'm just asking. Have you?"

"No. I've never in all my life been in love with a boy. I thought I was a few times as a teenager, but I was really just in love with the thought of being in love. It was liberating. And the alternative scared me to death."

Hanne had kicked her quilt halfway off and was lying with her hands under her head. Her entire upper body, half her thigh, and all of one leg were exposed. Her breasts were staring into the room, and just above her navel, Cecilie could see a pulse beating, quietly and evenly.

"But do you never feel a special . . . a kind of *benevolence* toward some man you like particularly well? The type of good feeling that means you want to be in his company all the time, do fun things, chat, play, the kind of things you long for when you're in love?"

"Yes, sometimes. But that's not a description of being in love. Don't you remember what it was like any longer, Hanne?"

She placed her hand gingerly on the gently pulsating spot on her lover's stomach.

"You want to do a whole lot of things more than that!"

Hanne turned around, looking at her earnestly. Car head-lamps formed a pattern on the ceiling, and in the fleeting shimmer of light Cecilie glimpsed a desperate expression she did not quite recognize.

"You must never, never leave me!"

Hanne snuggled close to her, almost on top of her, and repeated herself.

174

"You must promise you'll never leave me. Never never never."

"Never in this world and universe and all eternity," Cecilie whispered into her hair.

It was an ancient ritual. But it had been ages since they had resorted to it. Cecilie understood what it was all about.

Strangely enough, though, she did not feel threatened in the slightest.

CHAPTER
EIGHT

Although this was only Billy T.'s eighth day in his new post as detective, his office already looked like a pigsty. Papers were lying everywhere, some of them important, others scribblings and old newspapers. Beside the door, a pile of empty cola bottles was lying on the floor, and at least three of them toppled over every time someone entered the room. Above the door hung a little miniature basket, and two orange plastic foam balls lay in the center of the room. In addition, he had hung a bulletin board on one wall, directly facing the desk, with several snapshots of four small boys attached with staples from a staple gun. To make matters worse, the room was totally devoid of any item that might bring the slightest hint of hominess. The windows were filthy, though that was something Billy T. could hardly be blamed for.

"I don't really understand what we're doing," he said with resignation to Hanne Wilhelmsen, who by some miracle had avoided knocking over the bottles or trampling on something before taking her place. "Is the case solved now, or what? That's a bit of a disappointment, if I may say so. Plain and simple and boring: a divorced man with money problems dips his hand in the till, gets caught, murders his boss, and then slashes himself to death in a bout of regret and despair."

It was as though she had said the words herself. A disappointment. Maren Kalsvik had provided a statement that morning. Conscience stricken and shattered, she had given a full explanation of her deceased colleague's embezzlement. She herself had discovered it before Christmas and imposed as a condition for keeping quiet that he sort it out before Easter. All the money was to be paid back. Agnes had known about it. No, she had not spoken to the director about it, but she realized from Agnes's demeanor that her boss had surely known. Terje had admitted being there. He had insisted he was only looking for some papers. But he had told her barefaced lies for a considerable period of time, so she had no good reason to believe him. Neither had the police.

Still.

It could not be so simple.

"There's no suicide note," Hanne said thoughtfully, picking up one of the orange balls. Aiming for the basket above the door, she threw the ball in a gentle curve and hit the target. The ball lay dead on the floor. Stretching from the chair, she retrieved it and tried again. Two more points.

"Bloody hell, you're really good!"

"Used to live in the States, you know."

Billy T. lifted the other ball, tossing it into the air, where it hovered on the ring for a second before slowly teetering over on the right side.

"Two points," Hanne called, trying herself one more time. "Bingo! Hanny Wilhelmsen leads by four points!"

Grinning, Billy T. took up position as far away from the basket as possible, right over beside the window. For a few seconds he stood there, swaying up and down from the knees, before the orange ball drifted toward the basket, hitting the board and falling to the floor without even approaching the rim.

"I won," Hanne said, snatching both balls and placing them underneath her chair before Billy T. had the opportunity to continue the match. "I'm really missing a suicide note."

"Why? Do you actually think —"

"No, I don't mean that. I don't honestly think it's a murder. But we have to keep the possibilities open, don't you think?"

They exchanged glances and broke into laughter.

"Okay." Billy T. grinned. "But it's bloody tempting to come to the conclusion that Terje Welby killed Agnes. Difficult case solved within one week flat. Huge feather in the cap. Ready for fresh assignments. Fresh, *exciting* assignments."

"I haven't said that wasn't how it was. It's quite possible that it was Welby. It *probably* was him. But there's something that doesn't add up. Just a gut feeling. And if he was the one who murdered Agnes Vestavik, I damn well want better proof of the crime than him stealing some cash and taking his own life. And a question mark hangs over his reputation if he goes to his grave in the shadow of an unresolved murder."

Billy T. had good reason to take Hanne Wilhelmsen's gut feeling seriously. Especially when it mirrored his own.

"But where do we go from here, then?" he asked, somewhat daunted. "Strictly speaking, we're right back where we started!"

"Not quite. There are still some things to go on. A number of things."

They spent half an hour summarizing. First of all, they could wait for several pieces of technical information. Also, they had the husband. They had a lover of some kind who *might* have been rejected. They had a youngster, strong as an ox, on the run. Furthermore, they had somebody who had taken a large bite out of the victim's bank account, either by her giving the person in question large sums of money or by them being stolen. Both possibilities were equally interesting. Besides, there were several members of staff at the foster home who had been questioned only superficially. They had Tone-Marit and Erik's word, of course, that they were not of interest, but Billy T. should at least scrutinize them more closely. Four of the employees had not even attempted to produce alibis. Cathrine, Christian, Synnøve Danielsen, and Maren Kalsvik all lived on their own and had been at home alone on the night of the murder. The others' alibis had not been properly checked.

"And we really should look more closely at Olav's mother, Birgitte Håkonsen," Hanne said finally, sensing a faint unease when she mentioned the name. "There's no doubt she hated Agnes."

179

"How do you know that?" Billy T. leafed through the case files in front of him, finding nothing about Olav's mother.

Hanne waved at him dismissively. "I'll tell you later. But she really can't be excluded."

"Sounds a bit far-fetched to me," Billy T. mumbled, but he jotted something on a sheet of paper he retrieved from all the chaos on his desk.

"And one more thing."

Hanne rose to her feet and lifted one of the balls. Positioning herself where Billy T. had stood earlier, over by the window, with her back to the glass, she judged the distance to the basket and asked, "That number for Diakonhjemmet College. The one written on the other yellow note in Agnes's office. Have you checked what that was about?"

Swinging her right arm in a curved upward movement, she let the ball go once her arm was almost fully extended: it flew gracefully through the air, almost reaching the ceiling, and fell right into the basket.

"Can we play someday?" Billy T. said, impressed.

"Have you checked that number?"

"No, I haven't managed to do that yet."

"Then you can forget about it. I'll do it myself," Hanne said, suddenly throwing the ball right at him. "You need to practice first!"

Tone-Marit was extremely pleased with herself, with every reason to be so. In her eagerness, she had hunted high and low through the station for Hanne Wilhelmsen, but she was nowhere to be found.

180

However, nothing could spoil this for her, so she approached Billy T. instead, even though she was always a touch nervous in his company.

"What is it now?" Billy T. asked grouchily, peering up from the mess on his desk.

"I've discovered who cashed those checks," Tone-Marit said, looking forward to the scowl on the officer's face changing to anticipation and curiosity.

"No, fucking hell," he exclaimed forcefully. "Was it that grieving husband? Let me see!"

He waved his arms to reach for the document folder the young officer was clutching. She responded by hugging it close to her body and sitting down.

"No. But it was a man, and his name is . . ."

As she made a move to place the folder on her colleague's desk with a triumphant gesture, the documents fell to the floor. She blushed but picked them up in record time.

"Eivind Hasle. That's the man."

"Eivind Hasle? Do we have anything on him?"

"No, not at present. I checked every possible register. No criminal record, born in 1953, lives in Furuset, and works for a company in Grønland."

"In Grønland!" Billy T. laughed out loud.

"Haul the guy in at once. Phone and tell him it's a matter of extreme urgency that we simply must check out. Get him here! When was it, by the way, that those checks were cashed?"

"Two days prior to the murder."

Now Tone-Marit was smiling too.

"Well, shall we have a chat with Eivind Hasle, Tone-Marit, baby?"

It took only half an hour to bring the fortysomething man from his office in Grønland to the semicircular police station several hundred meters along the street. He seemed compliant but surprised when Tone-Marit phoned. Firmly placed on a seat in Billy T.'s untidy work space, it was difficult to determine whether he felt insecure or irritated.

"What's this about?"

"All in good time," Billy T. commented as he demanded his personal details.

"The first thing I'd like to know," he then said in as indifferent a tone of voice as he could possibly muster in his current state of emotion. "The very first thing is what relationship you had to Agnes Vestavik."

The man changed position in his chair, obviously feeling uneasy under the officer's sharp and penetrating gaze.

"Agnes Vestavik? I don't know anybody with that name. Agnes Vestavik?"

Then he looked thoughtful, and slowly a crimson flush spread around his ears. Eventually his earlobes, unusually large and awkward, were illuminated like traffic lights.

"Wait a minute. Is that the lady who was killed up in that day-care center? I read about it in the newspaper."

"Foster home. It was a foster home. And there's been very little coverage of it in the newspapers. Are you a conscientious reader of newspapers?"

182

The man did not deign to reply.

"You've never met her, then?"

Now the man seemed almost afraid.

"Tell me, what do you want? Why am I here?"

Now it was Billy T. who did not answer. He simply sat there, massive and broad, with arms crossed and eyes staring.

"Listen here," the man ventured, and now his voice was shaking. "I've no idea about this woman, all I've done is seen her name in the newspaper, and I'm surely entitled to know what you want from me."

"Let me see your driver's license."

"Driver's license? What do you want with that?"

"You really need to quit asking me a question every time I ask one of you."

Billy T. stood up abruptly. It worked this time too. The man cowered and fished out an elegant wallet in maroon leather. He searched and searched.

"No, it's not here," he muttered at long last. "Maybe I've left it in the car."

"Aha." Billy T. grinned. "So you've lost your driving license now. But you haven't discovered that until this very moment, I suppose."

"You don't use your driving license every day of the week! I can't remember when I saw it last. It's usually in here."

As though it would provide any proof at all, he withdrew his wallet again, folded it out in an almost indecent manner, and pointed at one of the pockets.

"Here!"

Billy T. did not look at him.

Instead he embarked on a two-hour interview so unpleasant that Eivind Hasle was beginning to threaten him with an action for damages.

"I think you should do that, Hasle. Sue us. It's become a national hobby. But do it bloody quickly, because before you can blink, you'll be sitting rattling the bars in that prison down there."

Unprofessional, though spoken in jest. Billy T. could have bitten off his tongue. But in two whole hours he had not come one single step closer to the question of who had killed Agnes Vestavik.

Hasle was allowed to leave. There was not a lawyer in the Western world would have dared to detain him for even twenty-four hours.

The man did not have his driver's license. He did not have a clue about either Agnes or the checks. He thought the signature on the forms seemed familiar but could quite credibly point out a couple of differences between his own and the signature he alleged was a forgery. And he did not bloody give in. So off he went.

By the time Billy T. had almost massacred the intercom apparatus without finding hide or hair of Hanne Wilhelmsen, his day was completely ruined.

The church was more than half full, with the congregation sitting in devout, decorous silence. The majority had chosen seats near the back, as though it was desirable to keep a certain distance from the tragic circumstances surrounding the central character's death. Agnes Vestavik's husband and children sat in the front row, with four additional people. Close relatives,

184

Hanne Wilhelmsen assumed. The two adolescent boys were wearing new suits and seemed uncomfortable in them. The little girl had problems sitting still and eventually wriggled away from her father's lap, managing to run all the way to the white flower-bedecked coffin before her eldest brother reached her and dragged her back into place, accompanied by screaming protests that echoed around the bare walls.

Behind the immediate family, five rows of pews were empty, then there was a scattering of grieving mourners with bowed heads, before the back rows, almost packed full. A church official, who was trying unobtrusively to persuade a few people to move forward, was met with whispered refusals and shaking heads.

Hanne Wilhelmsen held her post, standing beside the door under an overhang where she assumed the organ was located. The church official's long gray face wore an expression made for the job. He made an attempt on her as well, but she waved him away without saying a word.

Instead of an altarpiece, the front wall was decorated with an enormous montage so modern it took Hanne some time to discern that it was supposed to symbolize the Resurrection of Jesus. A simple bare cross stood in front of the huge picture, as well as a largish table covered in a white cloth, with a colossal candle in a silver candlestick on top. It had been ages since Hanne Wilhelmsen had been anywhere near a place of worship, and she was at a loss to interpret what she was witnessing. The low voices, the immense figure of Christ stretching his arms to his heavenly Father, the coffin decorated with flowers, the normally happy little girl trying to tear herself away from the entire situation, and the people clad in gray and black, all of it conveying some kind of reverence for death.

The minister entered from a door far forward at the side. At least Hanne assumed it was a minister, though her dress was white and adorned with a long, wide colorful scarf reaching right down below the knee. In fact she could not recall when she had last seen a minister in all the trappings of the trade. It had to be long ago, as she vaguely remembered an old man in black with a ruff collar.

Most of the staff of the foster home were present. Hanne recognized some of them and also noticed that the older children were there: Raymond, Glenn, and Anita. The young girl was wearing a frock; she was tugging at the edge of the skirt and obviously felt slightly uncomfortable. Glenn and Raymond were sitting beside each other, whispering. When Maren Kalsvik hushed them, they sat up straight.

There was no ordinary pulpit. The clergywoman with blonde hair styled in an irreverent ponytail stood with her back to the congregation, sending her prayers in the direction of the figure of Christ that was quite literally nailed to the cross. Hanne Wilhelmsen's legs were tiring, so she crept forward to the rear pew and sat down directly beside the aisle. Next to her sat an elderly lady in a Salvation Army uniform who seemed really devastated; sobbing as she sang, she clearly had no need of a hymnbook.

186

On the opposite pew across the aisle sat the Lover. Or whatever he should be called. Hanne was startled to see him and wondered if she was mistaken. She had glimpsed him only at the police station, on his way in to an interview with Billy T. But it was indeed him, she was almost certain. He was sitting at the far end, beside the wall, and kept some distance between himself and the people sitting nearest him. Hanne had not noticed him before now. Perhaps he had only just sneaked in. It was difficult to gain a true impression of him without leaning too far forward and to one side, and that seemed rather inappropriate, considering that the minister had embarked on a eulogy portraying Agnes Vestavik as something between Mother Teresa and Evangeline Booth. The Salvation Army woman beside her sobbed, nodding at every single word, clearly in full agreement with the minister that it was God's will for the little red-haired girl now running up and down the nave to grow up motherless.

Finally the minister began to wrap up. One of the boys, probably the elder of the two, rose to his feet and approached his mother's coffin with eyes downcast. In his hand he carried a rose, its head already starting to nod for lack of water, or perhaps it too was showing respect for the dead. Turning toward the assembled company in front of a microphone stand, he managed to stutter his way through a memorial speech. It was strange, stilted, and full of phrases that seemed unnatural in the mouth of a nineteen-year-old. However, it was a son's final greeting to his mother, and for that reason Hanne found it inordinately

187

moving. He finished by placing the rose on the coffin lid, before pausing silently and turning to return to his place, where his father embraced him before he resumed his seat.

Realizing the immediate family would come down the aisle before any others could leave the church, Hanne Wilhelmsen got off her mark quickly and, almost bent in two, slipped around the pew, where she positioned herself hugging the side wall to avoid being the first person to pass them on the way out.

The entire family stood in the doorway. The father had taken Amanda's arm, and she seemed placated by the thought of going home. One by one, the mourners passed by the four family members. Why were they so self-conscious? Was it death in itself that prevented them from looking the surviving family in the eye, or was it unseemly to be murdered while still the mother of a young child? Hanne felt miserable and tried to recall the uplifting atmosphere she had encountered on arrival, before the minister began her sermon, before everyone had been affected by close contact with what they had so elegantly attempted to avoid by assuming their places in the rear pews.

Almost everyone had gone now, and only Maren Kalsvik and the others from the foster home remained in front of the entrance. Hanne approached her and placed a friendly hand on her shoulder. The woman jumped so abruptly that her hand was literally slapped away. Maren spun around, her hand on her heart and mouth open.

"My God, you gave me a fright," she said, a fraction too loudly, flinching at the idea of having broken the second commandment in the Lord's own house.

"Sorry," Hanne mumbled. "Could you wait outside? I'd like to have a word with you."

Maren Kalsvik did not look pleased at the thought, but she nodded, placing her arm around Anita and stepping out to meet the grieving family. She gave the widower a long, sympathetic hug and kissed Amanda on the cheek. The two boys drew back, and she respected their feelings by simply offering them her hand.

As Hanne walked down the steps, she spotted the Lover as he sat inside a silver gray Mercedes with green license plates. Looking to neither the back nor the side, he smoothly levered the car into gear and let the vehicle roll forward onto the potholed road, exiting the gate several hundred meters farther on.

Poor man, Hanne thought, looking up at the skies.

The day was clear, and it had turned colder. The sun shone weakly and halfheartedly down on the churchyard, with little warmth to offer. The buzz of muted voices in conversation rose from the small huddles of humanity. Hanne Wilhelmsen approached the widower.

"Are you here too?" he asked in reedy, flat tones.

"Yes, as you see."

She smiled hesitantly. His boys had already crossed to the parking lot, and he had permitted Amanda to run after them. His gaze followed his daughter until she reached them, and then he turned his attention to the chief inspector.

189

"Do you usually attend the funerals of murder victims, Chief Inspector?" His voice contained a note of accusation and a large dollop of frostiness.

"No. But then this isn't exactly the usual kind of murder."

"Isn't it? What's so different about this one?"

His face did not disclose any particular expectation his question would be answered. He tugged discreetly at the sleeve of his suit, and she noticed his watch was an expensive affair.

"We don't need to talk about it here," Hanne said, signaling she wanted to go down to speak to Maren Kalsvik, who was standing on her own fifteen meters away, looking at them impatiently.

"Wait!"

He shot his hand out after her, taking hold of her arm as she started to walk off. When she stopped, he let go immediately.

"I was thinking of phoning you, but you know . . . There's been so much to sort out. Practical things. The boys. Amanda."

He stood up straight and took a deep breath. The sun caught his face. There was something terribly sad about the man's whole figure, with its perfect suit and his newly trimmed hair kept in place with hair spray, as though the only thing he possessed to keep him going was a formal appearance.

"That knife," he said finally. "The one used to kill Agnes. Was it an ordinary kitchen knife? A kind of . . . carving knife, is that what they're called?"

190

"Yes," Hanne confirmed, somewhat taken by surprise. "Or at least a large boning knife. Why do you ask?"

"It could have been ours."

"What?"

"It could have been our knife. The evening Agnes was . . . the night she died, she had taken four knives with her to the foster home earlier that day."

"What on earth for?"

Forgetting she was at a funeral, Hanne's voice had increased in volume.

"Whoa, take it easy!"

He raised his hands and waved them repeatedly at the ground, several times over, in an attempt to dampen her enthusiasm.

"They have a pretty deluxe electric sharpening machine at the foster home. She usually took her own knives there . . . our knives, I mean, now and again to sharpen them. That morning she brought four of them with her, maybe five, even. I remember it because she had to wash two of them before she left and cut herself slightly. I had to find a Band-Aid."

"Why didn't you tell us this before?"

"I didn't think about it! I was so sure she had brought them back with her that afternoon, she didn't usually leave them lying over there. And . . ."

He stopped, noticing that the people encircling them had gone quiet, and everyone's attention was fixed on the two of them. He drew her with him as he moved closer to the church wall.

"To be honest, my mother-in-law has been doing the house-work since Agnes died. She came right away. It was only yesterday evening, when she was complaining there were so few kitchen utensils, that I realized. I think there were four knives. Perhaps five, as I said."

"From Ikea?"

"No, I've no idea about that. I don't know where my wife buys . . . I mean, bought, knives."

"But I expect you would recognize the knife again if you saw it?"

He was too exhausted to notice the caustic tone.

"I suppose so."

"Then I reckon you should turn up at my office early tomorrow morning, at nine o'clock. On the dot. You have my sincere condolences."

She wheeled around. There was only one reason why she did not haul the man off with her immediately. It was *not* that he had just attended his wife's funeral, but that three children had just attended their mother's.

Maren Kalsvik's lips were blue and her teeth were chattering. She had sent the children over to the car, a large blue people carrier.

"What was it you wanted?" she said, her teeth rattling.

"It can wait," Hanne said. "But we need to talk to you tomorrow. Twelve o'clock, does that suit?"

"Just as inconvenient as any other time of day," Maren said, shrugging her shoulders. "At your office?"

Hanne Wilhelmsen nodded as she pulled up the hood of her duffel coat. Then she scurried over to the service vehicle, swearing like a trooper.

192

Billy T. was nowhere to be found. One or two people thought they had spotted him on his way out half an hour earlier, but they were unsure. Some were able to say that he had been looking for her. The receptionist spread out her arms in despair, complaining that no one saw the point in the established and frequently ignored system of reporting personnel whereabouts.

"We're the ones who get it in the neck," she said unhappily, expecting some sympathy from Chief Inspector Wilhelmsen.

But the chief inspector was preoccupied. First she popped into Billy T.'s office to find the telephone number previously attached to Agnes Vestavik's telephone directory, but it was impossible to locate it in all the uproar. She gave up after four or five minutes, reassuring herself that he had clearly told her it was the number of Diakonhjemmet University College's School of Social Work.

Returning to her own office, she grabbed the telephone directory before sitting down. "Diakonhjemmet, the Norwegian" was the nearest she found, but there was a long list of additional numbers, for a School of Social Care, a hospital, something called the International Center, and a foundation with its own phone number. "Diakonhjemmet University College" had its own entry. She dialed the digits, without knowing what the focus of her inquiry would be.

A considerable time elapsed before anyone answered the call. Eventually a nondescript, almost mechanical voice piped up, "University College, how can I help you?" and Hanne wondered for a moment whether it was an automatic answering service. She asked for the dean's office for lack of any better idea. There she spoke to a secretary whose voice was filled with sunshine and laughter, in stark contrast to the mechanical woman at the central switchboard.

Hanne introduced herself and endeavored to explain what she wanted without revealing too much. The lady was as quick on the uptake as her voice suggested, and she was able to confirm unequivocally that yes indeed, Agnes Vestavik, that poor, poor woman, had phoned several times the previous week. Or perhaps it was the week before that. In any case, she remembered she had called, and they had all been deeply shocked when they read about her murder. How was the family doing?

Hanne could reassure her on that point at least and asked what Agnes had wanted of them. Unfortunately, the secretary could not help her with that, but as far as she remembered, on one occasion she had asked to speak to someone in the examination office. Since they did not have an examination office, she had asked to speak to the dean. That was the first time, she thought. But what they had talked about, no, she was *very sorry* but she could not help her with that. It was also possible the dean had passed her on to someone else, though she knew nothing about that.

Hanne asked to speak to the dean, but was told that, regrettably, he was at a seminar in Denmark and would not return until Friday.

Hanne Wilhelmsen tried not to express her annoyance, as the woman had really been a great help.

Rejecting the offer of assistance to find out where in Denmark he was, she terminated the conversation. Before replacing the receiver, she nevertheless asked the secretary to find out as soon as possible whether Agnes Vestavik had ever worked at Diakonhjemmet's School of Social Work. The secretary promised, laughing, and chirped a good-bye after noting Hanne Wilhelmsen's name and telephone number.

Hanne's ear was still brimful of the happy secretary's voice when she put down the phone. It lifted her mood to talk to such people, but only for a few seconds.

She had to find Billy T.

Restlessness had taken its grip on Olav again. It was true he was calm when eating and sleeping, both activities that consumed a great deal of his time, but he was having increasing difficulty between meals. She had bought him some comics, but they did not succeed in holding his attention for longer than a few minutes at a time. The initial subduing fear had obviously deserted him, and he no longer listened to her.

"They're going to find you if you go out. You're reported missing. On the TV and radio and in the newspapers."

He smiled that strange smile of his.

"Just like in the movies. Will they give a reward?"

"No, Olav, they're not offering a reward. They're not searching for you because you've done something wrong. They just want you back at the foster home."

He frowned.

"Fuck no," he said vehemently. "I'd rather *die* than move back to that dump."

She couldn't resist a slight smile, a tired, weary smile. Catching sight of it, he vented his fury.

"You're laughing, you bitch! But I'll tell you one thing: *I'm not going back there! Do you understand?*"

She tried desperately to calm him down by making hushing gestures and pointing to the wall through to the neighbor's apartment. It did not perturb him in the least. However, he was at a loss for something to say and instead padded through to the kitchen and started to pull out all the drawers. He yanked them all the way out, tipping the contents onto the floor and yelling piercingly with every single drawer he grabbed hold of.

She knew it would pass. There was nothing to do other than sitting quite still, closing your eyes, and waiting. Tears spilled down her cheeks. She had only to wait. It will pass. In a little while, it will pass. Sit still. Don't say anything. Don't do anything. Don't, for heaven's sake, touch him. Soon, soon, it will pass.

It took some time to empty out all the drawers. She could not see him, but from the noises she knew he was kicking the kitchen utensils about and making a dreadful racket. The neighbors would notice it. She had hardly begun to think of an explanation when the doorbell rang.

The boy immediately stopped in his tracks. He suddenly stood in the doorway, and fear had returned to his eyes. He looked at her, not in a plea for help but with a command for her to wait until he had hidden himself before opening the door. Without a word, he disappeared into her bedroom. She crept after him, closed the door, and dried her eyes on the way to the front door.

It was the downstairs neighbor, an elderly lady who knew most of what transpired in the apartment block. This was not strange in the slightest, since she spent all her time either sitting at the kitchen window where she had an excellent view of all the comings and goings, or at people's doors with complaints: about noise, about music, about people who were not following the rota for the laundry in the basement or for washing the stairs when it was their turn.

"That was a terrible commotion," she said suspiciously. "Has your son come home?"

She craned her scrawny neck in an attempt to see inside the apartment. Birgitte Håkonsen made herself as tall and wide as possible.

"No, he hasn't come home. It was me, I dropped something on the floor. Sorry."

"Dropped something on the floor for a whole half hour?" the old woman exaggerated. "Yes, I'm sure I believe that. Have you got visitors?"

She extended her neck even farther, and because she was taller than Olav's mother, could discern the white rectangle at the end of the gloomy hallway. However, that told her nothing.

"No, I don't have visitors. I'm all on my own. And I'm sorry about the noise. It won't happen again."

As she was about to close the door in her neighbor's face, the old woman muttered about calling the police.

She hesitated momentarily before slamming it shut, turning the security lock as well.

Olav was sitting on her bed with his legs in the lotus position. He was remarkably supple for someone so stout. Now he looked more like a Buddha than ever before. She stood there observing him, and neither of them uttered a word. Then he moaned, almost a low howl, before stretching his arms and lifting his face to the ceiling, asking his question into empty space: "What'll I do?"

She did not answer, because he was not speaking to her. Whirling around, she shuffled back to the kitchen to tidy up. As absolutely quietly as possible.

It was impossible to get anyone to listen to me as far as the MBD was concerned. I took it up with the kindergarten first, but they simply smiled and said he would probably grow out of it. Again I thought I should talk to the child welfare service, as they could not possibly let me escape for a third time.

Then he started school. It had to go badly. As early as the first day, when all the parents were present, he got up from his desk in the middle of the first lesson and walked off out of the classroom. An odd expression crossed the teacher's face, and she looked at me in the expectation that I would do something. I knew if someone attempted to stop him, all hell would break loose. So I made the excuse that he needed the toilet and concocted a urinary infection on the spot. Shortly afterward, I sneaked out to find him, but he was nowhere to be found. It later turned out he had entered another classroom, declaring that he would prefer to be in that class.

It wasn't that he was stupid. On the contrary, he had a good head for math. And later, English. He was exceptionally good at English, but only orally. They said it might be because he was watching far too much television. Typical, really, when he hit upon something he was good at, something he mastered, they succeeded in turning that into something negative as well, something that was my fault.

Before the end of reception year, he was the school's outcast. The other little school pupils shunned him, the pupils in years five and six teased him and persuaded him to do the most unbelievable things. On May 17, the Norwegian National Day, he managed to lower the flag on the school's flagpole while everyone was listening to a speech given by a sweet blonde year-five pupil, talking about Wergeland, Norway's national poet, and the children's procession and freedom and the war, until suddenly she fell silent and pointed at the enormous flag now flying at half-mast. It had been cut into long strips, waving freely in the wind. Olav was standing beside the flagpole, jumping for joy and brandishing a pair of clippers, looking triumphantly at a group of class-six pupils who were standing doubled up with laughter at the back of the crowd. I couldn't bear any more and just left. Several hours later, he arrived home clutching a hundred kroner in his fist. He had a wager with the big boys, he explained. When I tried to explain to him that he could have asked me for money, he looked at me in surprise with that strange smile I have never quite been able to fathom.

In the beginning, he was invited to birthday parties. At least, for the first year. He was always good-natured and happy when he returned home, but I never actually discovered how things had gone. Then that came to an abrupt halt, and it broke my heart when he watched the other children in the neighborhood trooping off to parties, dressed to the nines and carrying presents under their arms. He sat at the window on the first few occasions, but when I tried to suggest we should find some fun thing to do, he pushed me away and switched on the TV.

That was the only thing that, strictly speaking, did not fit well with the MBD diagnosis. He could sit for hours in front of the TV screen. He was all consuming, and it was mind-boggling how much of it he understood. As a toddler he had been completely uninterested in children's television, even though I really tried to get him to watch it. By the time he commenced the year-two class, he was watching everything. It seemed as though he derived just as much pleasure from cartoons aimed at very young children as from the daily news and action films. I knew he ought not to watch all the films, but it didn't look as if he was ever scared. Apart from one occasion. I was going to bed, but he had started watching a film and refused to go to sleep. I attempted to lure him with a bribe of money, as he had to go to school the following day. But it was out of the question. The film was called Alien, and as far as I could see, a female was the central character. So I thought it couldn't be too dangerous and went off to bed.

In the middle of the night he came in and woke me. He was not crying but was clearly nervous and asked if he could sleep in my bed, something he had not done since he was tiny. I let him snuggle up to me and put my arms around him. He pushed them away but accepted me lying close to him. He hardly slept all night.

200

The next day, it was all entirely forgotten. I asked him what had been so creepy, but he only smiled.

At school he had been allocated an aide for fifteen hours a week. Though he had kept up with the work in most subjects in year one and the beginning of year two, his restlessness was so disruptive that he had started to fall behind. First and foremost, the task of the aide was to make him sit still, but he also worked with him on a one-to-one basis for a few hours.

Olav liked the aide, a young man, and he was friendly to me as well. I was afraid of him at the beginning, but he laughed a lot and at least gave me some impression that he liked my boy. Sometimes he accompanied Olav home, and the boy was almost unrecognizable. It was true he didn't listen to what I had to say any more than otherwise, but when the aide gave him instructions, he obeyed him without protest.

Once the young aide phoned me late one evening. Olav had gone to bed. He was running a temperature and was tired. It must have been when he had just started in year five. The aide wondered whether I found it difficult to set boundaries for my son. He was trying to tell me I was not quite "handling him properly," as he put it. If I was willing, he could come and talk to me in the morning, when he had no lessons with Olav and I would be on my own at home all the same. He had been in contact with the child welfare service, he admitted, and tried to adopt a light tone of voice as he informed me they had taken a positive view of him undertaking work as a kind of home consultant.

Child welfare service. Home consultant. The words were like knives in my heart. The aide, who had been a guest in my home, eaten meals here, laughed, ruffled my son's hair, and been pleasant and kind toward me . . . He had spoken to the child welfare service.

I simply put down the receiver.

Two days later, the representatives of the child welfare service were standing on the doorstep.

Facing Billy T. was a half liter of beer in a glass sparkling with condensation, with a delightful circle of froth on top. Hanne had contented herself with a Munkholm. Lifeless and lackluster, the top was a fine, white layer that could hardly be dignified with the name of froth.

"Talk about withholding important information," Hanne said quietly in order not to be heard at neighboring tables.

They had sat down at the table farthest back and on a raised area in the innermost recesses of the bar. A more pretentious proprietor had probably called it a mezzanine, but here it was simply known as the platform.

"Yes, it is fairly critical, to put it mildly," Billy T. conceded, diving into his beer. "Stupid of me not to ask when I had the guy in for the interview."

Hanne made no comment about his oversight.

"This means in all probability that the perpetrator did *not* come to kill Agnes," she continued. "It has been bothering me, this matter of the knife. It's a clumsy murder weapon. Not at all reliable. Unusual."

"Well, there is a lot of knife crime here in this country," Billy T. noted.

"Yes, but not deliberate murders! If you plan ahead of time to murder someone, a knife is probably not going to be your weapon of choice. Knives are about ... the city center on a Saturday night, fights, drunken nonsense, parties, cabin holidays in the pouring rain when people start to argue. And what's more, loads of stab wounds. And often a wounded culprit into the bargain."

"So you think the person in question came for some other reason, that things turned nasty, and he or she grabbed the knife almost on an impulse? For lack of anything better, so to speak?"

"Precisely. That's exactly what I mean."

The food arrived on the table. Hanne had ordered a chicken salad; Noah's Ark was the only place in the city where the chicken in the salad was served piping hot. Billy T. launched himself into a double kebab.

They ate in silence for several minutes, before Hanne grinned and lay down her knife and fork. Looking obliquely at her companion, she asked, "How's it going with that woman you met in the Canary Islands?"

He did not deign to respond, instead continuing to eat with undiminished enthusiasm.

"That golden tan of yours is starting to fade. Is it the same with your love affair?"

He prodded her in the side with his fork and spoke with his mouth full of food. "Now don't you be mean and rotten. I don't want to talk about it."

"C'mon, Billy T. Tell me more."

She waited patiently until he finished his meal, when he finally wiped his beard with his lower arm, emptied his half liter, and, signaling for another, planked down two fists in front of him on the table.

"It was nothing."

"It was not! You were so elated a week or so ago!"

"That was then, this is now."

She reconsidered and turned serious. "What's all that about, Billy T.?"

Appearing irritated, he put an unnecessary amount of energy into trying to catch the waiter's attention, since he had not responded to his earlier gesture.

"What d'you mean?"

"All that with you and women."

Billy T. had four children. None of them had the same mother. He hadn't even stayed with any of them long enough to be anywhere near deciding to move in together. But he loved his sons passionately.

"Me and women? Dynamite, that is!"

He finally received his half liter. Remaining seated, he etched hearts on the dewy surface of the glass.

"I can't stand any hassle," he added.

"Hassle?"

"Yes."

"What kind of hassle?"

"All that female hassle. That can't-you-pay-a-little-attention-to-me-as-well hassle. I like to do whatever I want. If a woman wants to do that with me, then that's great. After a while they don't want to do that any longer. Then the hassle starts. I just can't deal with that."

"Damage in early childhood," Hanne said with a smile.

"Probably."

"But you. Why ..." She broke off with a self-conscious smile.

He never learned what she had been about to ask, because something suddenly dawned on him. His gaze became distant, and perhaps to avoid closer interrogation about his wounded personal life, he returned to the latest information from the widower.

"What could have happened to the *other* knives?"

"What ..." She stopped as she realized the implication of the question herself.

"There should have been another three or four sharpened knives lying there. You're right about that. Can the murderer have taken them with him?"

"Of course he can. But why on earth would he do that?"

Hanne stared vacantly at her Munkholm bottle without receiving any help from that quarter. Then she turned her attention to a loud argument escalating at one of the entrance doors, where two exhausted characters from the park wanted to come in. The dark-haired waiter was employing all his reserves of tact and discretion, and in return was showered with crude racist comments. Immune to it, he succeeded in turning the old guys away.

"I think I know," she exclaimed. "If I'm right, we can really start to narrow down the search for the murderer."

Hanne was thoughtful rather than triumphant. Scanning the room, she managed to catch the waiter's attention again.

"Hi, do you think I could borrow four or five knives from the kitchen? Just for a moment. It's for . . . a bet."

The waiter looked surprised but shrugged his shoulders and returned with four large, well-used knives just a minute or so later.

Standing up, Hanne placed the knives on the table at Billy T.'s right side.

"Let's assume they were lying on that side. The principle remains the same. Sit as though you're concentrating on something in front of you."

Billy T. intently contemplated the crumbs on his plate. Stepping behind him, Hanne grabbed the largest knife from the table, drew it in a backward sweeping motion, and simulated a slow-motion movement toward her colleague's spine, allowing the point of the knife to stab him in the back.

"Ouch!"

He wheeled around and tried to massage the tender spot with his right hand. That gave him a sore shoulder. It became noticeably quieter in the premises, and curious bystanders at the surrounding tables were staring at the pair of them in alarm.

"Did you see that?" Hanne asked eagerly, replacing the knife on the table. "Did you notice what happened? When I grabbed the knife?"

"Of course I did," Billy T. answered. "Of course I fucking did. Hanne, you're a genius!"

"I'm fully aware of that," the chief inspector replied, self-satisfied.

In sheer enthusiasm, she paid the whole bill herself, though Billy T. had consumed far more alcohol.

206

"But, Hanne," Billy T. said, stopping suddenly when they reached the sidewalk, "if that stunt of yours in there has any relevance, then we can forget both the Lover and that guy Hasle without the driver's license."

"Well, Billy T.," Hanne Wilhelmsen said, "although we now have a bloody good theory, we must never box ourselves in. We still have to explore all avenues. That's elementary!"

"Okay, Sherlock," Billy T. said with a grin.

And then he could not resist smacking a kiss right on her lips.

"Yuck," Hanne said, wiping her mouth demonstratively.

But she was smiling broadly.

In a rather sad apartment in an even sadder neighborhood, an extremely frightened car salesman sat drinking beer. The twelve bottles stood like empty-headed tin soldiers in a circle on the table in front of him. He arranged them in patterns, changing the lineup every five minutes. His ability to move them into different positions without knocking them over persuaded him he was still not drunk enough to make any attempt to catch some sleep.

Directly in the center of the circle of bottles lay a checkbook. Agnes Vestavik's checkbook. There were only four checks missing. One had already been used when he stole the book, astonishingly easily from her handbag when she had been making a toilet visit. He had not afforded it a moment's thought; his hands had simply acted of their own accord. It was tucked in there, he knew, because she had used it when she paid for their meal shortly before. Without hesitation, he had pulled the leather wallet from her bag and stashed it in his own capacious coat pocket. Just as he was having second thoughts, she had emerged smiling from the restroom, asking whether they were ready to depart.

The three other checks he had used to withdraw three identical sums of money, from three different bank branches, in three different locations around Oslo. First in Lillestrøm. That had gone really well, although the pathetic false beard had almost fallen off because he was sweating like a pig. He had used a driver's license someone had left behind in a car he had loaned out for a test-drive. Age and facial features had matched to some extent, and the woman at the window had barely spared him a glance before counting out ten thousand-kroner notes on the counter and then ringing the bell for the next customer. He almost couldn't muster the temerity to lift the money, but the woman had looked at him impatiently, pushing them toward him with a gesture of irritation. Making an effort to control his trembling, he mumbled a few words of thanks and left the bank as slowly as possible. He had parked his car a couple of blocks away, closer to the railway station, in a parking lot where it was just another nondescript vehicle.

Yes, indeed, he was a car salesman and sometimes also sold a used car or two. He had cut a few corners here and there, and had occasionally felt he was something of a villain, but he had never done anything exactly criminal before. It was bloody easy. And absolutely awful. With ten rustling thousand-kroner

208

notes in his wallet, he had driven to Sandvika to cash the next check. It had to be accomplished before she discovered the loss of her checkbook and had the account frozen.

In bank number two, the procedure also went pretty smoothly. He had wiped himself thoroughly underneath the beard and managed to position it better. Choosing to park in the enormous shopping mall, he nevertheless strolled to a bank in the center of Sandvika, five minutes' walk away. The lady had looked slightly sternly at him, but that could have been because he hesitated when she asked him to produce his ID. In confusion he had almost handed her his own certificate but realized in time and put it back. Devastated by his uncertainty about whether she had spotted his two driving licenses, he fumbled so much with the other one that his behavior became suspicious. However, he obtained his money and decided he should stop.

Twenty thousand kroner. How much money did Agnes actually have? Did they check whether there was enough money in the account before they handed him the money? He tried to recall, but his memory failed him.

He headed now for Asker. At one moment he stuck to his decision to bring this to a halt, the next he was coveting more. Just one more check. The car kept its steady course, unaffected by the chaos overwhelming him.

As he entered the bank, it dawned on him that all banks had CCTV cameras. Of course he had known that, as this made it so convenient that the man in his photograph sported a beard. In addition he had donned an old cap, produced from a chest in his attic.

However, as he entered the third bank he was suddenly overwhelmed by fear, all the more so perhaps because he was the only person in the place.

"What can I do for you?" a smiling young man had said, coaxing him to approach.

It was too late to turn back, so he handed over the final check.

"The computers are down, unfortunately, so I'll have to phone," the young man said, smiling even more broadly as he scrutinized the check.

"I can come back later," he had stuttered as he held out his hand to retrieve the check.

"No, no," the man protested obligingly, withdrawing his arm. "It'll only take a moment."

It was true. The next minute he was leaving the building with ten more thousand-kroner notes and a piercing pain underneath his breastbone.

Now he sat drinking. The thirteenth beer bottle was empty, and he moved the bottles around in a new pattern: an angular shape, or a flight of geese heading south, or a gigantic arrowhead. The bottle at the front was pointing directly at him.

"Bang," he said softly. "You're dead."

He opened the fourteenth. Could he not knock over a bottle soon?!

Agnes had found out. That is to say, she had asked him if by any chance he had seen her checkbook. Straight out, just like that, without any kind of undertone whatsoever. Something that simply convinced

210

him she suspected him. Of course he had denied it, and of course she had known. She informed him she had asked the bank to investigate whether the checkbook had been utilized and would receive a response the following day.

Bloody hell. He had been so certain no one knew about their relationship. He had never written to her, quite simply because he never wrote anything other than contracts.

How long would it take until the police discovered those checks?

He abruptly rose to his feet, knocking over two bottles. One fell onto the floor but did not break.

Now he might attempt to get some sleep. Staggering into the bedroom, he collapsed onto the bed fully clothed. It took some time before he finally dozed off.

The checkbook was still lying on the table surrounded by thirteen empty bottles and one that had toppled over.

CHAPTER
NINE

This was the first truly beautiful day in ages. Although there was still a nip in the air and the temperature did not climb above zero degrees Celsius, there was a certain promise wafting in the breeze, indicating spring was not so terribly far away. The large grassy areas around Tøyen's swimming pool had begun to lose their covering of snow, and the occasional tuft of grass had tentatively peeped above the soil, though the coltsfoot flowers still had the good sense to keep their heads down. The azure of the sky was intense, and although the sun had only just struggled above the horizon, Hanne Wilhelmsen regretted not bringing her sunglasses.

On the little hill between a huge, hefty statue of pale stone and Finnmarksgata, in the shelter of some bushes and raised high enough above the road that motorists were not paying particular attention to what was afoot, several colleagues from the Traffic Section had positioned themselves and were setting up a speed trap. Malicious, Hanne thought, smiling. There were two lanes of traffic in both directions with a substantial barrier between, almost resembling a little motorway. Every reasonably experienced motorist automatically assumed the speed limit was at least sixty kilometers

212

per hour. Therefore, they drove at seventy. What they had failed to notice was there were no signs in the area, and so they were driving in a normal fifty-kilometers limit, as with everywhere else in a built-up area. Finnmarksgata was one of the state's most reliable sources of income.

Loitering in order to watch them hauling in the first two sinners, she then strode on, shaking her head. She crossed Åkebergveien at twenty past seven, and half a minute later she was standing in the elevator at the police station. The superintendent happened to be there at the same time. A big man, he was firm and muscular, but above all extremely masculine. His clothing was unfashionably tight, something that definitely seemed tacky, but the strength of the broad face beneath his bald head nevertheless characterized him as attractive, an impression intensified by his unusually calm and pleasant disposition. Usually. At this moment he did not even spare her a glance.

"The early bird catches the worm," he muttered to his reflection in the mirror.

"Yes, lots to do," Chief Inspector Wilhelmsen replied, tidying her hair at the same mirror.

"Pop into my office, would you?" the superintendent asked imperiously, glancing at his watch.

The elevator tinkled as its doors opened, and they both stepped out onto the gallery encircling the enormous foyer.

"Right away?"

"Yes. Bring me a coffee too."

She felt clammy, anticipating something unpleasant, when she called in at her own office to fetch the cup decorated with her star sign. In the reception area, no one had yet managed to activate the coffee machine, and she leisurely filled the tank with water and measured the requisite eight level spoonfuls. The receptionist appeared on the scene as the machine began to gurgle.

"Thank you sooo much, Hanne." She panted with such a display of gratitude Hanne thought she detected a touch of irony. So many jugs of coffee were made in that reception area that Hanne sometimes wondered whether this was the reason they never kept pace with all the things they should actually be undertaking.

Having poured out coffee for herself and a paper cup for her boss, she knocked on the door immediately adjacent to the reception. When she heard no response, she knocked once again, and when there was still no reaction forthcoming, though she was sure he was there, she ventured to open the door cautiously. A difficult task with a cup in each hand, resulting in her dropping the paper cup on the floor. The coffee splashed up her legs, scalding her even through her thick denim jeans.

The superintendent laughed heartily.

"Now you can see what happens when you don't mind your manners," he said, putting down the telephone receiver. "Astrid! ASTRID!"

The receptionist popped her head around the door.

"Pick that up and wipe up the mess, please."

"But I can do —" Hanne began but was interrupted.

214

"Sit yourself down."

She glanced apologetically at the secretary who, with rigidly pressed lips, squandered half a roll of paper towels wiping up the coffee with angry little movements before closing the door on the two police officers. Neither of them had uttered a word while she was cleaning. Hanne felt extremely uncomfortable.

"How are you enjoying being a chief inspector, Hanne?" he asked, now making eye contact with her.

She shrugged her shoulders slightly, unsure where this conversation was heading.

"All right. Sometimes very well, sometimes not so well. Isn't that the way it goes?"

She smiled gingerly, but he did not return the compliment.

He tasted the fresh cup of coffee Astrid had grumpily set before him, so emphatically that some of it spilled. Noticing a light brown circle outlined on the blotter, his podgy forefinger extended it into a face resembling Mickey Mouse.

"You were an outstanding detective, Hanne. You know that, as do I and most others here at the station."

A colossal *but* hovered, quivering, in the air between them.

"But," he said eventually, "you must remember it's different being a chief inspector. You have to lead. You have to coordinate. And you must *rely* on your subordinates. That's the whole point. When Billy T. is appointed lead investigator in the foster home murder case, then he's the one who has to do the investigating. It's all fine and commendable that you're interested

215

and want to chase things up, but take care not to undermine your people."

"He certainly doesn't feel undermined," Hanne objected, knowing he had a point.

"Of course he doesn't," the superintendent remarked, surprisingly tired and resigned, taking the hour of day into consideration. "You two are friends. He loves working with you. My God, the man would never have applied for a post away from the drug intervention unit if it hadn't been for you. But you have other detectives working with you as well. Smart people, even though they're young and inexperienced."

"Have they complained?"

Hanne realized she could easily be perceived as feeling hard done by and hoped he understood that was not the case.

"No, they haven't. But I sense there is something. And I notice you hobnob too much. For one thing, you're difficult to get hold of. Out and about far too often."

He yawned interminably, scratching his ear with a Bic pen.

"I supported you for this job, Hanne. There aren't many officers your age who get chief inspector posts. The only reason there hasn't been more grumbling is that everybody knows how clever you are. Don't give that grousing a reason to flare up again, will you? I still think, in fact I *know*, that you can become just as good a chief inspector as you were a detective. But you really must give the job a chance. Don't dash around like a chief inspector light or an officer deluxe, okay?"

216

They could hear loud chatter and laughter from the reception area beyond. The police headquarters was filling up, with people who would accept Hanne Wilhelmsen's job on the spot. A job she, right at this moment, would like most of all to jettison out the window. She felt downhearted, not so much because she hated being reprimanded as because she knew in her heart of hearts he was correct. She should never have agreed to apply for it. It was that *idiot* Håkon Sand who had persuaded her. Suddenly and unexpectedly, she missed him intensely. Billy T. was a great guy and they were well matched. They understood each other, often before either of them had said a word.

Håkon Sand, the police attorney she had worked with for so long, among other cases on a couple of dramatic and sensational murders, was a half-wit who stumbled his way forward through life one step or five behind everyone else. But he was wise. He listened. She let him down time after time, but he remained just as good-natured, just as obliging. The previous week, he had phoned and invited her to dinner and to have a look at his son, now barely three months old. The boy was even called after her, or almost, at least; his name was Hans Wilhelm. Håkon had asked her to be his godmother, an offer she had to turn down, although flattered, as she could not tell lies in a church. However, she had attended the christening four weeks earlier, though she had needed to leave early. Though disappointed, Håkon had smiled and encouraged her to phone him sometime soon. She had completely forgotten, until he, as happy as ever, had phoned again last week. However, she could not manage any of the days he had suggested.

She missed him. She would phone him today.

But first she had to devise something to say to her not very pleased boss. She had no idea how to begin.

"I'll make a real effort," she started. "Once this case is solved, I'll really make an effort."

"And how long is that going to take, Hanne?"

She stood up, but noticing an irritated gleam in his eye, sat down again.

"The best-case scenario, a day and a half. The worst-case scenario, one week."

"What?"

Now she had impressed him and felt her mood lift a couple of notches.

"If I get a nibble on a little hook I've cast out, then most of it will be concluded by the weekend."

Now the superintendent treated her to a real smile.

"Yes, yes, okay then," he said. "Then at least you'll have proved what we already know. You're good at *investigating!*"

He indicated that she could go, and Hanne offered up a silent prayer as she closed the door carefully behind her.

I just hope I haven't been too much of a bigmouth saying that . . .

An hour later, Agnes Vestavik's surviving marriage partner arrived in the police station at Grønlandsleiret 44 at nine o'clock on the dot. He was just as formally dressed as on his previous visit, but the past demanding week had cost him a couple of kilos in weight. This time Billy T. had more sympathy for the man, something he admitted to himself with a certain irritation.

However, the figure facing him would have forced the most hardened cynic to display a touch of sympathy. The man's hands were trembling, and his eyes had taken on a permanent red tinge, from the soft skin surrounding them all the way into the whites of his eyeballs. His skin was pale and clammy, and Billy T. persuaded himself the pores on his face had not been as prominent at their first meeting.

"How's it going, Vestavik?" he asked in such a friendly tone that the man stared at him in surprise. "Are things terribly difficult?"

"Yes. It's worst at night. During the day, there's such a lot to do. The boys are at home again; the eldest has taken a couple of weeks off from folk high school to help out with Amanda. Although my mother-in-law's fantastic, it's not really so easy . . . You know, mothers-in-law . . ."

Billy T. had never in his life needed to relate to a mother-in-law but nevertheless nodded in agreement. They were probably hardly any better than their daughters when things went awry.

"So now you'd prefer her to leave, is that it?"

The man nodded, grateful for all this unexpected understanding.

"Well," Billy T. said, "that can be quickly achieved."

Leaning to the left, he pulled open a drawer and fished out a large transparent plastic bag. Inside was a kitchen knife with a wooden handle that he placed

219

before Odd Vestavik, who instinctively recoiled in his chair.

"It's been washed. There's no blood on it," Billy T. reassured him.

The other man stretched a slim hand toward the bag, but stopped in midmovement, looking quizzically at Billy T.

"It's okay," the police officer nodded. "Just have a closer look at it."

The man scrutinized the object for a long time. Quite an unnecessarily long time. Billy T. shuddered. Here sat this poor man having to examine a knife that had been stabbed right into his wife's back. And that also had perhaps chopped up countless slices of meat for school sandwiches prior to that, at home in a cozy kitchen at the heart of a friendly nuclear family.

"Is it yours?"

"I can't swear that this one is ours," the man said quietly without taking his eye off the knife. "But we had one exactly like it. Absolutely identical, as far as I remember."

"Try to find some particular mark," Billy T. encouraged him. "On the handle, for instance. It's made of wood and might have some special characteristic. There are a couple of nicks there."

In order to be helpful, he leaned forward and pointed at the lower part of the handle.

"There, you see. It looks as if someone has whittled it."

The man gazed at the nick for a while before shaking his head sluggishly.

"No, I can't say I remember that."

Now he appeared almost embarrassed.

"But I wasn't in the kitchen drawers all that often. We were slightly . . . slightly old-fashioned in that way."

"I don't like cooking either," Billy T. consoled him. "I do it only because I have to. But you did at least have a knife like this?"

"Yes. It would have been easier if I could see some of the other knives. Then I would be able to be really certain."

He looked questioningly at the policeman. Billy T. took the opportunity to make and retain eye contact.

"The other knives are gone," he said softly.

The man did not bat an eyelid but did raise his eyebrows into an almost imperceptible expression of bafflement.

"We suspect the murderer took them with him."

"Took them with him?"

Now his astonishment was more obvious.

"What on earth would he want them for?"

"That will have to remain a secret between the killer and the police. At least in the meantime."

Billy T. returned the plastic-encased knife to the drawer and stood up.

"I'm really sorry you had to make another trip to the station," he said, holding out his hand. "I hope this is the last time we have to inconvenience you."

"Oh, it was nothing," the man replied, rising to his feet as well.

He seemed stiff and looked far older than his almost fifty years. Disconsolately, he shook the proffered hand.

"Will you be able to work it out?" he asked in a pessimistic tone of voice.

"Yes, you can certainly be sure of that. Quite sure."

As Mr Vestavik's back disappeared along the corridor, Billy T. experienced one of the welcome moments when it was a joy to be a police officer. A real joy. The next time he spoke to this man would be to tell him they knew who had murdered his wife. He was one hundred percent sure of that.

"Ninety, anyway," he muttered, correcting himself.

Hanne Wilhelmsen had not entirely recovered from that morning's mild reprimand, but she was trying not to take it out on Tone-Marit and Erik. The three of them were leaning over the railings, peering down into the foyer, where a TV team was on its way through the massive metal doors, laden with an enormous amount of equipment. A man was standing arguing with one of the boys on duty at the counter, and Hanne assumed it was the usual dispute about whether the state broadcaster, NRK, could park in a disability bay directly outside the door, or had to find a vacant legal space much farther away. The police officer won, of course, and the TV man disappeared out the door, shaking his head, to move the vehicle.

"The guys on duty here think they own the place," Hanne remarked.

Tone-Marit appeared about to defend her colleagues but let it go.

"Well, folks," Hanne said, changing the subject with feigned cheerfulness. "We've lots to do. I want you,

222

Erik, to haul in all the employees again. Fresh interviews. The most important thing is to bring in this Eirik what's his name, the one who found the body. I want that done immediately. He's still on sick leave, so you should be able to do that today."

"Do you want to interview him yourself?"

She was on the verge of saying yes but quickly changed her mind, smiling at the red-haired police officer.

"No, you do it. But I'll jot down some really imperative points we need to clear up. I'm relying on you to make a good job of it."

Tone-Marit was instructed to apply herself to summoning the others and informed that all the interviews must take place before the weekend, meaning they had a day and a half to get them done. The two young people exchanged meaningful looks, but before they could protest, Hanne added, "You sort it out as best you can. If there's too much to do, we can draft in a couple of trainees. But I'm confident you'll be able to manage it."

Billy T. came galumphing across the gallery.

"Hi! Hanne!"

She turned to face him.

"Maren Kalsvik phoned to speak to you. She said she had an appointment to come here today at twelve o'clock. Is that right?"

"Yes."

"It's fairly chaotic up there at the foster home just now. She asked if she could come tomorrow instead. Is that okay?"

It certainly was not. On the other hand, it was not at all surprising that work was making demands of the new boss since people were dropping dead like flies around her.

"Well, okay, but you'll have to speak to her. I've other plans for tomorrow morning."

He ruminated for a moment and then nodded his assent.

"I can phone and make a new appointment," he suggested obligingly.

Then they all went their separate ways.

Eirik Vassbunn was easy to contact as he was lying asleep at home. Erik Henriksen had let the phone ring twelve times before a lethargic voice said hello. Since he was taking sedatives, the police officer had authorized payment for a taxi to convey him to Grønlandsleiret 44.

Now Erik Henriksen was wondering whether the man was in any fit state to undertake an interview. He had not been anywhere near a razor for several days, and his face was grimy. His body smelled rank, and the odor filled the small room so rapidly that Erik Henriksen considered opening the window.

"I look awful," the man acknowledged, snuffling slightly. "And I stink. But you said it was urgent."

He reached for a paper cup of water the police officer had set in front of him.

"My mouth gets terribly dry from these medicines," he mumbled, drinking the entire contents at once.

The officer poured some more.

"Are you okay? I mean, will you manage to talk to me?"

The man lifted his arm and made a crawling motion. Then he bowed his head.

"I'll be fine. Might as well get it over with."

Eirik Vassbunn had worked at the Spring Sunshine Foster Home for only a year. By then he had four years of first-line service behind him, something that was a mystery to the police officer, but he dutifully recorded it with two hesitant fingers on the computer keyboard without revealing his lack of knowledge. Vassbunn was a qualified social worker, unmarried, with a daughter age seven from an earlier relationship. He had no criminal record but thought he had once been issued a speeding ticket sometime ago. He had been born in 1966 and had always lived in Oslo. He did not know any of the staff at the foster home prior to commencing work there. Apart from Maren Kalsvik, whom he had at least known vaguely, since they had attended the same college. He had left before her, so they were in different years and had not had much contact.

Thereafter they meticulously began to chart the events of the evening when Agnes Vestavik was killed.

"Were you on duty by yourself?"

"Yes, there's always only one person on night duty. Sleeping over. We have to be in the house, of course, but we have our own room where we can sleep."

"When did the children go to bed?"

"The youngest, that is to say the twins and Kenneth, are supposed to be in bed by half past eight. Jeanette and Glenn go to bed about ten, while Anita and

225

Raymond should in principle be asleep by eleven when it's a school night, but Raymond in particular is allowed quite a bit of leeway."

"But what about that particular evening?"

The man thought carefully and drank another cup of water.

"I think they all went to bed fairly early. They were worn out, because of the fire drill, and they had been roaming about because it was a day off school. Besides, Raymond wasn't feeling very well, I seem to recall. I would think they were all sleeping before half past ten. Perhaps even ten o'clock."

"When did they go to their rooms?"

"Well, the little ones are accompanied and tucked in. As far as the older ones are concerned, I didn't actually see them after . . ."

He halted, and an expression, almost an anguished look, crossed his face.

"Agnes arrived about ten o'clock, I think it was, and by then it had been awhile since I had said good night to the last one. Whether Raymond was actually *sleeping* at that point, I can't honestly know for sure."

"He says at least that he didn't hear Agnes come," the police officer informed him. "So he may have been. Sleeping, I mean. Were you sleeping?"

"No, I was sitting watching TV. As a matter of fact, I'd read some newspapers and so forth, and played some solitaire, as far as I can remember."

"Where were you sitting?"

The man seemed somewhat confused and frowned.

"In the TV room, of course."

226

"But whereabouts?"

"In a chair. A chair!"

Erik Henriksen placed a blank sheet of paper and pen in front of his almost namesake.

"Draw it for me."

Vassbunn fumbled with the pen but nevertheless succeeded in drawing a rough plan of the TV room at the foster home, with doors and windows more or less exactly pinpointed. Then he added chairs, the sofa, the table, and the actual television set, scattering a few circles at random around the "floor" to complete the picture.

"The beanbags," he explained. "And I was sitting there." He placed a cross on the armchair that had its back to the door.

"Oh, yes," the police officer commented, examining the sketch more closely. "Was the living room door open?"

"The dayroom," the other man corrected, slurring all his consonants. "We call it the dayroom. It was open."

"Are you quite sure?"

"At least it was open when Agnes turned up, and after that I wasn't out of the room until I did my rounds. At that point it was definitely open."

The police officer indicated they should pause while he caught up with writing his report. It took half an hour to hammer down three-quarters of a page. When he had finished, the witness was sitting sleeping.

This was something Henriksen had never experienced before. He was taken aback, feeling it was almost impolite to wake the man. On the other hand, they really needed to make progress. He sat there indecisively watching Eirik Vassbunn for a while. He was fast asleep, with his head on his chest and his mouth gaping. The police officer began to wonder what medicine the man was actually ingesting.

Finally he leaned across the desktop to shake the other man's arm.

"Vassbunn! You have to wake up!"

The man woke with a start and wiped some spittle from his unshaven chin.

"Sorry! It's these medicines. And then I can't sleep a wink at night!"

"It's okay," the police officer reassured him, as something suddenly struck him. "What kind of medicines are you taking?"

"Just Valium."

"Why?"

"Because I'm suffering from shock, of course!"

Now, for the first time, he seemed annoyed and dismissive.

"You've no idea what it looked like. Agnes with a huge knife sticking out her back, open, staring eyes, and . . . It was dreadful."

Naturally, Erik Henriksen could have told him he had seen the woman, both sitting in her chair and when she was placed in a cadaver bag addressed to the National Hospital, but he let it drop. Instead he brought out an ashtray and pointed to the Petterøe's tobacco packet jutting from the man's breast pocket.

"You're welcome to have a puff."

His hands were trembling so much it took an age for him to roll a cigarette, but he seemed grateful enough.

"Is it only now, since that experience, you've been on this kind of medication?"

Bingo. The man dropped the papers and tobacco, shaking even more.

"What do you mean?"

"Take it easy. We won't say anything to anybody, of course. But I'd like to know if you were taking Valium that evening. Is it something you take all the time?"

By now he had succeeded in composing himself sufficiently that it appeared he would be capable of producing something resembling a cigarette. He took his time answering, and inhaled deeply, clearing his throat before saying, "I have some trouble with my nerves, you know. A bit shaky. Don't entirely know what it comes from. But I manage fine. I use only a tiny dose, really."

His comment did not seem particularly convincing. Erik Henriksen waited to receive a reply to the question he had posed.

"Yes, it is. I had probably taken a pill or two that evening. Had argued with my ex-partner. The mother of my daughter. I was actually supposed to have her over the winter holiday, but then —"

"One or two?" the officer interrupted. "Did you take one or two tablets?"

"Two," the man mumbled.

"So you may in fact have fallen asleep in the chair?"

"But I wasn't even tired, for crying out loud! I needed to play some solitaire as well before I had any chance of sleeping!"

"But mightn't that be because you had *already* slept? Dozed off? Perhaps without actually remembering you had?"

The man did not respond. There was no reason to do so. They both remained silent, and the police officer spent the next quarter of an hour manhandling the computer keyboard again. This time the witness did not nod off.

"Well then," Erik Henriksen said so suddenly that Vassbunn flinched in his seat, "what happened when you found Agnes then?"

The witness's eyes almost glazed over, as though looking inward at himself.

"I became totally hysterical," he said calmly. "Absolutely hysterical."

"But what did you do?"

"Can you roll cigarettes?"

The police officer smiled crookedly, shrugging his shoulders.

"Probably better than that there," he said, pointing to the unfortunate trumpet-shaped object stubbed out in the ashtray. "Would you be kind enough to do one?"

Vassbunn shoved the pack of tobacco across to the policeman, who managed in an impressively short time to produce an entirely acceptable roll-up.

"I really didn't know what to do. I was already upset about Olav, who had vanished, and then Agnes was sitting there dead as a d — Dead. Right there and then

I felt it must be all my fault, and I was terrified. Then I phoned Maren."

"Maren?"

Surprised, Erik Henriksen leafed swiftly through the papers to find the one he was searching for. He stopped the witness, who wanted to continue, and finished reading. Then he slapped the bundle of documents together again and made a sign to the man to go on speaking.

"Yes. She lives nearby and is so much more . . . so much calmer and more restrained than me. She would probably be able to help me. So she arrived after only a few minutes. She was quite angry because I hadn't phoned the police. So she phoned."

"Okay. And then?"

"Nothing much happened after that. I sat down, as I couldn't bear to be in the same room as Agnes. Maren dealt with all the children and the police and everything. Then I went home.

"Can I go soon?" he added after a short pause. "I'm completely exhausted."

"I well understand that. But we need to talk about what happened earlier that day, as well. Can you manage that? Do you want some coffee?"

The man shook his head.

"More water, then? I can get you a cola, would you like that?"

"Water, please."

This time too he drank all of it at once, then waited for the next question with a resigned expression and closed eyes.

"When did you arrive at work?"

"Nine o'clock. After supper. All the youngest children were already in bed."

"Had you been at the foster home earlier that day?"

"Yes."

He opened his eyes, seemingly surprised this might have anything to do with the case.

"We had a meeting. Most people were there, as far as I recall. And then Agnes suddenly decided she wanted to have an interview with every single one of us. A kind of appraisal interview, or something of the sort. I didn't see the point and was none the wiser when it was my turn either. Terje went first, and that took an excruciatingly long time. Then it was meant to be Maren's turn, but she had to leave, because she had to go to the dentist's. And so it was Cathrine, I think, and then me. That didn't take long."

"What did you talk about?"

"Everything and nothing. How I thought things were going, how I dealt with Olav. Whether contact with my daughter was going well. My former partner and I had quarreled about —"

"Do you remember precisely how long it lasted?"

"No, maybe half an hour? Less, probably. In any case, I was in for a much shorter time than both Terje and Cathrine."

The police officer's fingers were battering away at the keyboard again, and the witness realized this would entail another break.

"Did you notice whether there were any knives lying anywhere in the room?" he asked after something — he had no idea what — caused the computer to take on a mind of its own.

"Knives? No, of course there were no knives lying there!"

"Is the office ever locked?"

"We rely on trust. No one is allowed to enter the office without Agnes's permission. Besides, there's a key hanging on a nail above the door, but as far as I know it's never used."

The screen facing Henriksen was filling up with rows of full stops, rows that were increasing at an alarming rate. He started to sweat.

"Turn off the computer," Vassbunn suggested, and Henriksen agreed that was a good idea and switched the machine off and back on again. He had not, however, remembered to save the last part of the interview and slapped his forehead in frustration. It took some time to rectify his blunder.

"But then it must be an easy matter to go into the office if you want to," he said at last. "Without anyone seeing you, I mean."

"In a house with eight youngsters and a total of fourteen staff? No, I can assure you it's not. You can never be sure someone won't turn up. Apart from during the night, when you're on duty by yourself. Then you would be reasonably safe, though there's always one or another of the children waking up."

"Does everybody work night duty?"

"No, only three of us. Plus Christian on occasion. He's really too young and inexperienced, if you ask me, but sometimes someone falls ill or that kind of thing."

"Did Terje Welby ever go on night duty?"

"No, not while I've been there, anyway."

"How was he?"

"Was? Terje?"

"Yes."

"Well, what can I say? He had excellent paper qualifications, you know. Master's degree and all that. Quite good with the very youngest children. But he got too easily involved in arguments with the teenagers."

"Maren?"

"Maren's the cleverest one of us all. She lives for that foster home. She has a hold on the youngsters that's completely unfathomable. Agnes thought really highly of her. We all do. She's actually quite old-fashioned, in a way. Her work seems to be a kind of . . . vocation!"

He savored the unfamiliar word.

"Do you socialize with her outside work?"

"No, not really. As I said, I knew her slightly from earlier, but we didn't meet up outside working hours. By the way, do you know any more about . . ."

He pulled a grimace and kneaded his neck.

"I've a thumping headache. Do you know any more about Olav?"

"Well . . . we know he was in a house in Grefsen until some point at the weekend. The boy's clearly able to look after himself. But obviously we're afraid something might have happened to him. We're searching."

"He's not really right in the head. I mean, I've met many damaged children in the course of the last few years, but no one comes anywhere near that boy."

"I see. Other people are taking care of his case. We might as well call it a day now, Vassbunn."

The final part of the interview was written with no full stops. It looked bizarre, but would have to do. Eirik Vassbunn was so obviously exhausted the police officer felt tempted to drive him home himself. But he did not have time.

"Take a taxi and send us the bill," he said in conclusion as Vassbunn virtually staggered out the door. "Send it to me. Hope you're feeling better soon!"

Erik Henriksen was sure Hanne Wilhelmsen would be hugely satisfied with the interview. Despite the missing full stops.

It was absolutely boring being inside all the time. Especially in the mornings, of course, when there was nothing on TV. It was now nearly a week since he had poked his nose outside the door. In a way he was missing the school a little. At least there was something to do there. Nothing happened at home. His mother was even quieter than usual. She was always so fucking silent.

Before they had held that meeting at the council committee when they decided he could no longer live at home, he had talked to a lady who said she was a kind of judge in the matter. She might as well have said it straight out. He knew it was called the chairman of the council committee, because his mother had explained everything to do with the case to him. He had even been to meet his mother's lawyer, and what's more, read loads of the papers concerning him.

The conversation had lasted quite a long time. They had not been in the council committee's office but instead a large room with benches and chairs only at one side. That was where the meeting was to be held, she explained. He thought it looked like a courtroom, and she had appeared surprised at his mentioning that. She did not look particularly Norwegian, more like an Indian, almost, with dark skin and completely black hair, but at least she spoke in an ordinary voice and had a Norwegian name.

She had asked him where he would want to live if given the choice. At home, he had said, of course. But then she wanted to know why. It wasn't particularly easy to explain *why* you wanted to live at home in your own house, so he had simply said it was the usual thing to do, and he didn't want to move. She had pestered him quite a lot. At least she had asked the same questions over and over again. The point of the conversation was somewhat unclear to him, for they decided he should move regardless. Finally she had asked him if he loved his mother.

What kind of question was that?! All people love their mothers, surely, he had retorted. He did too, of course he did.

It had not been difficult to say. It was true. Moreover, he knew his mother loved him very much. They belonged together, she used to tell him. But that did not seem so obvious when they *were* together. She was so scared of all sorts of things, of the neighbors, of his grandmother, of his teachers. And of that bloody child welfare service. She had made a fuss about the

236

child welfare service for as long as he could remember, especially if someone had complained about him.

He wanted to go out. He needed to go outside.

"I'm going out for a walk," he said suddenly, rising from the sofa.

His mother slowly lowered the newspaper she was reading.

"You can't, Olav. You know that. Or you'll have to go back to the foster home."

"But I can't stand being stuck inside any longer," he complained without returning to his seat.

"I appreciate that. But first we have to come up with a plan."

He placed his hands on his hips and spread his legs. A comical pose, but she did not laugh.

"A plan, what do you mean by that? When's that going to happen? When are you going to think up that plan you've been talking about all week?"

Instead of answering, she convulsively gripped the newspaper, now rolled tightly in her hands.

"You won't think up any plan, Mum. You never think up any plan."

He was not even angry. His strange contracted smile was almost sad, and he moved his hand toward her but stopped before reaching her.

"I will think of something," she whispered. "I just need some time."

"Honestly, Mum."

He did not say anything more after that but simply wheeled around and headed for the door. His mother rose from the sofa and hurried after him.

"Olav, my boy, you *mustn't* go out!"

She clung on to his arm. Although Olav Håkonsen was only twelve years old, he realized his mother was afraid. Moreover, he knew she was right to say it was stupid to go outside. In addition, he was certain she would be dreadfully worried the entire time he was gone. It was almost enough to change his mind.

But he *needed* to get out of the apartment. It was too small right now. He shook his mother off and grabbed a hundred kroner from a bowl on the hall table. Shutting his ears to his mother's sobs, he closed the door behind him.

By the time the cold February air blasted his face, he had forgotten his mother and was feeling almost carefree. To be on the safe side, he was wearing a large cap. And after all, it was already dark outside, so no one would be able to recognize him from a distance. As well as the hundred-kroner note he had filched, he had fifty kroner in his pocket, the pocket money for two weeks he had not yet touched. His mother had continued to give him an allowance even after he moved to the foster home. His mother had handed it to him when he had asked earlier that day, though she had looked at him strangely.

Most of all he wanted to go to the center. He had enough money to buy himself some goodies, or maybe play the slot machines. He could even do both. But of course he couldn't go there. So many people there knew him. However, what he *could* do was take the bus to another center, in a totally different part of the city. He had been to Storo a number of times. His mother knew a hairdresser there from the old days, and she cut both their hair quite cheaply. She was the one who had given him the punk hairstyle that was now growing out; he was now no longer completely shaved on one side of his head. It was really cool, he had thought himself, but a sad, tired look had crossed his mother's face when she saw him.

He would go to Storo. Although he couldn't remember whether he had seen any slot machines there.

The bus arrived only a few minutes after he reached the bus stop. He handed the driver the fifty-kroner note without a word and stuffed the change into his pocket before sitting at the very back of the almost empty bus. It was late afternoon, almost evening, but since it was Thursday there would probably be crowds of people at the shopping center. That was really for the best, when he thought about it.

The bus trip did not take very long. He had started to carve the bus seat with his pocketknife but was interrupted when a man sat down beside him.

Olav twisted his ankle when he jumped off the bus and let out a groan. The pain reminded him of his mother, and his good spirits abated.

There were no proper slot machines there, only a stupid lottery machine that he knew he would never win anything on, and a kind of one-armed bandit that wasn't much fun either. But there were two cafés on the ground floor, and he was hungry. One of them was quite a fancy snack bar, with meals and beer. The other was more like a tearoom. He chose the latter, where there were several vacant tables, and he bought himself a large bottle of cola and two slices of cake.

Storo Center appeared more old-fashioned than the center where he lived and was also certainly a good deal smaller. But it was fairly pleasant. At the table beside him, an unbelievably old man was sitting chattering away to himself, and Olav grinned at all the strange things he heard him say. He kept spilling his coffee too, and the waitress became annoyed when she had to come wipe the table for the third time. When the man discovered Olav listening in, he pulled his chair closer to his table, prattling even more about the war and the sea and his wife who had died long, long ago. Olav was enjoying himself and bought himself another cola and a fresh cup of coffee for the old man, who smiled and thanked him effusively.

He was so amusing Olav did not manage to spot them in time. Two uniformed police officers were approaching the café.

The boy remained seated, not moving a muscle. Not because he realized that was sensible, but because he was totally terrified. The chance of encountering the police had been only a distant, inconceivable possibility.

The waitress waved them over.

"He's been sitting here for four hours now, only drinking coffee. He's spilling it and interfering with the other customers," she complained, pointing toward the old man.

The man kept quiet for the first time since Olav arrived, trying to hide himself in his coffee cup. He moved closer to Olav, as though in an attempt to obtain some kind of protection. When the boy sluggishly stood up to perform a disappearing act, with his back turned to the two uniformed policemen, the old man grabbed his arm and whispered desperately, "Don't go, boy! Don't leave me!"

For someone so small and puny, his hands were strong, even though they were trembling. Olav felt the fingertips through the sleeve of his jacket and had to shake vigorously in order to make him let go. That took a few seconds, and in the meantime the police officers had crossed over to the table.

"Is he with you?" one of them asked.

Olav stared at the floor, pulling his cap even farther down over his ears.

"No, no. I don't know him at all," he said, starting to head for the exit.

He had nearly reached as far as the florist's store beside the automatic doors when he heard one of the police officers shout. As people were going in and out almost continually, he could already feel the cold draft of freedom beckoning beyond the door.

"Hi, you there! Wait a minute!"

He stopped without turning around. The cap was making his forehead itchy, but he did not dare pull it up. He had something inside one of his shoes, something that had grown enormous and was digging into his sole so much it was almost paralyzing his foot. Something had seized hold of his lungs, and he could not breathe. He saw all the people coming and going around him, men with wives and little brats in baby carriages, all of them with mouths smiling and moving about. Nevertheless, he could not hear anything except the fierce hammering of his own heart. He felt sick. Terribly sick.

Then he took to his heels. He judged it perfectly, as the doors were standing wide open, just about to close again. All the people on their way in and out of the center suddenly stopped, taken aback at the sight of the boy exploding through the doors like an enormous cannonball, heading for the parking lot. Consequently, they were standing blocking the exit when the two policemen came running in pursuit, and the doors closed before sliding all too slowly open again, with two cursing policemen standing on the inside. When they finally emerged, the boy was nowhere to be seen. Choosing to chase after him in two different directions, they took off. One of them dropped his cap and had to watch impotently as a car drove over it before he ran on.

The other one had more luck. As he reached the multistory car park, he saw a figure making its way up the external staircase. The cap and quilted jacket, barely visible above the edge of the railings, matched. He wanted to get hold of his partner before continuing the chase but concluded there were so many exits from the car park that he did not have time. He dashed off after the boy up the stairway.

His colleague, although making his way toward a Statoil gas station a couple of hundred meters along the road, recognized the situation and ran toward the car ramp at the end of the parking lot in order to cut the boy off from there. He arrived on the story above only a few seconds after his partner, but the boy was nowhere in sight. The elder of the two made a zigzag movement with his hand, mimicking a shark hunting. Then they searched the entire floor. They checked all the vehicles. They checked between, in front of, and behind them, and even examined underneath every single car, though neither of them thought for a moment that a gross twelve-year-old could fit under an ordinary car. Eventually they had to admit what was staring them in the face, no matter how embarrassing it was for two well-trained police officers in the prime of life: Olav Håkonsen, the missing boy, had vanished without trace.

Disheartened, they continued their search for another half hour, both inside and outside the shopping center. Then they sat down, shamefaced, in their police vehicle to report that the boy had been spotted and pursued but had disappeared. Since the last trace of him had been found in a house in Grefsen, the police were able to conclude quite wrongly that he had been staying in the area the entire time. Thus they were able to discard the dawning suspicion that he had been at home with his mother, a suspicion bolstered by several neighbors, promised total anonymity, who declared their conviction that Olav Håkonsen was in hiding in his own home.

But at least the boy was alive. That offered some comfort.

Two days after the aide phoned, the child welfare service representatives were standing there. Olav had just turned eleven. I was not expecting them. I thought they would call me in for a meeting and had already looked in the Yellow Pages for an attorney. You're entitled to that, free of charge, I knew that from before. But there was so little information listed about what they specialized in, and there are so many different kinds of attorney.

And so they were standing there. Two of them, a woman and a man. I hadn't met either of them previously, but then it had been many years since I'd had any contact with child welfare. They were friendly enough, I suppose, though I don't recall very much about it. An investigation had been initiated, they told me, on the basis of something they called "reported concerns."

Reported concerns! Here I was with continued concerns about the boy for more than eleven years, and then they turned up now! They asked if they could come in and looked around in the same way as the lady from social services had done that time long ago, when Olav was still a little baby. Stolen glances, in a way, but at the same time so barefaced.

It was a Thursday, and I had just cleaned the whole apartment. They certainly wouldn't be able to get me for that. I put out coffee and cookies, but they didn't touch a thing. Did they think I would poison them?

Then they told me everything I already knew from before. About Olav's deviant behavior and aggressive conduct, and that the older children lured him into doing all sorts of strange things. About his erratic school attendance, and that he spoiled things for the others. About him being excessively overweight. They wondered what we were eating. I became furious, I remember that quite clearly. I dragged the woman with me out to the kitchen and opened the refrigerator door.

244

Milk, cheese, fish cakes from the previous day. Margarine and onions and a bag of apples.

She jotted notes on a writing pad, and I could see she had written "full-fat milk." Then I gave up. The boy refused to drink semi-skimmed or skimmed milk. Did they think it was better that I didn't get any milk into him at all?

They stayed for a long time, and as I say I don't remember much about it. Fortunately Olav was out, though they began to glance at the clock when it turned evening and he still had not appeared. They wanted to obtain information from various sources, they said, and it might take several months. Then they wondered whether I had any objections to an expert assessment being conducted. A psychologist or a psychiatrist would talk to both of us, so the child welfare service "would be in a better position to find out what we required."

Objections? I had tried for more than five years to persuade someone to examine the boy's head, without receiving help from anywhere. Of course I didn't have any objections. I already knew there was something wrong. Something that should have been discovered ages ago. "Better late than never," I said, and noticed that they exchanged a look. But why a psychologist would want to talk to me was completely incomprehensible. Going along with something like that would be admitting it was all my fault. So I turned it down flat.

When the expert eventually set to work, I nevertheless went along with her being present in the apartment with Olav and me on a couple of occasions. "Observations of interaction" was what she called it in her subsequent report. I did not recognize myself at all. Everything was twisted and distorted. I tried to get my lawyer to understand it wasn't my fault that Olav went to bed so late. I could certainly try to force him, but that only led to a shouting match, and it was obviously better that things were pleasant and quiet than that the boy should toss and turn without being able to fall asleep. "Serious boundary-setting issues" was what the psychologist wrote.

Precisely as I had expected, they discovered he had minimal brain dysfunction, MBD. To be sure, only that "symptoms were found consistent with a minor degree of MBD," but my attorney assured me this was simply the way they normally expressed it.

I had known that the entire time. No one had listened to me. Now, when it had been scientifically proved there was something wrong with the boy, the child welfare people were insisting that in any case I could not take care of him. He was so difficult. Besides, they thought it was not certain he was ill, all the same, since the symptoms of MBD could also indicate a failure of parental care.

They were insistent that they wanted to saddle me with a home consultant. I said I was open to anything at all to help Olav, but that I didn't need any help myself. I wasn't the one who was sick. I'm not the one there's something wrong with.

Finally the case ended up at the council committee and they wanted to take the boy from me.

I hadn't slept for several nights. When I arrived there, I noticed I smelled, even though I had showered that morning. I felt as though my clothes were too small and regretted wearing the blue polyester blouse rather than something made of cotton. But the attorney had said it was important that I was smartly dressed. For the first hour, I was totally

246

preoccupied by my awareness of the odor gradually worsening and the rings of perspiration under my arms becoming increasingly noticeable. I felt dizzy. A large, plump woman with a ponytail and glasses and a confused mixture of dialects droned on about everything that had gone wrong down through the years. She was the lawyer for the child welfare service. There were five people serving on the committee, four women and one man. Three of them took notes, while the man farthest to the left nodded off through the entire procedure. One of the women, who had to be more than sixty years old, sat the whole time gazing at me with a look that made me feel even more dizzy. I had to ask for a break.

My lawyer took far less time than the one representing the council. That was probably a bad sign, but I didn't have the temerity to ask why that was so. Besides, the council had loads of witnesses. I had none. My attorney said it wasn't necessary. I couldn't think of anybody, either, when he asked me in advance.

After two days it was all over. The chairman of the committee, who had been friendly the entire time, asked me if I felt that everything of significance had been discussed, or whether I had anything I wanted to add. Inside me there was a massive lump of words that had not been spoken. I wanted so much to make them understand. I wanted to take them back in time, show them all the good things, get them to see how much Olav and I love each other. I wanted them to understand that I had done everything for my boy, that I had never drunk alcohol, never taken any kind of drugs either, that I had never slapped him, that I had always, always been afraid of losing him.

247

Instead I shook my head and stared at the floor.

Twelve days later I was informed that they had taken my son away from me.

Olav Håkonsen was sprawled in a garbage container behind the multistory car park at the Storo Center, wondering how long he had been lying there. He had a thumping headache and was aware of a terrible stench. He tried to raise himself but collapsed back onto all the trash bags. It had become totally dark. When he attempted to see what time it was, he realized his Swatch had disappeared. It was impossible to remember whether he had it with him earlier. He was overwhelmed by nausea when once again he endeavored to balance himself in an upright position, and he puked out the cake and cola. That alleviated matters slightly.

The container was half full, but the garbage was unevenly distributed, and he was lying so high up he almost reached the ice-cold metal edge. His mittens were gone as well. Eventually he succeeded in hauling himself up but quickly lost his balance on the squashy layer beneath him. He tried to recall what had happened.

He had jumped. Six or seven meters above him he glimpsed the edge of the top story. It had been the only solution, he remembered. Then he remembered nothing more.

Instead he dug himself deeper down among the black stinking bags of garbage and dozed off into a blessed, dreamless void.

248

★ ★ ★

Erik Henriksen's working day had been long, and it was going to be even longer. They still had five interviews left, and it was something of an illusion to believe that they would have them finished by tomorrow, as Hanne Wilhelmsen had requested. At least not if Tone-Marit and he were to manage them on their own.

God only knew how Hanne and Billy T. actually passed their time. Not that he in any way suspected them of shirking their duties, but it would have been uplifting to know what they were up to. They weren't in the office very often, and even Billy T., who should really have been just as actively involved in dispatching the interviews, was constantly impossible to locate. Sometimes Erik Henriksen felt that he was not properly *included*. That they didn't entirely trust him. Not particularly inspiring. Now and again he felt a stab of irritation, almost anger, directed toward Hanne Wilhelmsen. That was something quite novel, and he did not know how to deal with it.

Tilting his head from one side to the other, he felt his neck muscles contract. He was exhausted, out of sorts, and fed up. Now he longed to go home.

Tone-Marit was standing in the doorway, saying nothing and simply smiling.

She was very ordinary. Quite sweet, really. Her face was round, even though she was slim. Her eyes were narrow and lopsided, and when she smiled, they disappeared altogether. Her hair changed color from time to time; during this year he had known her, it had changed from blonde to copper red to dark brunette, as

249

it was currently. He did not know whether the curls were her own, or whether they had been purchased too.

She did not usually say very much. He did not know very much about her. But now she was standing here, and it was late in the afternoon. Billy T. was out and about. Hanne Wilhelmsen was a lost cause. Tone-Marit stood in the doorway smiling.

"Shall we go to the cinema?" he suggested before he had time to consider it deeply, and she did not even seem surprised.

"Yes, we could," she said. "What would you like to see?"

"It's all the same to me," he answered, feeling less tired already.

They sauntered into the city center, too late to make the seven o'clock screening and with all the time in the world until the one at nine.

Tone-Marit walked beautifully. A determined, self-assured gait, with a little feminine swing of the hips that did not seem to be an affectation. She carried her head erect, although she was almost as tall as he was, and he was a six footer. She was wearing a short leather pilot's jacket over painfully tight denim jeans, and quite pointed shoes with laces that disappeared up under her trouser hems. She was not saying very much now either, but that was of no consequence.

It took them half an hour to reach Klingenberg. By then he knew at least where she stayed and that she lived alone. What's more, she played soccer in the premier league, trained five times a week, and had played in six international matches. He was extremely

250

impressed, and taken aback that he had not known these scraps of information before.

As they rounded the glass cases beside the cinema entrance, he spotted Hanne Wilhelmsen. The old familiar feeling of his heart beating just a tiny bit faster caught him off guard, but for the first time it was combined with something negative, almost depressing, that anger he had not quite managed to shrug off. Slowing his pace, he rubbed his freckled face with his finger and weighed the possibilities of going to the cinema at Saga instead. However, they had already decided on this movie.

Hanne Wilhelmsen was standing fiddling with her cinema ticket and chatting to three other women. Two of them had cropped hair and looked quite similar, one in an old anorak and the other in a dun-colored shapeless jacket and rubber boots folded over at the top, just like an old sea dog. Both were wearing old-fashioned student glasses. The third woman was totally different. She had midlength pale blonde hair and was almost as tall as Hanne. Underneath an open maxicoat in some kind of expensive-looking fabric, she wore a dark red dress with buttons down the front. The two top buttons were unfastened, and the collar was turned up. Now she was throwing her head back and laughing at something one of the short-haired women had said. Hanne, standing half turned toward Erik and Tone-Marit, nudged her shoulder and smiled in a way he had never seen before. Her face was so open, she seemed younger, she seemed happier, more uncontrolled, in a sense. Suddenly, she caught sight of him.

Erik was here. And Tone-Marit. She had of course experienced this on many previous occasions. Colleagues out and about in the city. Oslo was not such a huge place. She had her strategies. A brief nod or a slight wave before hurrying off in the direction of something or other that seemed a very important destination. Something urgent that prevented any intimate conversation. It occurred frequently, although Cecilie usually became annoyed, or at least dismayed.

But here, outside a cinema where the movie would not begin for another twenty minutes, casually huddled together with all the other people standing waiting, waving their cinema tickets, it would be no use. They were her immediate subordinates. People she worked in close contact with. Day in and day out. She had to talk to them.

She beat them to it by taking the initiative and leaving her friends to approach her two colleagues. Too late, she discovered Cecilie had followed her. Karen and Miriam fortunately read it all so rapidly that they headed for the doors, departing the scene. Why on earth they insisted on looking so much like lesbians was unfathomable. And sometimes uncomfortable.

She had no idea what she was going to say. So she said it like it was.

"This is Cecilie."

The earth stood still for three whole seconds before she added, "We share an apartment. We live together."

"Oh, yes," Erik Henriksen said, holding his hand out to Cecilie. "I'm Erik. We work together."

252

His left hand made a circular motion that included himself, Hanne, and Tone-Marit.

"Are you a colleague as well?" he asked doubtfully, scrutinizing Cecilie's face.

"No, far from it." She laughed. "I work at Ullevål Hospital. And so you're Erik. I've heard a lot about you."

Hanne noticed Erik was struggling with his perennial blushing and said a thank-you to higher powers that she was therefore more easily able to conceal her own. She did not even dare to look at Tone-Marit.

"Did you manage to complete most of those interviews?" she asked cheerfully, taking an imperceptible step to one side to avoid standing too close to her girlfriend.

"Five left to go," Tone-Marit replied. "We'll probably finish them tomorrow. By the way, the boy was spotted this afternoon."

Hanne pulled herself together.

"Was spotted? By our people?"

"Yes, at the Storo Center, but he made a successful escape," Erik confirmed. "He's a tough little nut. He's been on the run for a fortnight now. They're searching the entire area up there. It's not far, you see, from that villa where he spent a few days. The boys think he's found himself a new hiding place, so they're investigating abandoned farmhouses and that kind of thing. Farms scheduled for demolition."

"Well," Hanne said lightheartedly, trying to bring the unwelcome encounter to a conclusion, "I want to get myself a poster!"

"She's hopeless," Cecilie said apologetically with a smile. "She loves movie posters!"

"That last remark was bloody unnecessary," Hanne hissed when they were out of earshot.

"I thought you were clever, Hanne," Cecilie said calmly, taking the cinema tickets from her to hand over to the inspector.

"I'd no idea Hanne shared an apartment with anybody," Erik whispered once he and Tone-Marit had found their seats. "Really lovely girl too."

Tone-Marit fiddled with a straw that refused to fit into her carton of juice.

"I don't exactly think they just share an apartment," she said serenely, finally managing to push the reluctant straw into place.

But by then Erik was already tucking into a bag of chocolates and had started to look forward to the movie.

CHAPTER
TEN

At ten o'clock on Friday morning, Maren Kalsvik phoned Billy T. again. Kenneth was unwell. He was crying and did not want her to leave the house. Normally he would have to accept it, she explained, but there had of course been so much lately. The boy was afraid, brokenhearted, and was running a temperature of thirty-nine degrees Celsius. She realized it was a lot to ask, but since the other members of staff were sitting in a queue at the police station waiting to be interviewed, she thought she would take the liberty of asking if he could come over to conduct her interview there. At the foster home.

Billy T. liked Kenneth. Besides, he knew what sick children could be like.

At twenty minutes to eleven he parked his own car on the road leading down from the Spring Sunshine Foster Home. He had not been able to contact Hanne, and that made him slightly ill at ease. He had been on the point of phoning her home to check whether she was there but had rejected that idea.

As he opened the gate on his way up to the large house, a skinny woman emerged from the main door.

Catching sight of him, she halted and waited until he reached her.

"You're from the police?" she asked skeptically, looking him up and down.

When he confirmed her supposition, her eyes affected an expression of concentration, as though struggling to call something to mind. Then she shook her head briefly, obviously casting the thought aside. Without another word, she held the door open until he was inside before scurrying away along the gravel path.

Raymond came thundering down the stairs, almost colliding with Billy T. as the police officer was about to pop his head around the door of the dayroom.

"My goodness, are you not at school?" he asked.

"I'd forgotten my gym clothes! Maren's in the conference room," the seventeen-year-old called out, slamming the front door so violently behind him it could have wakened the dead.

Fortunately it did not wake Kenneth, who was sleeping on the first floor.

"Finally. He hardly slept a wink all night," Maren Kalsvik said ruefully, offering him a chair.

"It doesn't look as though you did either."

She smiled faintly, squinting her eyes and shrugging her shoulders.

"It's okay. But I'm worried about him. This is affecting the children, you know. Children who should be spared any anxiety. That's one of the reasons for them being here. Oh, my! A murder and a suicide. In ten days."

She covered her face with her hands and remained sitting like that for a few seconds until, with a start, she sat up straight and in an exaggeratedly cheerful voice suggested they should begin.

"Since we're doing this here at your house," Billy T. said, placing a tape recorder in the middle of the table, "I'm using this. Okay?"

She did not answer, so he presumed it was acceptable. After some initial fumbling, it even worked, although it was at least fifteen years old and made a ticking sound like an old-fashioned clock. It belonged to Oslo Police Station, and someone had ensured it would not be forgotten by plastering it with OPS labels in six different places. Beside the tape recorder he placed a cell phone belonging to him, only two months old. He had received it as a Christmas present from his sons, meaning that their respective mothers had somehow collaborated on the gift.

"Have to have this on," he said somewhat apologetically. "It's the tackiest thing, I know, but we're in the middle of an investigation and all that. The others have to be able to contact me."

She still said nothing. So that was probably okay as well.

"We need to return to the evening of the murder," he commenced.

"I do that every single night," she said impassively. "When I'm finally able to sit down and relax. Then it hits me. All of it. That dreadful sight."

Actually, he admired her. So young, and so much responsibility. Enough bucketfuls of love for a whole flock of children.

"Are you living here now?" he asked.

"Yes. Just for a while. Until things settle down."

The old wreck suddenly stopped ticking, and he fiddled some more with the buttons, clearly reluctant to remain depressed. Eventually the recorder seemed to be functioning again.

"Can you recall precisely when Eirik Vassbunn phoned you?"

"It must have been just before one. At night, that is." She smiled wanly.

"How was he behaving?"

"Totally hysterical."

"Hysterical? What do you mean by that?"

"He was sobbing and stammering and couldn't manage to explain anything at all. Going completely to pieces."

Her face had taken on a hard expression, and she pulled the elastic band from her hair, gathering her ponytail together once more and putting the band back on.

"He says you arrived before he had called the police."

Billy T. stood up and crossed to the window. Placing his hands on his back, he asked, without looking at her, "Why did you not say that when you were interviewed the first time?"

Then he turned around abruptly and fixed her with a stare. All he could read there was genuine astonishment.

"But I said that quite clearly then," she said. "I'm one hundred percent sure of that."

Billy T. stepped toward the table to produce a copy of the previous interview. It was five pages long and signed by both Kalsvik and Tone-Marit Steen.

"Here," he said, reading aloud, " 'The witness says she was phoned by Eirik Vassbunn circa 01:00 hours. It could have been ten minutes before or ten minutes after. She thinks it did not take longer than a quarter of an hour for her to arrive on the scene. Vassbunn was extremely upset, and the police had to drive him to the emergency doctor for medical attention.' Full stop. Nothing about it being you who had phoned. Nothing about the police not being here when you arrived."

"But I really *did* say that," she insisted. "Why wouldn't I have said so?"

Billy T. rubbed his hands over his skull. He needed to shave. It prickled and felt itchy. He knew she was probably telling the truth. The previous interview did not mention that she had arrived before the police, but neither did it mention that she had *not*. Tone-Marit was promising, but she could obviously still make mistakes.

The phone rang. They both jumped slightly.

"Billy T.," he barked, angry at the interruption. His anger increased when he heard it was Tone-Marit.

"Sorry, Billy," she said. "But I —"

"Billy T. Billy *T.*, I've told you. A hundred times."

He turned halfway around, away from the table, and Maren Kalsvik raised her eyebrows and pointed toward the door. He nodded, somewhat disconcerted, but she seemed grateful to be able to take a break so early. She carefully closed the door behind her, and he was left alone.

"What is it?"

"We've found out who committed fraud with those checks."

He said nothing. He heard the *whooshing* sound of water in a pipe and assumed that Maren Kalsvik was in the kitchen next door making coffee. But it might also be something wrong with his ears.

"Hello? Hello!"

"Yes, I'm here," he said. "Who was it?"

"The Lover. The videos show it clearly, even though he's wearing a stupid false beard."

Hanne's theory in the bar disintegrated, though it did not matter in the least.

"One more thing," she said, her voice fading and almost disappearing in the grating and crackling from the phone. "Hello? Are you there?"

"Yes," he shouted. "Hello?"

"The Lover has disappeared. He's not been at work for a couple of days but hasn't phoned in sick or anything like that. The friend he told us he was with in Drøbak on the evening of the murder can't be found either."

The *whooshing* noise became even louder. Now he was not sure whether it came from the water pipes, the telephone, or his own head.

"Hello?"

"Yes, okay, I'm here," he shouted irritably. "Find out where the guy is now. Don't do anything else. Do you understand? Nothing! Just find out where he is. I'll be at the station in twenty minutes."

He shut the lid of the cell phone, threw on his jacket, and barely had time to say good-bye to Maren Kalsvik, who was left standing, looking taken aback, with a jug of coffee in one hand and two cups in the other.

Billy T. forgot the tape recorder, of course.

Hanne could not remember when she had last slept so well. All the same she was dog tired. It took her several seconds to work out what day of the week it was. She resisted rising to face it. For safety's sake, she felt to see whether she had a sore throat. Or stomach. When she examined herself really thoroughly, there was a faint ache somewhere behind the small of her back. But that simply meant she would have her period soon. She dragged herself up to surface from the quilts. And swore like a sailor when she saw it was more than half past ten.

Cecilie had already left. The kitchen table had been set for her, with knife and fork, napkin, and the prettiest dishes. On the plate lay a loving note wishing her a good day. That at least improved things slightly.

The Diakonhjemmet School of Social Work was situated logically enough at the end of the street called Diakonveien, extending from the roundabout at Volvat to an enormous parking lot. The college itself was situated in an attractive open layout, almost at the top of a rise, but it was a patchwork of different architectural styles. The entrance was tucked into a corner between a two-story brick building and an enormous yellow block of indeterminable vintage.

"Just as unwelcoming an entrance as the one at Oslo Police Station," Hanne Wilhelmsen muttered to herself as she walked the thirty meters from the car park to enter the college through double glass doors.

A notice board on her right-hand side promoted a folk song concert on Saturday evening, causing her to shudder. Three female students descended a little concrete staircase, or perhaps they were teachers. Just as Hanne was about to ask the way to the dean's office, she caught sight of another notice board indicating she should climb the stairs and walk to the left and through the atrium. On her way, she was invited by another couple of notice boards to morning prayers, and they also even offered to pray for her if she wished.

Not such a bad idea, she thought. *But I doubt the offer applies to the likes of me.*

Hanne was greeted by a woman by the name of Ellen Marie Sørensen. The lady showed her where the cloakroom was. Her face was sharp and efficient, her words friendly, but her voice was shrill and demanding. The clothes she wore were not particularly expensive, and not especially tasteful either, but formal and suited the rest of her. A gray pleated skirt and frilly blouse beneath a darker gray suit jacket making her appear older than she probably was. Her hair was cut in a simple but very feminine style, with faint streaks of color from a tint that must have been applied long ago. Ellen Marie Sørensen was the kind of woman in whose company Hanne Wilhelmsen always felt clumsy. She regretted not wearing something more official than velvet trousers and a traditional Norwegian sweater.

The woman made her feel she should have worn her uniform.

Mrs Sørensen was able to confirm that she had spoken to Agnes Vestavik recently. She could not provide an exact date, but in any case it could not have been more than three weeks ago. She remembered the circumstances so well because she had been surprised by the inquiry. At first she had declined to answer.

"You can never know," she said, puckering her mouth meaningfully. "Anybody at all could phone claiming to be anyone at all, you see."

But when the dean had come in shortly afterward and requested that she respond to the inquiry made by Agnes Vestavik, who was an old friend of his, she had phoned her back and provided the information she sought.

"And what was that?" Hanne asked, folding her arms.

Perhaps it was something to do with the place. A Christian college ought to predicate itself on being a place where God was more present than usual. Or perhaps it was simply because she was grasping at every least straw in the hope of influencing the answer to why Agnes Vestavik had phoned Diakonhjemmet University College's School of Social Work the week she was killed.

"Dear God," she said to herself, glancing at her knuckles, white with anticipation. "Let the reason be what I think it is."

He heard her. She did not even say thank you. She was far too busy.

It was broad daylight and he felt at death's door. This was at least how he thought it would feel to be at death's door. His arms and legs were totally numb. His head was on fire. The rest of him felt cold as ice. Maybe that was why he had hardly been able to move. He could hear the constant rumble of vehicles, and often voices too. He had to get away from here.

It became even colder when he shoved aside the garbage bags covering him. But then it became slightly easier to move. Two seagulls perched on the edge of the container, peering down at him. They tilted their heads and emitted several piercing screams of complaint. Perhaps this was where they lived. Maybe he had stolen their house. He shooed them away, but they did not fly away farther than the parking garage, from where they continued to look down at him, protesting.

Eventually he fought his way out of the container, having to lie with his stomach on the edge and almost roll himself out. He hurt himself in the fall, but that no longer mattered so much, and he was brushing the worst of the muck off himself with sluggish movements when a man suddenly leaned out from the ground floor of the car park to ask if he needed help. He shook his head and toddled off.

He had no idea how many hours he had elapsed while he lay there. He had been sleeping mostly. Dozing, at least. The short spells he had been awake had been spent making a decision.

264

He needed help. He could not manage by himself. But there weren't really many people who had ever actually, genuinely helped him. The aide, perhaps, at least a little, but then he had got mixed up with the child welfare service. Gone behind their backs.

And Mum, of course.

He felt a stab of pain when he thought of his mother and realized more clearly just how difficult things were for him. His skin was prickling, and his head was thumping harder than ever.

However, at least he was not hungry.

Most of all he wished his mother could help him. That would be the right thing to do. Because it was true what she used to say: they belonged together.

But she never succeeded in doing anything. And this was something she certainly could not sort out. It was slightly unclear *what* exactly needed to be sorted out, when he considered it, but someone really had to do something. It simply wasn't possible for his mum to be that person.

There was only one person left. Maren. She had helped him. She had said it so distinctly: if ever he had a problem, he must come to her.

Befuddled and weary, he began to set his mind to how to find his way to Maren.

They almost ran into each other outside the staff entrance. They had parked their cars totally illegally, managing to reach the door despite the obstacle of traffic to and from the gas pumps for squad vehicles behind Oslo Police Station.

"Where the fuck have you been?" Billy T. asked, but Hanne Wilhelmsen could tell he was elated rather than enraged.

"I've discovered who we're looking for," Hanne said.

"So have I," said Billy T.

They stopped.

"Why do I have a feeling we haven't arrived at the same person?" Hanne said softly.

"Because we probably haven't," Billy T. said just as quietly.

So they both kept their mouths shut until they were sitting in their chairs in Hanne's office.

"You first," said Hanne, taking a swig from an old bottle of cola.

Making a grimace, she put down the bottle.

"It's the Lover," Billy T. said tentatively, grabbing the cola.

"I advise you against trying that. It's ancient." She waved toward the half-empty bottle.

"What makes you think the Lover did it?"

When she was given the explanation, she fell completely silent before lighting a cigarette. It took her seven minutes to contemplate what she had been told. Billy T. let her think in peace.

"Haul him in as quickly as possible," she said eventually. "Immediately."

"Yessss," he exclaimed triumphantly, banging his fist on the desk.

"But make sure you get a blue form first. For fraud. And passing forged checks. And theft."

"Not for murder?"

She shook her head almost imperceptibly.

"But fucking hell, Hanne, why not for murder?"

"Because he didn't do it."

She stood up and grabbed hold of a statute book. Remaining on her feet, she flicked through it to the penal code. She could not quite recall whether theft of a checkbook was grand or petty larceny.

"Who the fuck did it, then?"

Now almost roaring, he spread his arms wide in despair.

"Who does Her Highness Hanne Wilhelmsen believe is the sinner? Or is that a secret she would prefer to keep to herself?"

"Maren Kalsvik," she said impassively. "Maren Kalsvik did it."

Before she managed to give the reasons for her assertion, there was a knock at the door. Billy T. stepped across and yanked the door open.

"What is it now?" he spluttered at Tone-Marit.

"More news. This here."

She lowered her head to go under Billy T.'s arm and walk over to the chief inspector.

"Look here, Hanne," she said, handing her a sheet of paper.

It was a copy of a nuptial settlement. Signed by Agnes and Odd Vestavik.

"Odd Vestavik has not been telling the whole truth to Billy T.," Tone-Marit said. "This was delivered to the city registrar's office two days before the murder. It had simply not yet been recorded."

"What does it entail?" Billy T. said impatiently, attempting to grab hold of the paper Hanne had not yet finished reading and therefore kept him at arm's length.

"It entails him not being able to divide the estate. Meaning in practice he remains sitting with the whole lot and can do whatever he wants with it. Everything goes to him."

"Good heavens," said Hanne, wheeling around to face Tone-Marit. "How have you managed all this? Check fraud, papers, nuptial settlements, and God knows what . . . Here we've been rummaging about for a fortnight looking for motive and opportunity, and then we end up with a bountiful superabundance in one day!"

"We organize our time," Tone-Marit said, fixing Hanne with a look. "Because unfortunately we have a chief inspector who can't be bothered leading her troops effectively. So we do the best we can. Erik and I."

It was far from being a hostile look. Not even challenging. But it was steady and did not budge an inch.

Billy T. had stiffened on the spot. He did not dare to move anything other than his eyes, and he thought it seemed as though the second hand on the wall clock had stopped in pure and simple fright.

"Touché," Hanne said, smiling wryly. "Bull's-eye, if I may say so."

Billy T. breathed a sigh of relief and grinned broadly.

"Young people nowadays, Hanne. They've no respect."

"You can just keep your mouth shut."

Her forefinger tapped him on the chest.

"From now on I'll be leading. Bring Erik here. *At once.*"

It did not take long to have an arrest warrant issued for the Lover. An inexperienced and rather dull-witted lawyer had been assigned to the case, and the interest he had shown for Agnes Vestavik's homicide had been lukewarm until now, to put it mildly. He shrugged his shoulders and furnished two officers from the training section with the necessary formalities, before Hanne Wilhelmsen quietly gave them the instructions they needed and sent them on their way. They had already ascertained that his disappearing act was no more serious than sitting at home drinking.

She returned to her office, where Billy T. had acquired some cola of more recent vintage for all four of them. She sat down in her usual seat and drank half her bottle. Then she looked from Tone-Marit to Erik and back again to the young female officer.

"You're quite right. I haven't been on top of things. I'm sorry about that."

Feeling abashed, Billy T. and Erik attempted to brush her off. Tone-Marit sat in silence, looking at her.

"I'm really sorry."

Tone-Marit continued to stare at her, but the suggestion of a smile was lurking in her narrow eyes. Hanne smiled back and went on. "Now we need to try to find our way in this tangle of murderers we've become embroiled in."

269

She had divided the contents of a green-covered folder into four bundles. They were sitting neatly in a row front of her, and she placed a slim hand on one of them. Her wedding ring shone up at the three others on the opposite side of the desk, and an old reflex was urging her to pull her hand away. However, something held her back.

"This is Maren Kalsvik," she said, giving the bundle a little smack before moving on to the next one. "And this is the Lover who robbed the woman blind before she died. Here . . ."

Her hand slapped down on the third bundle.

"Here we have the husband who lied to the police about what he gains from his wife's demise."

The fourth bundle, still inside the green cover, was placed right at the end of the desktop.

"This is all the rest. Olav Håkonsen, his mother, Terje Welby, and —"

"Why have you actually written off Terje Welby?" Tone-Marit interrupted. "Despite everything, he's still of great interest, is he not?"

"It's too simple, Tone-Marit. It's far too obvious and simple. And I don't like there being no suicide note. The crime scene technicians have no doubt that it *was* a suicide. If they ever were in doubt. Terje Welby was killed by his own carpet knife. From regret and depression, most likely. Because he had been a villain and a crook and stole money from his employer. But we haven't found *anything* else that confirms he murdered Agnes. All my experience suggests there would have been a letter there. A letter that either protests his

270

innocence of the murder and begs forgiveness for whatever else he must have done, or confessing to all of it. This is a suicide committed in the deepest despair. Both escape and atonement. It would not have been accomplished without letting anyone *know*. What he had done, and what he had *not* done."

"But now we know he did not write a letter," Billy T. said with a long, loud belch.

"Yes, oh yes, I think he did," Hanne said quietly. "I'm pretty certain he wrote a letter of that nature. But someone removed it."

Erik spilled cola down the front of his shirt. Tone-Marit's mouth literally fell open. Billy T. whistled.

"Maren Kalsvik," he said, mostly to himself.

"But it could have been any person at all," Erik protested. "Why precisely her?"

"Because she wanted us to content ourselves that the killer was dead. Because her world would fall down around her if she lost her job. A job she lives and breathes for, and a job she obtained by falsifying documents and telling lies."

Now it was Tone-Marit who whistled. Low and long drawn out.

"Maren Kalsvik went to the Diakonhjemmet School of Social Work," Hanne continued, folding her hands behind her head. "That's quite true. But she failed her final exams. In the spring of 1990. That wasn't so critical, because you can resit in the fall. The problem was simply that she failed again. And made one of her life's most stupid choices. Instead of repeating her final year, and so having two fresh opportunities to sit the examination, she chose to take another resit. And she damn well failed again."

"Is she stupid, or what?" Billy T. mumbled. "She really seems so clever!"

"It's one thing to be clever at practical things, but theory is something quite different. There might be a thousand reasons for it going so badly. The dramatic point is that after a second resit you're barred from another attempt. Forever. There is no Maren Kalsvik in the examination records of Diakonhjemmet School of Social Work. Neither in 1990 nor in 1991. Or indeed in any other year either, for that matter. She must have needed to produce a diploma when she got the job, but it's a forgery, there's no doubt about it."

"Oh, fuck," Billy T. said.

"She probably felt something like that, yes. When she failed, I mean."

"But do we know that Agnes had told Maren she knew about it?" Tone-Marit asked.

"No, we don't," Hanne replied, shaking her head. "But *if* she had told her, then Maren knew her life was going to crash down into the famous ruins. And that would be a hundred times worse than sitting in the cooler for stealing thirty thousand kroner. It's worse than being homeless and penniless too. And besides, I have more . . ."

Half an hour later all the cola was finished and the temperature in the chief inspector's office was approaching a dangerous thirty degrees Celsius. Erik was sweaty and excited, Billy T. was smirking, while Tone-Marit once more concluded to herself that Hanne

272

Wilhelmsen was the best detective she had ever encountered.

None of them any longer harbored any doubt. The Lover was a scoundrel who would receive his comeuppance for theft. The widower was a poor soul, a wimp who had been afraid of telling the truth when it was nowhere near threatening him.

Maren Kalsvik was a killer.

But however they twisted it and turned it, it was impossible to prove.

Cathrine Ruge was standing beside the fruit counter trying to remember whether she had some carrots, or whether she ought to buy another pack. They did not look particularly tempting at this time of year in the middle of winter. Perhaps she should take kohlrabi instead. She stood weighing a grayish-yellow oval root in her hand when a noisy gang of teenagers in red quilted jackets with white felt cats sewn on the backs came shrieking into the store.

My God, the student celebrations begin earlier and earlier, she thought. In her day they were reading furiously right up until, at the earliest, one week prior to the Norwegian National Day, perhaps with the exception of a gathering for coffee in a café on the occasional Saturday. She herself had not dressed up other than possessing a student cap, and that she had worn only on May 17.

The teenagers emptied a refrigerated cabinet of soft drinks and helped themselves to huge piles of chocolate. They pocketed candies from a pick 'n' mix stand, and one of the boys, a skinny guy whose voice was shriller than all the others' put together, was so keen to impress the two girls in their company that he ended up tipping over the entire rack. Chocolate, hard candies, and jelly babies overflowed onto the floor, and suddenly everything went completely silent before they burst out laughing. The young female checkout operator looked devastated; she was probably younger than they were and had never been closer to a student cap than she was at this precise moment, and she did not even dare to launch into a rebuke. Instead she locked her cash register and left to fetch a dustpan and brush. Before she returned, the teenagers had taken all they could carry of both the cola and chocolate, and vanished out the door.

Cathrine contemplated for a moment the possibility of stopping them but was almost as frightened of the noisy, wild gang as the young girl at the checkout had been. They surged out of the store like a troll with a multitude of heads, leaving four adults standing shamefaced, making an effort to avoid looking at one another, without lifting a finger to stop the monster in its tracks.

However, she could at least help the checkout operator to tidy up. Hesitantly, she crouched down and started to retrieve the candies. They were mixed together with rubbish and winter mud, and had to be thrown out. The young girl gratefully held out a large garbage bag and whispered, "They come here often. They make a lot of noise, but they don't usually steal anything."

My God, she's trying to excuse them, Cathrine thought, getting to her feet. "You should certainly report them!"

"The boss will deal with that. He'll be here soon."

The girl seemed even more frightened of the boss than of the teenagers who had demolished the store, and Cathrine offered to wait until he arrived to help her to explain what had taken place.

"No, no, not at all," the girl refused. "That would only make it worse."

It took them ten minutes to clean up. A quarter of a garbage bag full of spoiled candies.

"If you tell the school about this, they'll get into trouble," she said in an unsuccessful attempt to cheer up the checkout operator who was now back at her post in the little booth. "That cat means they attend the Cathedral School. I can certainly . . ."

"No, no," the young girl replied. "Forget it."

Shaking her head, Cathrine paid for her groceries and went out the door. She had purchased the kohlrabi, even though it looked soft and spindly. She was almost sure she had carrots in the refrigerator.

Then it suddenly struck her. The thing that had seemed so important when Christian had talked about Maren having possibly killed Agnes. Enormous, freezing drops of rain splashed her face as she stopped to think more closely about whether it was something the police ought to know. She deposited the plastic carrier bag on the sidewalk and kneaded her cold, wet face.

It probably meant nothing. Because it must have been Terje, of course, who had murdered Agnes, although it was disconcerting that the police had called them all in for interviews again. Stupid that she had not remembered it yesterday, when she had been down there giving a new statement. Then she could have mentioned it quite naturally, and the police themselves could judge whether it was significant. Now it would be like stabbing Maren in the back if she phoned simply to tell them. It would be a way of expressing a suspicion. And she did not really suspect her. No way. Perhaps that was why she had forgotten about it.

She lifted her bag and started walking. The kohlrabi bumped against her leg with every second step she took.

She would have to think about it.

Quite oddly, he was no longer freezing, though his skin felt exactly as it did when he was chilled to the bone, numb and strange with goose bumps. It was even more bizarre that he was not hungry. He had not eaten since yesterday, and he had thrown up the cakes long ago. Instead of the usual feeling of hunger, he felt a faint nausea, but not as bad as last night.

His head was bothering him most. It was pounding and thumping, as though someone had inserted a screwdriver just behind one of his temples. Now and again he took hold of his ear, as it was so painful you would almost think there was a large hole there.

Besides, he was thirsty, terribly thirsty. Whenever he had walked past a kiosk or gas station, he had bought a soft drink. But the entire world was probably out looking for him now. There were police cars everywhere; he had never in all his life seen as many patrol cars as he had today. It delayed him considerably, and he became even more exhausted with the effort of constantly having to hide. They did not have their sirens on either, so he had to be on the lookout all the time. Some of them drove excruciatingly slowly. He was the one they were hunting. At one point a police car stopped quite suddenly no more than a hundred meters away from him. A man had emerged from the car and put his hands up to his eyes, peering over toward where he was walking. He had to take to his heels again, and by good luck a basement door had been lying open into a car workshop or something of the sort. By the time he was thrown out — when a bad-tempered, gray-haired man discovered him sitting down in a repair pit — the police had fortunately disappeared again.

But it was taking an awfully long time. He had to reach there before evening fell. When he was closer to the foster home, he might perhaps be able to travel the final stretch by bus. Perhaps. He'd have to see. He hadn't made up his mind yet.

"There are loads of cars out hunting for him. They've spotted him twice. Here . . ."

Erik Henriksen pointed with an improbably badly bitten fingernail at a spot on a fairly large map of Oslo lying on Hanne Wilhelmsen's desk.

". . . and here."

The chief inspector was fidgeting with an empty cigarette packet, fashioning a stork from the silver paper. When it was completed, she bent over the map and drew vague circles with her pinkie before finding what she was looking for. Then she attempted to make the stork stand there.

"The foster home," she said.

The stork fell over.

"He's making his way to the foster home."

Using a broken pencil as a pointer, she outlined the route from Storo to Spring Sunshine. The points Erik had indicated to her lay in a more or less straight line between the two places, though closer to Storo than the foster home.

"Why the hell's he going there?" Erik Henriksen asked, making an effort to force the stork to stand upright again. "He ran away from there!"

"It must be completely level underneath it," Hanne instructed. "Make its feet a fraction bigger."

"Why do you think he's going to Spring Sunshine?" Erik repeated, finally managing to stand the paper bird on its legs.

Hanne did not answer. She had no idea why Olav Håkonsen was returning to the foster home. But she did not like it. It bothered her. A grumbling unease had settled somewhere between her navel and diaphragm, and was growing gradually more intense. She felt it again. It was the feeling she always had when something cropped up that she did not understand, though it obviously had some kind of significance.

278

Something she was unable to anticipate, something she could not weave into her theories. She really disliked it.

"I just sincerely hope they get hold of him before he reaches there."

"Of course they will," Erik said reassuringly. "They've got five squad cars out looking for him. It can't be *that* difficult to catch a twelve-year-old!"

It was well past two o'clock in the afternoon, and they were running out of time. At least if they were going to fulfill the optimistic promise of having the case all wrapped up before the weekend. Hanne Wilhelmsen was already dreading having to phone Cecilie to tell her she would probably be late. They were expecting guests, and she had sworn she'd be home in plenty of time.

"Oh, shit," she suddenly exclaimed when it dawned on her she had promised to buy fresh asparagus and eggplants at the green-grocer's in Vaterland.

The superintendent raised his eyebrows quizzically.

"Nothing," Hanne said quickly. "It was nothing."

She turned to face the police attorney, who was half sitting, half sprawling on the chair and at this precise moment was extremely preoccupied by something that seemed to be located inside his ear. First he tried to poke his finger in after it, but when that did not help, he picked up a paper clip and straightened it out to form a little spear he inserted all the way into his head.

Hanne knew she ought to warn him but could not muster the energy to do so.

"You're quite sure there's not enough evidence to support an arrest?" she asked for the third time.

"Yes," the police attorney responded, withdrawing the spear.

A yellowish-brown lump had attached itself to the tip, and he looked delighted. Hanne turned away.

He tucked the paper clip into his breast pocket and straightened up in his seat.

"All you have is a pile of good theories. Nothing tangible. She has a motive, but there's certainly no shortage of those in this case here. People with motives, I mean. What's more, you know nothing about whether Agnes had in fact *confronted* Maren with evidence of the fraudulent diploma. If you can come up with some confirmation of that, I'll make a fresh evaluation. Then at least we'll be approaching something resembling grounds for an arrest. I need more, Hanne. Substantially more."

"But we know at least that she had falsified a diploma. Can we not haul her in for that?"

The police attorney smiled indulgently at her and pulled out his ear picker again. Now he set to work boring into his other ear.

"There's probably sufficient evidence for that charge," he said with his head tilted. "But that will be done quietly and calmly and without any arrests. Totally undramatic. Ouch!"

Pulling the mistreated paper clip from his ear, he stared at it in dissatisfaction. Then he rubbed the end of it between his thumb and forefinger, before wiping the earwax on his trouser leg and standing up.

"My advice is to invite her to another interview. Present her with the facts you have and cross your

280

fingers for a confession. She must be quite worn out by now."

Then he smiled and left the room.

"Filthy pig," Hanne said under her breath as he closed the door behind him, and hoped he had heard it.

The superintendent did not crack a smile at all but left them behind as well.

"But he's right, you know," Billy T. said dryly as the door closed for a second time.

"I hate it when people like that are right."

"You hate it when anyone other than you is right, if you ask me."

"Psssh!" She tapped him on the head.

"But what'll we do?"

"We could invite her to come here and give the excuse that yesterday's interview was interrupted," he suggested without any visible enthusiasm.

"And then she'll ask again to be interviewed up there, and then we'll insist that she comes here," Hanne intoned in an affected monotonous voice. "And then she won't understand why we can't wait until Monday, and then we'll be even sterner and instruct her to come here at once, and then we'll risk her getting the picture. And taking all the time in the world to eliminate whatever proof exists in this . . ."

She exploded.

"*. . . damn case!*"

The map of Oslo on the desk, quite new and completely serviceable, in the course of a few seconds was transformed into a crumpled ball of paper. Hanne flung it at the wall, before picking it up again, a little embarrassed, and slowly began to investigate whether the map could be rescued.

Suddenly shouts, yells, and loud cheering could be heard from the corridor. They looked at each other and competed to see who was less curious. They were speedily relieved of waiting for a decision, because the door was thrown open, and Sergeant Synnøve Lunde came bounding into the room.

"We've caught the guy! The double murderer from Smestad! He was arrested on board a ferry to Denmark!"

Then she bounded out again.

Hanne Wilhelmsen and Billy T. exchanged glum looks.

"We'll go and pick up Maren Kalsvik," Hanne decided.

At Spring Sunshine Foster Home, the situation was far from satisfactory. All the duty rosters had gradually broken down as people died or went on sick leave, and Maren Kalsvik had her hands full organizing the entire menage. The children knew how to capitalize on this disarray and were noisier, quarreling more, and stretching all the boundaries with any scope for flexibility. Raymond was virtually looking after himself, less worrying than Glenn, who had been caught shoplifting earlier that day. Anita, grouchy as a toad, was not speaking to anyone. Maren suspected that her boyfriend had dumped her. The twins had made up their minds to drive Jeanette to distraction, and had almost succeeded the previous evening by peeing in her bed without her noticing it before lying down in all the mess. Kenneth was more anxious than ever and had become convinced that a pirate was living in the basement.

"Now I want you to be quiet!"

She was yelling at the top of her voice.

An uncontrolled outburst from Maren Kalsvik was so infrequent that she achieved the result she wanted. All at once. After a few minutes, however, they started all over again.

It was three o'clock, and only an hour since the first ones had begun to arrive home from school. Her headache had started two minutes after Kenneth turned up, and since then it had become steadily worse.

She moved into the TV room, closing the door behind her. Christian would have to deal with them for a while. He was quite good with the children, although sometimes he allowed them to do far more than they should.

Air. She needed some fresh air. She walked over to the window and opened it wide. It felt beneficial, and she gulped down deep breaths. Her nostrils moved in time to her breathing, out and in, out and in. She closed her eyes.

In a way she wished she never needed to open them again.

"There! There he is again!"

The trainee police officer had his face plastered to the car's side window and was attempting to point in the right direction, but it turned into more of a vague thumping on the glass.

"There he is, in that garden!"

"Call up the nearest patrol car and get them to cut him off at the other side of that housing estate. And tell them to turn off those bloody sirens!"

Several seconds after the trainee had relayed his superior's orders, they could hear the distant sirens disappear.

"If we don't succeed in catching that boy now, I'm going to fucking hand in this badge," the older man in the car said obstinately, executing an unnecessary, illegal, and extremely effective skid to turn the car around.

He had managed it. If he hadn't been so exhausted, he would have been proud of himself. Maren was going to be proud of him. Twice he had plucked up the courage to ask for directions. In a few places he had spotted buildings he recognized, and now he had reached his destination. But it was crawling with police around here. There had been more and more of them, and in the end he had tramped through gardens and over bushes in order to be as invisible as possible from the road.

He had managed it. But how would he make contact with Maren without the others seeing him?

Uncertain, he sheltered underneath some bare overhanging trees. It was still light enough for him to be seen from a distance, so he positioned himself as close to the trunk as he could manage. There was only one road, one gate, and one garden path separating him from the entrance door at Spring Sunshine.

About fifty meters.

Eventually Maren Kalsvik opened her eyes. Slowly and hesitantly. She covered her face with her hands. Her skin was cold, but she did not feel chilled. She leaned in toward the window frame. It squeezed her pelvis, but the pain was in a sense welcome, as it reminded her that she was still alive. Her head was empty and yet chaotically full at the same time. She was overwhelmed with dizziness and noticed in astonishment she had been holding her breath for a long time. Gasping, she managed to breathe in some reviving air.

It was just beginning to grow dark; the shadows were no longer as sharp and here and there seemed to merge into the dark earth. Someone had left the gate open. It should always be kept closed.

Something was moving underneath the trees on the other side of the road. The contours of a figure were just beginning to become clear when a delivery truck with a carpentry firm logo on its side appeared, blocking her view for a moment. Once the vehicle had driven past, she had to screw up her eyes to verify whether she had seen correctly.

Although the figure — because it was definitely a person — had pulled in closer to the tree trunk encroaching on the sidewalk, the outline was now quite obvious. Not particularly tall, but all the same it appeared to be large and broad.

"My God, it's Olav," she said aloud.

Rushing toward the door, she almost slid on Lego bricks scattered across the floor as she headed for the stairs in her haste to reach the front door. However, she kept her balance, and without even putting on any shoes, she thundered down the stairs and out onto the gravel path.

"Olav!" she shouted, holding her arms out wide. "Olav!"

As she saw him step from the shadows to become more clearly visible, she noticed the car. She did not realize at first that it was a police vehicle; she registered simply that it was driving far too fast.

The boy crossed the sidewalk and took a preliminary step onto the road. She herself had reached only halfway down the garden path.

"Stop!" she screamed, halting abruptly herself in the hope that it would have an effect on the boy.

But he ran on.

Now she could see his face, only fifteen meters away. He was smiling, a completely different smile from what she had seen before. He looked happy.

Two meters across the road he staggered feebly, starting to raise his arm in a gesture probably intended as a greeting.

The car was traveling far too fast. Too fast for the speed limit of thirty kilometers an hour, and far too fast to have a chance to stop for a twelve-year-old suddenly tottering out into the road.

The brakes squealed. Maren Kalsvik screamed. An elderly lady, who lived four houses farther down the road and who was out to let her poodle do his business in the remaining daylight, shrieked as though possessed.

The front of the car hit the boy at knee height, and both bones broke instantly. He was thrown up onto the hood, and his heavy body smashed the windscreen before continuing up onto the roof. The police officer driving lost his grip on both the steering wheel and the road, and the vehicle swerved sideways ten meters farther down the gravelly asphalt before colliding with and demolishing a meter-high metal fence and juddering to a sudden stop at a tree stump. Both car doors were badly dented and the two police officers tugged at their door handles in agitation.

Olav still lay on the road.

Maren Kalsvik reached the boy at the precise moment he opened his eyes.

"Lie still. Olav, you must lie quite still."

He smiled once more, that unfamiliar, genuine smile. She sat down on the ground beside him, wanting more than anything to lift him up and hold him. But he could have broken his neck, so instead she bent her face right down toward his head and stroked her fingers, light as a feather, across his cheek.

"It'll be all right, Olav. Just lie completely still, and everything'll be okay."

Saliva was dribbling from his mouth, and she pulled her sleeve down to wipe him carefully on the chin.

"I saw you, Maren," he whispered, almost inaudibly. "You were running. In the garden. Did you hear . . ."

He pulled a slight grimace, and she hushed him.

"Did you hear that I ..." he moaned after all. "You ..."

Maren Kalsvik was feeling terribly cold. The chill came flooding over her and had nothing to do with sitting in her stocking feet, wearing no outdoor clothes, on a muddy road in Oslo one February afternoon. The bitter blast came from inside her, from a room she had locked, sealed, and then thrown away the key. Now the door was wide open. Her teeth were chattering as she hushed the boy.

"Lie still, Olav. You have to lie still."

In desperation, she raised her upper body and screamed, "Ambulance, has nobody phoned for an ambulance?"

The old lady had sat down on the sidewalk and was crying so vehemently that the poodle was going crazy around her, whining and barking. The police officers had still not managed to extract themselves from the wrecked car. Another car arrived around the bend and screeched to a standstill as soon as the driver realized what had happened.

"Phone for an ambulance," Maren yelled again, this time directed at Christian, who was standing like a pillar of salt on the stairs, clutching the door handle as five youngsters tried to pull it toward them from inside.

"You were crying," Olav whispered, so faintly she had to place her ear right down beside his mouth. "You ... I saw you running, Maren."

Then he smiled again and whispered something indistinct into her ear.

288

Just as Hanne Wilhelmsen and Billy T. arrived, having sprinted the fifteen meters from their car that was now blocking the road, Olav Håkonsen sighed softly, almost inaudibly, and died.

After an hour and a half of questioning Maren Kalsvik, Hanne Wilhelmsen had not achieved anything other than making Cecilie inordinately cross. It had taken time to sort things out at the foster home. Staring at the almost black windowpane, Hanne thought morosely that by now their guests would have finished eating the first course. If Cecilie had been capable of concocting something different from the asparagus that had unfortunately not reached home.

If only Billy T. would arrive soon. It was his turn to have his children for the weekend, but he had promised to return as soon as the boys were all tucked up in bed. His sister would babysit. Hanne rumpled her hair and massaged her scalp.

She was making no progress whatsoever.

Maren Kalsvik had relinquished her right to legal counsel. Hanne Wilhelmsen had stated explicitly that Maren was charged with falsifying her diploma, but provisionally only suspected of the murder of Agnes Vestavik.

"So she doesn't have any rights at all as far as that's concerned, not yet anyway," Billy T. had quite correctly pointed out.

She was entitled to an attorney, regardless, but she said no thanks. As far as the diploma was concerned, she acknowledged all of her wrongdoing in an impassive tone and without batting an eyelid. She had sat like a wooden doll during the entire interview, confining herself to answering in single syllables as truthfully as possible. When Hanne, more from personal curiosity than professional necessity, inquired why Maren had failed so many times, her facial features became, if possible, even more dispassionate. She would not answer that question.

There were two things she denied repeatedly, every single time Hanne thought she had enticed her into a corner: that Agnes had told her she had exposed her, and that she had anything to do with the director's murder.

"I'd no idea she had found that out," she said. "I had absolutely no reason at all to kill Agnes."

Lighting a cigarette, Hanne Wilhelmsen propped her feet up on the desk, then stared into midair before letting her eyes slide closed. Olav's heavy, dead body had fixed itself to the inside of her eyelids, so she quickly opened them again. She scrutinized the other woman.

"You were actually quite fond of that boy," she said softly.

Maren Kalsvik shrugged her shoulders, not allowing herself to be tempted into changing her countenance.

"I saw it in you. You were fond of him, weren't you?"

She had not shed any tears. She had held the boy tightly, but when they finally made her understand he was dead, she had released him, risen to her feet, and composed her features into the stiff expression she had retained ever since. It was beginning to get on Hanne's nerves.

"Well," she said when Maren Kalsvik had been given two minutes to respond without taking the opportunity to do so, "we're not getting anywhere with this and it's becoming late now. So I'll tell you what I believe and you can sit down in a cell to contemplate it overnight. Contemplate whether it isn't best to confirm what we already know."

"Cell" was not strictly true. But it worked: a tiny, almost imperceptible trembling appeared at the corner of the woman's mouth, and remained there. For a considerable length of time.

Hanne stood up and stepped around to the opposite side of the desk. Perching her posterior on the desktop edge, she crossed her legs. Maren Kalsvik was sitting a meter away, staring at a point in the center of her stomach.

"You had a dental appointment that day. Agnes's discussion with Terje took so long you had to be excused. You had to get to the dentist's in time. It strikes me that Agnes would not have been pleased about that. She must have been in a bad mood that day. Very understandable. One untrustworthy member of staff after another."

Maren was still staring at a spot or something on her sweater, but Hanne noticed the trembling in the corner of her mouth was no longer visible.

"Perhaps Agnes did not want to make a fuss. Perhaps you had plans for the rest of the day as well. I don't know. But I think it's likely she asked you to return later in the evening. Late in the evening. She would put her own child to bed first. And have peace and quiet at the foster home too. What do I know? Perhaps you had some inkling there was something unpleasant in store. Probably you did, because she must have insisted on holding the meeting. In any case . . ."

She left the desk and returned to her seat once more. Taking a blank sheet of paper from a drawer, she started to make a paper airplane.

"In any case, you came back. About half past ten, perhaps. You were quiet, because you knew fine well some of the children would be going to sleep at that time. Maybe you popped your head in to say hello to Eirik Vassbunn, but when you saw he was asleep, you did not bother. That may have been because you wanted to show consideration."

She folded and refolded.

"But it might also have been for other reasons. Anyway, he did not notice that you had arrived."

The plane was almost completed. Taking a fresh sheet of paper, she tore it carefully to form a splendid tail.

"Then you learned what it was about. Or what proof she had obtained. Or that you were being fired. Something totally upsetting."

Hanne shifted her eyes from the paper plane to the other woman's face. Still completely expressionless. Still as though hewn from stone. It no longer irritated Hanne. Now it was a good sign. A damn good sign.

"You obviously kept your voices fairly low. There were children sleeping on that entire floor. Even though several rooms separated you from them. But to be honest . . ."

Hanne Wilhelmsen broke off and sent the airplane in a beautiful curve up toward the ceiling, where it hovered, almost still, as it reached the top of the arc, before flying in a lightning loop and coming in to land on the window ledge. Maren Kalsvik did not allow it to disturb her composure, offering the plane not a single glance.

"I've tried to step into your shoes," Hanne said in a friendly tone. "Tried to think about what it would be like to be discovered. That my boss found out I hadn't been to Police College after all. That everybody got to know about it. That I got sacked and became unemployed."

Dripping a few drops of coffee into the overflowing ashtray, she poured the wet contents into the wastepaper basket before stretching her hand into a drawer and withdrawing four Kleenex tissues to wipe the ashtray. She then lit another cigarette.

"I would quite simply have fallen apart. I mean, after so many years, after demonstrating I was really competent at what I was doing, for a trivial piece of paper to turn my whole life upside down."

She shook her head and smacked her lips.

"I'm not making fun of you, Maren," she said gently. "I mean it. I would have fallen completely apart. And though my job means so much to me, I think yours is even more important to you. That's obvious from the way you handle the children."

A chain of smoke rings dissipated on its journey to the ceiling. The two women remained sitting in silence for a while. The only sounds they heard were footsteps coming and going in the corridor outside. The station was about to empty for the weekend.

"Tell me if I'm wrong, then," Hanne suddenly encouraged her, finally making eye contact with the other woman, who changed her sitting position and shook her head, muttering something that Hanne did not catch. Then she returned to her role as Sphinx.

"You begged for mercy, perhaps. I would have done that," Hanne continued indefatigably. "But Agnes . . . Do you know, by the way, what the name Agnes means? Pure or virginal. Saint Agnes was maidenly but stubborn. It cost her her life. Was our Agnes equally stubborn?"

Maren naturally made no reply, but her face was now almost transparent and livid.

"She probably was," Hanne said for want of a verbal confirmation from Maren. "And then something happened, something I'd like some details about. Look at me!"

She banged both fists on the desk, causing Maren Kalsvik to flinch. They glanced at each other fleetingly, before looking away. Hanne shook her head.

"There were some knives lying there. Agnes's own newly sharpened knives. On the desk, possibly, or perhaps on the bookshelf. It's not so important where they were. Anyway, you moved across the floor, around the desk, and were standing behind Agnes when you suddenly snapped. It happened in the blink of an eye.

Before you've had time to think, it happened. You grabbed a knife and thrust it into her back. You were furious, you were desperate, and you were completely out of control. There's an enormous amount here for a defense counsel to work with, Maren. An enormous amount. Perhaps someone will even come to the conclusion that you were suffering from impaired mental capacity at the time of the attack. A lawyer might help you."

She rolled her chair over toward the window to open it. The room was gray and foggy with cigarette smoke. Now it turned chilly instead.

"Shall I phone for an attorney?"

"No."

She had been sitting motionless for so long her vocal cords were almost paralyzed, and the reply was more of a cough than a word. Hanne cursed Billy T. Still no word from him.

"Are you sure?"

"Yes."

"Okay. Then I'll continue. You probably couldn't fathom what you had done. Murder, you understand, is almost always committed in the heat of the moment. You hadn't planned anything of the kind. More sustenance for the defense!"

Hanne took out the Yellow Pages for Oslo, and leafed through it to the list of attorneys. She then threw the open catalog toward Maren.

"I would really recommend you get hold of one."

The woman did not answer, just shook her head faintly.

"I don't have the energy to say it again," Hanne said with a sigh, taking the directory back. She closed it with a smack.

"It might well be that you decided to report it to us at once. But then you soon thought of other alternatives. You knew where the desk key was, so you fetched it and opened the drawers to look for the compromising papers. I've no idea whether you found anything about yourself. But it's likely that you found some about Terje. You left them there, in the hope that the police would find them."

Hanne laughed, a short, hollow laugh.

"It wasn't strange that you knew Terje had been there after you! I should have placed more emphasis on your amazement that the key was not lying underneath the plant pot when we were talking the day after the murder. Because you had of course put it back. When Terje was not arrested, you realized we hadn't found anything. Ergo . . ."

She tapped her temple meaningfully with her left forefinger.

Maren Kalsvik was still sitting like a zombie, motionless and with her gaze directed at something Hanne Wilhelmsen could not fathom. Something beyond this world. Her eyes were pale steel gray, almost inhuman, more like a dog or a wolf. Hanne could not recall anything other than that they had seemed much bluer before. On the other hand, the entire office seemed gray now. The footsteps and voices from the corridor, which had broken up the monotony of her monologue, had now disappeared. Most of the

Homicide Section had gone to celebrate the solving of the double murder with a beer or four. At home Cecilie was probably standing making coffee, having used up all her excuses for why Hanne had never appeared. What had become of Billy T. was a mystery. Erik and Tone-Marit had been given permission to leave around seven o'clock, after the Lover had tearfully admitted to check fraud. His friend, finally tracked down, had confirmed the coffee-drinking episode until late on the evening of the murder, something the staff of the café had hesitantly, but nevertheless convincingly, also confirmed. He had been allowed to go. He was probably feeling like hell.

Hanne Wilhelmsen was not feeling so hot herself either.

But Maren Kalsvik was feeling far, far worse. She sat stock-still, without uttering a word, without looking at anything, without reacting to anything that was said. It was the only method she had of maintaining a hold on life and reality.

Something inside her was about to collapse. Her innards were churning into a chaotic mixture. Her abdomen was thumping and beating, as though her heart had fallen all the way down. She managed to breathe only with the very top part of her lungs, as though they were squeezed right up into her throat, where there was not enough space. Inside her head there was not a single thought. Instead her emotions were whirling around inside her stomach, desperate to escape. Her arms and legs had disappeared; they were simply there, dead and numb and serving no other purpose than to constrain everything that was aching and exploding inside her torso.

The only thing she succeeded in clinging on to was determination that she must survive. The only way to survive was to sit totally still and hope it would all pass. There was no one in the entire world who could help her. Apart from herself. By keeping her mouth shut. She must not unravel. Must not believe God had turned his back on her. She clutched a red point somewhere inside her stomach, held tight, and refused to let go.

The suicide letter had arrived in the post two days after he had killed himself. She tore it open and spilled her coffee on it, a letter addressed to her. "I did not kill Agnes," it had said. He begged her to believe him. There was something else there too. "Be careful, Maren. Agnes knew about your fraudulent diploma. I knew as well. Be careful. I have done so much that was wrong. But so have you."

She had burned the letter. It was not addressed to the police. It belonged to her.

My God, she thought, as a rumbling sound came from somewhere inside her stomach. *Forgive me. Help me.*

Chief Inspector Wilhelmsen had left the suspect to her own thoughts for a lengthy period. She did not know what she was waiting for. She was sinking into a kind of indifference, a defense against the unbearable fact that she knew she was sitting across from a murderer and did not have the foggiest idea how she was going to see to it that the woman received her well-deserved punishment. Prove that she had committed the crime.

She chased the feeling away but appreciated it would return if something did not happen soon.

"You didn't need to fear fingerprints. Other than on the knife, that is, but they were swiftly disposed of. Just a wipe. All other prints belonged there quite naturally. You'd been there hundreds of times. That was how we realized why you'd taken the other knives with you."

Maren Kalsvik moved for the first time during the entire interview. Stiff and sore, she leaned forward toward the coffee cup, its contents thick, cold, strong, and bitter. She blinked vigorously a couple of times, squeezing her eyes shut as though there were a speck of dust in them. The smallest tear hung on the eyelashes of her left eye, before falling and running slowly down her cheek. It was so tiny that it was used up before it reached her mouth. Then she sat back, returning to her wooden doll position.

"For now," Hanne said, rising from her seat, "I'll show you what I think. I'll show you how, quite early on, we realized the murderer had to be someone who spent his or her daily life here, someone who didn't need to be afraid of fingerprints in the rest of the room."

She crossed to the door and opened it. Outside, the corridor was deserted and gloomy.

"Now I am you, okay?"

She pointed first to herself and then to the other woman.

"I've just killed someone. I'm incensed, I'm desperate, but the most important thing of all is I don't want to be caught. I have a hard job getting out of it. But then perhaps I suddenly remember what happened when I grabbed the knife I stabbed into Agnes."

Maren Kalsvik made no sign of watching her. She just sat still, with her profile to the door. Hanne sighed, approached her, and took hold of her beneath the chin. Her face was cold as ice, but her head was limp and the chief inspector had no difficulty forcing her to make contact.

"When a person takes hold of a knife that's lying in a pile of other knives, it's extremely difficult not to touch the other ones. It's well nigh impossible, if you don't take your time to pick out only one. Look here!"

She took out four long items from a drawer, a letter opener, a slim leather pencil case, a felt-tip pen, and a ruler, and laid them on top of the desk.

"If I lift one of them without knowing exactly which one I want to take hold of, this is what happens!"

As she quickly grabbed the letter opener, her point became clear. She had touched all three other items as well. As she had demonstrated to Billy T. in the bar in Grünerløkka.

"You didn't have time to mess about. You were acting on the spur of the moment. A moment's rage and desperation. The remaining knives were the only place your fingerprints preferably should not be. You could have wiped them. But that would have taken time."

She let go her face and approached the window.

"Of course everyone would have been afraid of fingerprints on the knives. But you see . . ."

The palms of her hands touched the cold glass, and she paused before turning to continue.

"If it had been an outsider who had done it, he or she would have had to fear fingerprints in *other* places too. As far as a stranger is concerned, we have two theories. If he was planning to do something illegal, the outsider would have known to wear gloves. No reason to bring any knives. Or else he committed an unplanned murder. In the heat of the moment. Then the knives would have been the least of his problems. He would have had to wipe down the whole place. The door handle. The desktop, perhaps. The armrests on the chair. What do I know? But you always touch somewhere or other when you enter a place. And that was how I knew."

Maren Kalsvik still did not move a muscle. It seemed as if she was not even breathing.

"None of the surfaces in that entire room had been wiped. There were marks and dust and scraps of dirt everywhere. No sign that anyone had taken the time to clean up. The person who killed Agnes and took the knives did not need to bother about anything other than them. The person concerned belonged to the Spring Sunshine Foster Home. The fingerprints belonged in Agnes's office. Except for on the knives, for no one could have claimed to have touched them."

The chief inspector crossed over to the door again, pantomiming her role as a murder suspect.

"Perhaps I hear someone coming. Perhaps I'm simply terribly afraid. In any case, I have a difficult time getting away. The simplest thing is to take the knives with me. That's what you did. And then you chose to disappear down the fire escape. The lucky thing was . . ."

Hanne laughed out loud.

"Quite resourceful of you to haul it up again when you came back. Before the police arrived. Caused us a good deal of trouble, that did. Well."

She walked slowly back to the chair behind the desk, and as she passed the suspect, she let her hand slide lightly over her back.

"Like that," she said emphatically and with a demonstratively satisfied smile as she returned to her seat again. "That's the way it happened. Approximately, at least. Isn't that so?"

Some of the blueness had returned to Maren Kalsvik's eyes. She raised her hand and stared at it as though incredulous that it could still be lifted. Then she ran her fingers through her hair and stared Hanne Wilhelmsen directly in the eye.

"How have you thought to prove all that?"

Where the hell was Billy T.?

Billy T.'s little boys had fallen asleep long ago, after a great deal of fuss and three chapters of *Mio, My Son*. His sister smilingly chased him away before settling down with a pizza and beer and the remote control.

Instead of traveling directly to Grønlandsleiret 44, he called in at Spring Sunshine Foster Home. The receptionist at the police station had delivered a message from Cathrine Ruge just before he had left to collect the youngsters, informing him she could be contacted at the foster home all afternoon. Since the home was not very far out of his way, he thought he might as well drop in.

It was quiet and peaceful in the dayroom. Raymond, Anita, and Glenn were out, and Jeanette was staying the night with a classmate. The twins were sitting watching TV, while Kenneth and Cathrine were assembling a jigsaw on the huge worktable. Kenneth was excited and restless and Cathrine was having difficulty persuading him to sit still.

Billy T. joined them on the puzzle for a few minutes and then had to wait for three-quarters of an hour for Kenneth to fall asleep. Cathrine groaned as she descended the stairs again.

"That boy's having a dreadful time just now," she said. "God only knows how Christian managed to keep them all inside until Olav's . . . until Olav was taken away."

She was unbelievably skinny. Her head was a spectral skull glazed with nothing but skin. Her eyes became enormous in her tiny, narrow face, and Billy T. could discern a kind of beauty if it hadn't been for the woman not being endowed with a single scrap of fat.

"I really haven't a clue whether it has any significance," she said half apologetically as she removed two sheets of paper from a folder she had brought down from the first floor. "But on the day Agnes was killed . . ."

Billy T. turned the two sheets to face him.

"I was up there with her. Immediately after Terje had been there. Maren had been there too, but only for a couple of minutes. We talked about a whole lot of things to do with work. Perhaps it took about half an hour or so. A bit about Olav, a bit about Kenneth. Yes, we're struggling with Kenneth, you see. He's been placed with three different families, poor thing. His mother —"

"Okay, okay," Billy T. interjected, waving her one. "Get to the point!"

"I wasn't really meaning to be nosy, you know. But there was a diploma lying on her desk. From Diakonhjemmet. I recognized it, of course, because I got my qualifications there myself . . . But after a while Agnes lifted the paper and stuffed it quickly into the drawer. It was exactly as if it had suddenly dawned on her that it was lying there, and she didn't want me to see it. I noticed it was Maren's before she put it away. It was actually quite bizarre, you see, that it was lying there and that Agnes seemed so abrupt and so on. What's on it is not exactly a secret, of course. There aren't any marks or anything like that, it only says 'pass.' But I didn't think much of it. In fact I had completely forgotten about it. But there was something that . . . something that struck me and that I didn't recall until today . . ."

Cathrine rose to her feet and stood behind Billy T. She leaned over him and pointed at the certificates.

"Do you see that they are different?"

They were indeed. At the top of one it stated DIAKONHJEMMET SCHOOL OF SOCIAL WORK in broad capital letters. Underneath was printed "Diploma of Social Work Examination." Whereas the other one had a symbol at the top, a circle with a thick line forming the upper half and the lower formed by the word "Diakonhjemmet." In the center of the circle stood a kind of cross, reminiscent of a Nazi Iron Cross.

"Horrible, that Nazi cross," Cathrine preempted him. "And as you see, they changed the heading to 'Diploma of Social Work Education,' not 'Examination.' The first one is from 1990; it belongs to a friend of mine. The other one is from 1991. It's mine."

A bony forefinger directed his attention to the date near the foot of each page.

"And what's terribly odd, you see," Cathrine continued once she had returned to her own seat. "It's that Maren's diploma had that iron cross at the top! But she has always claimed she took the exam in 1990 . . . I asked Eirik about it to be sure, earlier today. He was in the year before her, and he graduated in 1989. I just *can't* understand it, really . . ."

Now she was staring at her hands, folded on the tabletop.

"It's not my intention to make difficulties for anybody, but it is quite strange, isn't it?"

Billy T. did not utter a word but nodded faintly. Without taking his eyes from the two diplomas, he asked, "Did you see Maren when she left Agnes's office? Or later that day?"

The spectral skull was deep in thought.

"Yes, I met her as she was coming downstairs. She told me it was my turn."

"How did she seem?"

"She was quite grumpy, and I remember thinking she had probably had an argument with Agnes again. They were good friends, really, I didn't mean it like that, but they disagreed fairly often. About things to do with the children, you see. Agnes was stricter, more old-fashioned, in a way. Last year Maren wanted to take the children abroad on holiday, but —"

"Cathrine!"

A desperate, feeble voice was calling from the top of the staircase. Billy T. did not get to hear what happened about Maren's plans for a foreign holiday, because Cathrine Ruge stood up and dashed off upstairs. It was twenty minutes before she reappeared.

So Agnes *had* confronted Maren with her deception. It couldn't have been accidental that her diploma was lying out. If this lanky skeleton had told them what she knew at her first interview . . . It had damn well been the *day* after the murder! The day after! Who knows, Terje Welby's life might have been spared. Maybe even Olav's too. Billy T. fought his rising rage. Then the scrawny skeleton reappeared.

"He's having a dreadful time, you know. Kenneth, I mean. Now he's got it into his head that there's a pirate living in the basement. Every night this imaginary pirate comes upstairs to eat all the children. My God . . ."

306

Her voice was shrill, and the only reason Billy T. did not interrupt her was he was so furious he simply had to keep his mouth shut.

Cathrine continued. "This evening he came home with four big knives, to add to the mess. Anita had taken him over to the playground to divert him when things were at their worst here. He had found them among some stones and insisted it was the pirate who had stashed them there so he could cut the children up. God Almighty. He's just having a terrible time."

Billy T. fleetingly shook his head, and his anger disappeared.

"Knives? Had he found some knives?"

"Yes, four horrible, huge knives. I threw them away."

"Where?"

"Where?"

"Where did you throw the knives?"

"In the garbage, of course!"

He stood up so fast the chair toppled over.

"What garbage can? The one in here, or did you take them outside?"

Cathrine Ruge looked exasperated.

"No, I wrapped them up well so the refuse collectors wouldn't injure themselves, and then I threw them out there." She pointed over her shoulder with her thumb.

Billy T. stormed out to the kitchen and tore open the door of the cabinet underneath the sink. Almost at the top, among potato peelings and two discarded sausage ends, lay an oblong parcel wrapped in newspaper. He clutched it carefully and held it up to Cathrine, who

307

was standing in the doorway with her hands by her side and a disgruntled expression on her face.

"This?" he asked, and she nodded briefly.

Eighteen minutes later he was at Oslo Police Station, where an exhausted and disconsolate colleague was sitting, longing for the weekend.

Ten o'clock had come and gone, and she would have to give up soon. Billy T. would hear about it. It was awful to spend a Friday evening in this way. What was worse was that Cecilie was going to be bad tempered all day tomorrow. And worst of all was that she would have to let Maren Kalsvik go.

"It's funny, you know," she said quietly to the silent woman, sighing almost inaudibly. "It's odd how it always turns out that there's so much turbulence in people's lives. It happens almost every time."

She stretched her arms above her head and yawned, before taking a pair of scissors from the desk drawer and starting to cut out a figure from the cardboard of a used writing pad.

"It's me," she said, almost to herself. "My fingers have to be busy all the time. That's why it's so difficult for me to quit smoking."

She peered in embarrassment over at the second cigarette packet of the day.

"Take a completely ordinary human being. An average person."

She had fashioned a lady with a full skirt. With her head tilted to the side and a satisfied expression, she began to draw a face. After that she colored the dress with a pink highlighter pen, and when that was finished, she propped it up against her coffee cup. It stood lopsided, stiff, and straight with a broad blue smile.

"Agnes Vestavik, for instance," she said dispassionately, pointing at the cardboard doll. "We start to poke around in a seemingly boring, normal, and straightforward person's life. Then it turns out that the reality is something different. There's always something more there. Nothing is as it seems to be at first glance. We all have our dark side. If I was murdered, for example . . ."

She stopped. It was late. She was dog tired. The person facing her was a stranger. She continued.

"If anyone murdered me, the detectives here would be as surprised as can be."

She chuckled quietly.

"The world is one colossal illusion. A distorted image. Look at yourself, for example."

The cardboard doll fell to one side, without Maren Kalsvik paying any attention to it.

"I like you, Maren. I think you're a good person. You do something that's important. Something meaningful. Then a number of things take place that you're not in control of, and suddenly you're sitting here. Having murdered someone. The ways of the Lord are truly mysterious."

Hanne Wilhelmsen no longer had any idea whether Maren Kalsvik was listening to her at all. There was a knock at the door.

It was Billy T.

She was about to give him a murderous look, but when she caught sight of his face, she changed her mind. He had come up with something. And it was of enormous importance.

"Can I have a word or two with you out in the corridor, Hanne?" he asked quietly in a friendly tone.

"Of course, Billy T.," Hanne Wilhelmsen replied. "Of course."

They were away for what seemed an age. Red-and-white specks were dancing behind her eyelids, and there was a faint *whooshing* sound in her ears. Besides, it was deathly silent. When she gingerly raised her bottom a fraction, she noticed her legs had gone completely to sleep. Her muscles were tingling painfully, and she felt stiff and sore when she stood up.

The story of the falsified diploma had entirely slipped her mind in the course of the past four weeks. It had all been a catastrophe. It was true, she had always had trouble with examinations, ever since she was at junior high school. Her high school diploma had been hell. Excellent continuous assessment, dreadful examination results. It only became worse and worse.

Her weeklong home assignment had gone well. The snag was the final examination. Something happened to her as soon as she entered an examination hall. The desks spaced out at regulation distance, the stone-deaf old bats who were supposed to ensure there was no cheating, all the lunch boxes, thermos flasks, pencil cases; the whispering silence, the atmosphere before the exam papers were issued; the anxiety experienced by the majority combined with anticipation into a mixture of childish excitement. Only not for her. Maren Kalsvik became frightened and paralyzed. Her last chance disappeared when she resat the spring after she should actually have graduated from college. She had not been able to afford to repeat an entire additional school year. That was what she should have done. When she stood there, one summer day in 1991, and learned that all her hopes of being a qualified social worker were dashed, she had at first felt nothing but a vast, gray emptiness. Almost the same as now. One hundred and forty thousand kroner in student loans and nothing to show for it. All avenues closed. No fresh opportunities.

It had been so simple. A borrowed diploma, a small amount of correction fluid, and a photocopying machine. She hadn't dared to create an original, but it was frighteningly easy to superimpose a "Genuine copy confirmed" stamp and scrawl some illegible initials.

It was a crime. It was the only thing she could do.

Since then, she had forgotten about it. Now and again — at night perhaps, or just before her period or when both occurred simultaneously — the knowledge that she was living and working on the basis of a lie pricked her conscience mercilessly. Then she had to clench her teeth, work on, demonstrate how clever she was, and prove to both God and herself that she really deserved that diploma. Then she forgot about it again. Often for months at a time.

Until that fateful day.

The two police officers returned abruptly to the room; she heard them but did not turn around. The huge man asked her to sit down. An indistinct mark surrounded by condensation was visible on the windowpane where her forehead had rested on the cold glass. She went back obediently to her seat and resumed her stiff, motionless posture.

The man, whose only designation she had learned was his first name, was sitting in Chief Inspector Wilhelmsen's chair. The policewoman crossed to the window and fingered the mark where her head had been resting. They were both terrifyingly silent.

Then she noticed the parcel. An oblong parcel wrapped in newspaper, quite dirty, and with a strong smell of . . . was it garbage? The policeman left it lying unopened in front of him on the desk and stared at her. It was impossible to make him look away. He caught her gaze; his eyes were more intense than any she had ever seen, frightening, fascinating, and totally different from their previous meeting. They were almost how she had imagined God's eyes to be, when she was a child and believed he could literally see her everywhere.

"You have lied, Maren Kalsvik," he said in a deep, quiet voice, reminding her even more of God. "Agnes *had* confronted you with your deception. We have proof."

Keep quite silent, keep your mouth shut, the words thundered inside her head, and she felt devastated as she felt her face grow hot.

Her grip on the armrests became even tighter, and her jaw felt as though it would break. But she said not a word.

312

"We know that the diploma was in Agnes's office on the day she was killed. No one has clapped eyes on it since. One point for us. Minus point for you."

Suddenly he changed. He smiled, and his eyes were friendly. Normal.

"Not that I want to bother you with details. We'll have plenty of time for that later. In the meantime I just want to bring your attention to it. That we know you're lying. That's how we get by. People tell lies. When they lie about one thing, then we know they can lie about something else. Such is life. And so we have a little surprise for you."

His enormous hands carefully touched the newspaper.

"Haven't even had time to put them in an evidence bag. So you can only have a tiny little glimpse. For the moment."

The *whooshing* sound in her ears increased. She shook her head feebly, but it did not help any. Not her blushing either. She forced herself at the very least to breathe normally.

Her lungs refused to cooperate any longer. They were expanding energetically and then collapsing. She gasped for air, and there was a burning pain in her chest.

"Four knives. Found in a children's playground. By a child!"

He chortled. The chief inspector at the window had turned to face them, and Maren looked at her. She obviously did not think the situation was amusing in the slightest.

313

"You're smart enough to know we haven't yet managed to have these checked for fingerprints. But they were shoved far down in between some stones, and you must have taken a really good grip of them. Perhaps you were wearing gloves. Perhaps there won't be a single print. But now we've progressed much further than where we were a couple of hours ago. First and foremost because we know you lied. Now we've come so far that we can go home for the weekend."

"So far that we can charge you, Maren. You know what that involves?"

Hanne Wilhelmsen had not a trace of the man's triumphant tone. She only seemed sad. Of course Maren Kalsvik knew what it involved.

"We'll bring you to court to be remanded in custody on Monday. In the meantime, you'll stay here."

She wrapped the knives up carefully again.

"And we'll be *able* to put you in prison, Maren. Don't spend the weekend hoping for anything else."

It was over.

The *whooshing* noise in her ears vanished. The steel band around her lungs loosened slowly. Warmth spread through her body, pleasant and almost intoxicating. Her body felt at the same time both light and yet heavy as lead. Her shoulders dropped, and she suddenly noticed how painful her jaw felt. Deliberately, she opened her mouth wide, several times. There was a cracking sound.

It was all over.

She was guilty. She had defrauded her way to a meaningful life. Olav was dead. He was a boy of only twelve years of age. Twelve dreadful, miserable years. He had come to her, and he died. It was her fault.

It didn't really matter what these people were saying. It no longer mattered what happened to her. There was only one way forward. She would have to pay. She could pay with her own life.

"I want to sleep now," she said softly. "Can we talk about this again tomorrow?"

The two police officers stared at each other before the chief inspector glanced at the clock.

"Of course we can," she said. "Besides, you have to speak to an attorney. Now I must insist."

Maren Kalsvik smiled, pale and exhausted.

"We'll arrange that early tomorrow morning," Hanne Wilhelmsen continued. "Now you'll be able to get some sleep."

It took some time to arrange the formalities with the officer on duty. Furthermore, Hanne did not want to leave until she had ensured that Maren Kalsvik would receive medical attention. From bitter experience, she knew the staff on cell duty could not always be relied upon, especially on a Friday night.

As a matter of fact, it was now the early hours of Saturday.

"Can you drive me home, Billy T.?" Hanne asked once Maren was safely installed in the rear building. "Can't you come home with me to Cecilie?"

He actually could not do that, but after a quick phone call to his sister he put his arm around her and escorted her to the car, parked in a disability bay without anyone on the crime desk daring to grumble. She wobbled weakly, sinking down heavily into the seat, and they did not exchange a single word until Billy T. had squeezed the car into the world's smallest parking space twenty meters away from the apartment block where Hanne lived. She made not the slightest sign of leaving.

"There are two things I really wonder about," she said wearily.

"What are they?"

"First of all, do you think she'll confess?"

"Definitely. We'll have her remanded in custody for at least four weeks. You could see it in her. The relief. She even damn well had some color in her cheeks. A couple more interviews, and it'll all come tumbling out. Maren Kalsvik isn't evil. On the contrary. What's more, she believes in God. Her whole soul is burning to confess. Then we only have to make it as easy as possible for her. She'll confess. Without a doubt."

"Will we get a conviction if she *doesn't* confess?"

"Doubtful. You know that yourself. But she'll confess. That's the best evidence in the world. A confession."

His fingers were drumming on the steering wheel. Then he looked at Hanne.

"What was the other thing that you were wondering about?"

"I really wonder so bloody much," Hanne began quietly, clearing her throat.

Then she put more emphasis into her voice.

"I really wonder what that *T* in Billy T. stands for."

316

He leaned his head back and guffawed.

"There's no fucking person apart from my ma and me who knows that!"

"Please, Billy T. I promise not to tell anyone. No one at all."

"No way."

"Please!"

He continued to hesitate, but then placed his mouth right beside her ear. She leaned sideways toward him, his beard tickling her earlobe.

Then she smiled. Had it not been for the day having been so excruciatingly long, she would have laughed. Had it not been for a boy having died right in front of her face, and for knowing that a mother was sitting somewhere having lost her son and she should really have paid her a visit, she would have roared with laughter. Had it not been for a young, capable child welfare worker on the basis of a pile of unfortunate circumstances sitting in a fucking remand cell and about to stay there, she would honestly have split her sides laughing. But she only smiled.

The *T* stood for Torvald.

He was called Billy Torvald!

They sent a minister: I've never had anything to do with ministers. All the same I could tell immediately, even though he wasn't wearing that bizarre collar of theirs. In fact he was wearing jeans. Open-necked shirt, with a forest of dark hairs sticking out. I kept staring at those hairs.

He wasn't particularly old, maybe about thirty. It was obvious he wasn't accustomed to such tasks. He stuttered and stammered, and looked all around for help. In the end I had to say that I knew why he was there. There couldn't be any reason for them sending a minister to little old me other than that Olav was dead.

He didn't want to leave. I had to virtually throw him out. He looked at me oddly, as though it disappointed him, or even shocked him, that I did not cry. He asked me if I had anybody to talk to, or if he could call someone who could come and stay with me. I gave up answering his questions; he wasn't listening to me anyway. Nobody ever has. Finally I managed to lock the door behind him.

In many ways I've known it all along. Perhaps I've been waiting for it since that very first day in the delivery room, when his enormous, abnormal body rolled over on top of my stomach. In a sense he was not meant to be. Perhaps that was why I didn't feel anything for him during the first few months. I knew I wasn't going to be allowed to keep him.

Even when I watched his back yesterday afternoon, I knew it. I hung out the window in the hope that he would see me and turn back. I couldn't shout. The neighbors would hear it. When his bulky figure disappeared around the corner at number 16, I could feel it inside me. He was gone.

I started to tidy his belongings. The games, most of them broken. The clothes, so enormous, so unflattering, I could never find anything nice to fit him. Some of his schoolbooks were still scattered about, the exercise books with his big crooked handwriting, the arithmetic books with every answer wrong. Now they're all stored down in the basement.

He was carrying Flipper in his rucksack. A little dog with long ears that my mum gave him for his first birthday. It's the only thing she has ever given him exactly on the right day. He loved that dog, and at the same time he was ashamed of him. But he brought it with him from the foster home.

There were four knives lying there as well. In the rucksack. I've no idea what they were doing there, but he must have taken them with him from the foster home. He's always had a peculiar inclination toward knives. They're not the first knives I've removed from his rucksack. Did he want to take something with him to defend himself? In any case, they should be handed back. They didn't belong to me.

I went there yesterday evening. Now I don't really know why. Of course I wanted to return the knives. Perhaps honesty in connection with the knives was an excuse to look at the place again. That dreadful place. Now, twenty-four hours later, with everything that's happened, it dawns on me that somehow I had realized this was where he would go. Some sort of attraction.

When I was approaching the foster home, there was something holding me back. I stopped beside a playground and could make out the outline of the dark building against the sky.

The director there was killed with a knife. A kitchen knife. I had four kitchen knives in my handbag. That I had found in Olav's rucksack. My boy. I couldn't hand them back.

I had to get rid of them. The police find out everything.

The playground was in complete darkness, and between it and a neighboring garden was an old knee-high stone wall. I was able to push the knives in between some of the stones. Far in. First I wiped them thoroughly. Probably they would never be discovered. But I had to protect him. As I have always tried to protect him.

He's been taken from me so many times. Bit by bit. In the kindergarten, at school, by the child welfare service. I've never succeeded in keeping hold of him.

But by God I've tried. I've loved him more than my own life.

And when I sit here, on his bed, smelling the scent of his pajamas, sweet and quite strong, and realize he's gone forever, and it's night and darkness has fallen and everything is completely silent, I have nothing left. Nothing.

Not even myself.

CHAPTER
ELEVEN

Maren Kalsvik was standing in a witness-box in Oslo's new courthouse, shivering slightly. The judge was about to sign his name on some form or other that a besuited attorney had placed before him. Hanne Wilhelmsen appeared exhausted and struggled in vain to conceal a yawn behind her slim hand. She was more formally dressed than Maren Kalsvik had ever seen her previously: a black skirt and blouse with a dark gray suit jacket on top and a silk scarf in subdued earth tones.

The chief inspector had treated her with respect. She had shown compassion. She had never become impatient, although she had repeated her theories over and over again throughout the weekend, without Maren being willing to offer as much as the movement of a facial muscle to confirm or deny what had taken place in Agnes Vestavik's office on that fatal evening more than a fortnight earlier. Maren Kalsvik had chosen to remain silent. She had refused to talk to an attorney.

It was correct that she had been there. Eirik was sleeping, something that had confirmed a dawning suspicion he was taking something or other that he shouldn't, at least not when he was given the task of looking after eight sleeping youngsters.

The meeting with Agnes was, however, shorter than Hanne Wilhelmsen assumed. It had lasted only ten minutes. First she had considered begging. All her pride vanished when she realized she was about to lose her job, forfeit her entire existence.

Agnes had told her about Terje. About knowing that Maren knew. Her voice was unfamiliar and quietly distorted, filled with rage that had to be suppressed because of eight sleeping children. Agnes could understand the business of the diploma, she had said. She could make sense of that. In a flash she showed something resembling sympathy, and her voice returned to something like normal. It did not last long. She could not forgive the real betrayal. Maren had gone behind her back to cover up embezzlement. Agnes waved the papers furiously, the fraudulent diploma in one hand, the statement detailing Terje's malpractice in the other.

Maren Kalsvik wanted to beg. Then she caught sight of Agnes's eyes and realized it was futile.

She had given her a week to write her letter of resignation. There was nothing more to be done. She had turned away and quietly left the office.

On the landing outside she had stood still for a moment, as tears got the better of her. She attempted to smother her sobs, and when she thought she heard movements from one of the children's bedrooms, she had crept down the stairs. Eirik was still fast asleep. When she came outside, she started running. She had to flee. She sprinted around the house, crashed down through the back garden, stumbled over the fence, and somehow managed to reach home.

When Eirik phoned a couple of hours later, she battled against a feeling of relief that overwhelmed her in a wave of guilt. When only a few minutes later she was standing on her own in Agnes's office, it was lying there. The diploma. On the desk, together with other papers. Eirik had not spotted it. She folded it over and placed it in her pocket. Totally without thinking.

She had thought it was Terje. Until the suicide letter arrived. Then she feared the worst. Then she had it confirmed. Olav had seen her running. He had seen her crying. He had told her the truth before he died.

It was all her fault.

"Are you willing to make a statement?"

The judge was staring at her over a pair of reading glasses, perched so far out on his crooked nose that they were about to fall off.

"No," she said aloud.

He sighed before whispering a message to the secretary, and then rasped a horrible, racking cough. He continued his questioning of the prisoner: "Do you plead guilty or not guilty with respect to the charge?"

Maren Kalsvik gazed yet again at Hanne Wilhelmsen. The chief inspector was leaning forward across the desk, touching her silk scarf as she tensely returned her gaze. When Maren Kalsvik shifted her weight from left foot to right before replying, she did not look at the judge. Instead, she smiled faintly as she looked the chief inspector in the eye.

"I'm guilty," she whispered.

Straightening her back and dropping her eyes from Hanne Wilhelmsen's scrutiny, she cleared her throat before repeating, more loudly this time: "I am guilty."

Also available in ISIS Large Print:

Blessed Are Those Who Thirst

Anne Holt

It is only the beginning of May but the unseasonable heat already feels tropical. Criminal investigating officer Hanne Wilhelmsen is sent to a macabre crime scene on the outskirts of Oslo: an abandoned shed that is covered in blood. On one wall is an eight-digit number written in blood. There is no sign of a victim — is it just a kid's prank, or foul play? Is it even human blood? Hanne has a bad feeling about the numbers, but without further evidence, she can do nothing.

As more bloody numbers are found throughout Oslo, Hanne's colleague Hâkon Sand discovers that the eight-digit number corresponds to the filing number of foreign immigrants waiting to be granted Norwegian citizenship — all female, all missing. When a dead body is finally unearthed, Hanne and Hâkon fear they have a serial killer on their hands.

ISBN 978-0-7531-9116-3 (hb)
ISBN 978-0-7531-9117-0 (pb)

Babylon

Camilla Ceder

A flat in Gothenburg holds a nasty surprise for Inspector Christian Tell. Anne-Marie Karpov, respected academic, lies murdered alongside a much younger man. The dead man is Henrik, her student and lover.

The obvious suspect is Rebecca, Henrik's partner. Rebecca's volatile behaviour has brought her to the attention of the police before. But when Rebecca's flat is burgled, and strange artefacts are found among Henrik's things, Tell must cast the net wider.

Does the answer lie with Karpov's shifty ex-husband, a man with a professional interest in ancient treasures? Or is there another suspect? As the mystery takes Tell from the icy streets of Gothenburg to the alleyways of historic Istanbul, the troubled detective and his team will be tested to the very limit of their powers . . .

ISBN 978-0-7531-9188-0 (hb)
ISBN 978-0-7531-9189-7 (pb)

The Blind Goddess

Anne Holt

A drug dealer is battered to death on the outskirts of
Oslo. A young Dutch student, covered in blood, walks
aimlessly through the streets of the city. He is taken
into custody, but refuses to speak. Five days later a
shady criminal lawyer called Hansa Larsen is
murdered. The two deaths don't seem related, but
Detective Inspector Hanne Wilhelmsen is unconvinced.
Soon, she uncovers a link between the bodies: Larsen
defended the drug dealer.

But there are powerful forces working against Hanne; a
conspiracy that reaches far beyond a crooked lawyer
and a small-time dealer. The investigation will take her
into the offices of the most powerful men in Norway —
and even put her own life at risk . . .

ISBN 978-0-7531-9114-9 (hb)
ISBN 978-0-7531-9115-6 (pb)

Fear Not

Anne Holt

The snow-covered streets of Oslo are the very picture of Christmas tranquility. But over the tolling bells for Christmas day, a black note sounds. As first light breaks, Bishop Eva Karin Lysgaard is found stabbed to death in the quiet city centre. DI Adam Stubo heads up the police investigation, but it is Johanne Vik, criminal profiler, who infers an unlikely pattern from this shocking murder, and who suspects that a bitter and untempered hatred has been unleashed upon the city of Oslo. A hatred that is not yet satisfied . . .

ISBN 978-0-7531-8938-2 (hb)
ISBN 978-0-7531-8939-9 (pb)